A Candlelight Regency Special

# A GAME OF HEARTS

*Marlaine Kyle*

*A CANDLELIGHT REGENCY SPECIAL*

Published by
Dell Publishing Co., Inc.
1 Dag Hammarskjold Plaza
New York, New York 10017



ISBN 0-440-12912-5

Printed in the United States of America
First printing—May 1982

*FOR MARK AND KYLE*

# A GAME OF HEARTS

## *CHAPTER ONE*

Emma Robinson stood in the drafty vestibule of the building that housed the offices of her father's solicitors. Mr. Raymond, the elder partner, had worn a grave expression and his words had been carefully chosen, as though he sought to soften their impact, but a whole cadre of gentle phrases would not change the stark reality of her situation. She was penniless—an orphaned young woman of twenty-two who must now depend upon the continuing generosity of her aunt and uncle, Lord and Lady Parton, for even the barest of life's necessities. Knowing well her parents' carelessness with money, she had not expected them to leave more than a modest estate; but to be told that, after the gambling debts and the dressmaker and all the other bills were paid, there would be *nothing* had been a rude shock, indeed.

Yet she could not bring herself to feel any resentment. Her mother, Georgina, had been a sweet-tempered, pretty woman, but, alas, somewhat featherbrained. As for poor papa, with his cheerful, good-hearted, overly optimistic attitude toward everything, he had undoubtedly felt assured of living, if not forever, at least to a very ripe old age. It would not have occurred to him that his only child might ever have need of anything but her loving, indulgent papa and, at some future time, an equally loving, indulgent husband.

Clutching the gray woolen folds of her Spanish coat about her in anticipation of the frigid February gusts outside, Emma walked to the door, fighting down an inner alarm. Since her nineteenth birthday, she had turned down two young men who, willing to overlook her lack of a dowry, had offered for her. She had not fancied herself in love with either of them, and fortunately her father had been more than willing to keep her at home a while longer. Perhaps, she thought wryly, she would soon come to rue her romantic fancy that a loveless marriage was quite unacceptable.

She shook her head and told herself firmly, feeling sorry for yourself is nothing to the purpose. One small gloved hand pushed open the door, and she descended the steps to the bustling London street, where she paused and the wind caught at curls escaping her snug fur cap, whipping them into a red-gold tangle.

The carriage in which her cousin Charlotte awaited was no longer standing in the spot where she had left it. Given Lottie's impatient nature, this was not altogether surprising. Probably her young cousin had grown restless with waiting and had instructed the groom, Benjy, to take a turn through the streets before returning to meet Emma.

Lady Parton had remonstrated with Lottie about the latter's disinclination to take her abigail along on the afternoon's jaunt, but she had been won over to her daughter's point of view upon being reminded how very sensible and trustworthy Cousin Emma was. Lottie's unexplained absence now caused Emma to wonder, for the first time, if her cousin was indeed up to some mischief. However, preoccupation with her own utterly impoverished state, of which she had just been informed, took precedence in her thoughts over any potential impropriety of Lottie's.

Thankful for the thickness of her coat and the warm lining of her half boots, Emma paced back and forth in front of the brownstone building at a fast clip. She was quite slender and small-boned; this made her seem more delicate than she actually was and now, in the drab gray of her coat and the black of her mourning beneath, she looked wan and frail. Yet her agile movements belied any such condition. The paleness of her complexion was in vivid contrast to pink cheeks, their hue heightened by the biting wind, and large dark-lashed eyes of a blue-green color. Her Aunt Claire would have been scandalized had she known that Emma was alone on a London street, and Emma herself might have thought to return to the vestibule to await her cousin had she considered it, but her mind was elsewhere.

How was she to go on? She could remain with the Partons, acting as a genteel companion to her Aunt Claire, hovering in the background as her nineteen-year-old cousin, Charlotte, whirled through her second London season. This prospect did not appeal to her, but the only possible alternative would be to try to find employment, perhaps as a governess in a family with young children. That held no more attraction for her than staying with the Partons, except for the fact that she would be earning her own way.

Emma had grown up in Bristol, where her father had been a woolen merchant. Although they had never lived in luxurious style, their small house had been cozy and attractive, and her father had been generous to a fault when it came to his wife and daughter. Emma and her mother had always had large wardrobes of clothes in the latest fashion, several household servants, and whatever else they required.

Looking back, Emma was amazed that the atmosphere in their home had been ever lighthearted, since she now knew that her father's finances must have been strained for some time. Indeed, they had been in such a tangle that it had taken the solicitors eight months to straighten them out. Yet her father had managed somehow to keep the unpleasant reality from his wife and daughter.

Her comfortable, protected existence had come to an end abruptly eight months earlier when both her parents had taken ill and quickly died of cholera. Emma, miraculously spared, had gone to live with her mother's sister, Lady Parton, and her husband, Lord Randolph Parton, at their country estate in Sussex. She had never lived in the country, but Emma found, in her grief, that the quiet setting soothed her. Even her aunt's constant complaints and varied, often imaginary, ailments had not spoiled for Emma the rustic surroundings, where she had taken frequent solitary walks and indulged a passion for reading and a secret desire to write poetry.

Recently the Partons had traveled to their house in Bedford Square for the season, and since she had no other choice, Emma had come with them. But always, at the back of her mind, was the vague idea that, when her father's estate was settled and she had means of her own, she would manage to change the circumstances of her life; the role of the poor relation was irksome to her. She had even entertained the daring notion of hiring a companion and moving into her own quarters; although, in her more practical moments, she realized that her aunt and uncle would never allow her to live alone. Still, with money of her own, she might have found a way to have a more independent life. Now that would not be possible.

I cannot remain with Aunt Claire and Uncle Randolph forever, thought Emma darkly, turning on her boot heel and stopping suddenly in her pacing, almost colliding with an elderly gentleman who had been walking behind her. After a while I shall have to find work, she decided with a stubborn determination that caused her spine to stiffen and her small chin to jut forward.

The February afternoon was gray with a frosty bleakness, yet there was an exhilaration in the air caused by the hurrying people, the clattering carriages, and the bustle of business being conducted all around her.

"Emma!"

She turned to see her cousin descending from the Parton carriage a few yards away. In the drab street Lottie's scarlet fur-lined cloak was a brilliant splash of color that drew the eyes of passersby. A few wisps of dark hair could be seen at the edges of the cloak's hood. As Lottie came toward her, the carriage moved off slowly.

"Poor Cousin, have you been waiting long? I thought I had time for a ride through the park."

"Not long," Emma replied, looking after the departing carriage, her suspicion of a few moments before returning. "Why have you sent the carriage away, Lottie?"

"Benjy will meet us here in an hour." Lottie's brown eyes twinkled with mischief. "I told him you would not have completed your business until then. What did Mr. Raymond have to say? Is everything settled at last?"

"Quite settled," Emma replied with irony. "I find I have not a feather to fly with."

"Oh, pooh, it is nothing to signify." Lottie passed this off with the careless indifference of an extremely pampered young woman who had never wanted for anything in her life, nor ever would. "Papa will provide for you." She linked her arm through Emma's. "Pluck up, Cousin. We have an hour to spend at the Frost Fair."

The reason for Lottie's refusal to bring along Joan, her gossipy abigail, was at last apparent. Joan would not have been able to keep silent about her young mistress's imprudent visit to the Frost Fair. The abigail's tittle-tattle belowstairs would quickly have made its way to the family apartments. Emma walked along beside her cousin, protesting, "Lottie, you know Aunt Claire would not approve of our going there alone."

"But we aren't alone, Emma dear," Lottie said with a tinkling laugh. "We are with each other, and it's only for an hour. Don't put yourself in a fret. Mother won't be aware of how long we are away. She was coming down with one of her headaches when we left."

"She might think to question Benjy," Emma equivocated. "I cannot like this, Lottie."

Lottie's brown eyes regarded her cousin with supreme impatience. "Why should she question Benjy? Stop quibbling, Emma, do! Everyone at the Massingales' party last evening was talking about the Frost Fair. This is our opportunity to see what all the excitement is about. It's only a short walk. It will help take your mind off your troubles."

Emma was not gulled by this last statement tacked on to Lottie's argument as an afterthought. "How considerate of you to concern yourself with my state of mind, Cousin! Tell me, when did this burst of compassion strike you?"

Lottie's eyes met her cousin's and she smiled. "You cannot give me a set-down, you know," she said reasonably. "I am very thick-skinned."

"I would never have suspected that!" Emma told her archly.

"I am determined to have an adventure," Lottie went on, "with or without you, Emma. Admit it now, aren't you the slightest part curious to see a frost fair? We may never have another opportunity in our lifetimes."

"A fate not to be contemplated," said Emma dryly. "I will own it would be a pleasant diversion, but we shall be in a dreadful coil if Aunt Claire finds us out. She will have a spasm and—"

Lottie was already headed in the direction of the Thames. "Leave Mother to me."

Emma was not excessively consoled by this since, in spite of her words, Lottie usually left it for others to set things right when they went wrong. Yet she could not but laugh at her cousin's wide-eyed eagerness. "I see you are not to be deterred." Emma hurried to keep up with Lottie's quickened steps. "Well, in that case, I might as well find what enjoyment I can from this."

Lottie bestowed a charming smile as she did when she got her way. "I have always said you are sensible."

This year of 1814 had begun with plummeting temperatures and the hardest frost to grip London in centuries. As the icy days continued, Londoners began to refer to the "Great Frost" and cheerfully set about making the best of it. By the beginning of February, when the *haut ton* began to arrive, the Thames between London Bridge and Blackfriars had become a solid surface of ice thick enough to be safely used as a roadway, and it was promptly dubbed Freezeland Street.

The air of festivity was due in great part to the news from France. The war against Napoleon, which for a long while looked as if it might go on for years and years, seemed now to be coming to an end. Wellington had entered France in October and from that time his armies had moved steadily forward. Even though Napoleon had, in December, turned down generous peace terms, his empire seemed clearly to be falling apart.

As the two girls joined the crowd milling from one

booth to the next, Charlotte squeezed Emma's arm conspiratorily. "Look, there is a sweet hawker!" She thrust her gloved hand into her reticule and came up with coins to pay for two squares of hot gingerbread. Handing one square to her cousin and taking a bite of the other, Charlotte rolled her brown eyes. "Sweets always taste better at a fair. Don't you think so?"

"Oh, indeed," Emma said readily. She was beginning to catch some of Lottie's enthusiasm for the Frost Fair.

Charlotte finished her gingerbread and announced, "I must see the toys in that booth. What fun it will be to have children of my own to shop for!"

Emma managed an agreeable murmur at this, but she was thinking that her cousin had a good deal of growing up to do before she would make a proper mother, in spite of the fact that Lady Parton was determined to see Charlotte safely affianced to some lord of the realm by the end of the season. And indeed there were a number of attentive young men from whom the wealthy and pretty Charlotte might choose, a decision the flighty young girl seemed in no hurry to make. Lottie was enjoying all the favors she was receiving too much to limit them to the attentions of one gentleman, it seemed.

"I see you have remarked the bookstall," said Charlotte, following Emma's lingering gaze. After a thoughtful pause she added magnanimously, "Very well. You browse through your dusty tomes while I examine the booths more to my liking. I shall meet you at the bookstall in a half hour."

"We should stay together," Emma said with vacillation, torn between the impropriety of abandoning her young, gently reared cousin and the magic lure of the books.

"Fiddle!" Charlotte exclaimed. "What could happen to either of us in this merry crowd?"

"Well . . ." Emma hesitated. "No more than a half hour then."

Charlotte nodded, her brown eyes glowing with the excitement of the Frost Fair, with which Emma herself was fully infected by that time. Then she hurried toward the toys, and Emma lost sight of her cousin's scarlet cloak as the jostling crowd surrounded her.

The bookstall was a tent with one side open, containing crudely made counters where volumes of varied description were stacked. Emma's uncertainty about separating from her cousin was pushed aside as she succumbed to the drawing power of the printed page. She moved to one of the counters and leafed through a slender volume, a romantic novel by an author unknown to her. The action was accompanied by a deep pang of regret as she remembered her now impossible dreams of her own cozy rooms, one of which would have been lined with books, with an escritoire in one corner where she could pen letters to her friends and record her observations and poetry in her journal.

The bookstall proprietor, a round little man with a woolen cap pulled down over his ears, had a fire going in a small iron stove in a back corner of the tent. The fire took the edge off the chill, and Emma removed her gloves so that she could handle the books more easily.

She was laying aside a novel reluctantly when she heard a faint mewing sound behind her. Turning, she saw the head of a kitten appear beneath the tent wall near her feet.

"Poor kitty," she cried with dismay and bent to extricate the small furry body from the weight of the tent, lifting it in both hands. The kitten was gray, wretchedly thin, and trembling with fear and cold and, doubtless, hunger.

The tiny creature sniffed at her woolen coat and gave a faint, plaintive cry of distress. Making soft sounds of sympathy, Emma tucked the kitten beneath the folds of her coat, leaving only the small head exposed. Gradually, the trembling in the little body subsided as Emma's body warmth enveloped it.

Looking about, she spied the proprietor and made her way around a few book buyers to his side. "Sir, is this your kitten?"

The man squinted at the furry face protruding from the front of Emma's coat and shook his head. "Another homeless beast. They are attracted to the Frost Fair by the smell of food." With a careless shrug, he turned away to wait on a customer.

Emma stood where she was, looking down at the kitten, and wondered what to do with it. She could not bring herself to abandon the poor creature to what would most likely be death by starvation or freezing. But what a fuss there would be if she took him back to the house in Bedford Square. Uncle Randolph would grumble about the danger of disease and pestilence brought on by picking up stray animals. Aunt Claire's nerves would be affected and she would take to her bed, if she were not already there with the headache she'd complained of earlier. As for Sir Humphrey, Lord Randolph's eccentric old uncle who made his home with the Partons, he would pronounce the beast "a demmed nuisance."

Making her dilemma worse, the kitten was now purring in her arms in the most contented way. Emma sighed and murmured, "What shall I do with you?"

"Did you drop this, miss?"

Startled by the deep male voice behind her, she turned to face the immensely tall figure of a man wearing a many-caped great coat and fine Hessian boots, one hand extended with her glove grasped in long brown-gloved fingers.

"Why, yes." She flushed, taking the glove with her free hand and tucking it into the pocket of her coat. It had evidently dropped out as she was rescuing the kitten. She looked up at the man, whose face was partly hidden by a woolen scarf drawn across his chin. Dark hair and rather prominent brows shadowing brown eyes could be seen between the scarf and a curly-brimmed beaver.

"Thank you, sir. I must have lost it when I picked up the kitten."

His dark eyes moved to the small furry head, and a smile flicked across his face. "Is he yours? It is a he, I presume?"

Emma felt herself blushing furiously. She was behaving in a way that was totally unlike herself. She had never been a goosish female. "No—I mean, he isn't mine. As to whether it is a he or a she, I cannot say." She managed to ignore the warmth flaming in her cheeks and meet his dark eyes. "I'm afraid it's a hungry stray. I can feel sharp little bones through its fur."

What she could see of his face, she decided, was very strong with a straight nose and firm mouth. His skin had the clear, deep glow provided by good food and being often out of doors. His hair, she saw now, was raven black and curled slightly across his forehead. His eyes were a deep shade of brown made more striking by the darkness of his eyelashes which were long and thick.

"Th-thank you again for returning my glove," said Emma, finding that she was slightly overawed, another reaction that was rather foreign to her.

He lifted a finger to stroke the kitten's nose, while the tiny creature purred even more vigorously. "Where did you find this draggle-tailed fellow?"

"He came in under the tent," Emma told him, "just at my feet. Do you like cats? Most men prefer dogs."

"Cats are clever beasts. Look how this one managed to land at the feet of the most kindhearted person in the booth." Unaccustomed as she had become in the past eight months to receiving compliments, Emma was momentarily at a loss for a suitable reply. She had the odd feeling that she was alone with this imposing man, in spite of the crowds of people on all sides. It occurred to her suddenly to recall her aunt's repeated dire warnings about men whose wont it was to accost young women who were unwise enough to go about unchaperoned. Such men had a way with sweet words, said Aunt Claire, by which they squeezed their way past a lady's defenses.

She said at last with a tart edge to the words, "You can not know if I am kindhearted or not."

"I heard you commiserating with the kitten before I spoke to you and judged from that." After a slight pause he added, "Will you take him home with you?"

"That would not do. I am staying with my aunt, who dislikes cats intensely. They make her sneeze."

The dark eyes were amused. "What is your aunt's name? It may be that I am acquainted with her."

Emma looked into his eyes and cast about for an appropriate reply that would tell nothing without being rude. She had a brief mental picture of this man approaching her aunt at the next ton party and saying offhandedly that he had run into her niece in a bookstall at the Frost Fair. That would not do at all.

He seemed to sense her dilemma. "Perhaps you will tell

me your name then." There was curiosity under the amusement.

Another silence, during which Emma could hear her heart thumping and hoped he could not hear it, too. "Sophia." She heard herself supplying her second name, so that it was not really a lie.

Then he asked abruptly, "Do you live in London all year, or are you up for the season?"

"I—I do not know how long I shall be in London. For the time being I am with relatives in their town house. Which is why I cannot take the kitten with me." She glanced about with a distracted look. "Oh, I do hate to abandon the little thing." There was unconscious pleading in the blue-green eyes and she added darkly, "He will surely perish."

"Surely," agreed the stranger with a muscle twitching at one corner of his mouth. "It may be that I can find a home for him."

Emma's blue-green eyes flew to his face and she saw that he was serious. "Oh, sir, would you? How very kind of you!" She lifted the kitten from the folds of her coat and he took it, pressing it against his cloak.

"I can promise he will be fed and cared for."

"How shall I thank you?"

"Help me choose a book for my sister. I collect you are a book lover, else you would not be in this particular booth."

"Yes." Emma moved to pick up a novel she had noticed earlier. "Has she read Miss Austen's *Pride and Prejudice?*"

He took the volume from her outstretched hand. "I do not think she has. Do you recommend it?"

"Oh, yes! Miss Austen's Elizabeth is the best heroine

the English have been given since Shakespeare—and Darcy is quite the most dashing hero. I am sure your sister will admire him."

The brown eyes narrowed, studying her. "It seems you have fallen in love with the mysterious Darcy. I suggest you exercise more discretion where mysterious gentlemen of flesh and blood are concerned. They are not always as admirable as the fictional ones."

Emma did not like the note of condescending amusement. "I am sure you would know more about that than I. But do not think I am easily duped. I assure you, sir, I am not."

"Nor did I mean to imply that you are a shatterbrain, Sophia." Such equivocation, spoken as it was in a humorous tone, did nothing to enlighten Emma as to his true impression of her. Not that it mattered. She would not be likely to be in the company of this gentleman again.

"I—I must go now, sir."

"Back to the nameless aunt who sneezes at cats?" He smiled directly into her eyes.

Emma could not but smile, also, at the engaging twinkle she saw in the brown depths. He stepped back courteously as she left the bookstall to stand nearby and wait for Lottie. Once she glanced over her shoulder and saw him, the kitten clutched in one hand, and the other hand leafing through the novel she had recommended for his sister. The rotund proprietor had appeared at his side and was speaking in an ingratiating tone, as if the man were a person of some importance.

Then she saw her cousin at a booth across the frozen thoroughfare and hurried to her side. "Come along, Lottie. Benjy will be waiting."

"Fudge!" The exclamation was filled with Lottie's

reluctance to leave the fair and her chafing at the punctilios that regulated the behavior of young women of good family; but she did not resist when Emma took her arm and urged her back toward the solicitors' offices where their carriage was waiting.

When they were tucked inside with a laprobe covering their legs, Charlotte wailed, "We were too rushed by half. Somehow we must contrive to return to the Frost Fair."

Emma was remembering a handsome face and twinkling brown eyes. "Yes," she mused, only half hearing Lottie's words.

Lottie brightened. "Do you mean to say that you will help me think of a way for us to pay a second visit?"

Emma came out of her reverie abruptly. "No, I didn't mean to say that at all," she said firmly. After all, another chance meeting with the tall stranger would be extremely unlikely. "We shall be more fortunate than we deserve if Aunt Claire does not learn of this afternoon's peccadillo. I have no wish to add another to the list."

"Lud!" Lottie muttered with a quelling glance. "You are too inclined to look for trouble, Emma."

That may be, thought Emma wryly. A penniless young woman was frighteningly vulnerable to the vagaries of fate. She was like the stray kitten, she thought, dependent upon the benevolence of more fortunate beings than herself.

## *CHAPTER TWO*

Sir James North's look-in at White's was a sudden decision, uncharacteristic of the marquis, who was not a gentleman who ordinarily acted on impulse. It was, he reflected as he glanced at the kitten curled on his knee, the second impulsive thing he had done that day, and this gave him brief pause. Nevertheless, he tucked the bedraggled gray kitten, which a cursory inspection had revealed to be a female, into a fold of the laprobe, instructed his driver to wait, and entered the gentlemen's club where he was greeted enthusiastically by two of his acquaintances.

"I say, James," Lord Robert Ryerson exclaimed, "you were missed at the Massingales' rout last evening."

"I was otherwise engaged," Lord North replied, not feeling called upon to attempt an explanation of his preference for a good book to an evening spent evading the wily traps laid by matchmaking mamas. A preference which his own mother had been heard to remark upon despairingly as a habit that would one day cause her to go *quite* distracted. "When a man has reached James's age," Lady North had been heard to add on one occasion, "it is of no use to press matrimony upon him, for it will not do. He will not marry until he is ready, and no strategem will be anything to the purpose." Sir James only wished she would not vacillate from that opinion upon occasion and press him concerning his duty as the only son.

"Nor can I feel," Sir James said now with asperity, "that the gathering was any less gala because of my absence."

Lord Ryerson shrugged his elaborately padded shoulders and flipped the long tail of his coat with a careless hand. "The ladies were disappointed, I believe. As for me, I managed to go on deuced well without you," said his lordship with a good-natured quirk of one light-colored eyebrow.

Sir Charles Emberland, a tall gentleman with hair of a bright copper color, whose manner and style of dress proclaimed him to be a Tulip of the first order, remarked lazily that Lord Ryerson's satisfied air was due to his having contrived to claim the supper dance with Miss Parton the previous evening.

"Miss Charlotte Parton," Lord Ryerson pronounced in a reverent tone. "James, have you ever seen such a dashed enchanting creature?"

Lord North's expression was one of attempting to call to mind more clearly a very vague memory. "Do you refer to that dark-haired daughter of Viscount Parton, the one who threw you over last season?"

"She did no such thing!" Lord Ryerson protested. "I don't deny I came dashed close to offering for her last season. Knew her mama didn't care for me, though."

"Not to dress it up in clean linen," Sir Charles drawled, "Lady Parton has an eye out for a great fortune, my man. If I were you I should set my sights elsewhere. Miss Parton's mama will never give you the nod."

"I can but try," said Ryerson hopefully. "Devil of it is, I can't blame Lottie's mama excessively." He looked morose for a moment, then perked up. "I fancy Lottie has *some* tender feeling for me. She did go into supper with me last evening and she was extremely pleasant about it, too."

"What is that to the purpose?" inquired Emberland languidly. "I daresay Miss Parton is pleasant to her father's groom, but she don't mean to marry him. Her hand will not be exchanged for a paltry sum. That, old friend, is the bald-faced truth of the matter where your Lottie is concerned."

"Devil take it!" Sir Robert retorted. "I am not a poor man."

"But not nearly as wealthy as some other gentlemen I could name," said Sir Charles, eyeing Lord North significantly.

That gentleman regarded Ryerson's exaggeratedly stylish clothes and observed, "I daresay you would find yourself in better straits, Robert, if you were not so intent upon being a frippery dandy."

"Hell's teeth, James! One must keep up appearances."

"Precisely my point. The truly wealthy do not worry about appearances. Take that great-uncle of your fair Lottie's. I'm told his dress is quite unstylish and, by all accounts, he's as rich as the king—if not as mad."

"Sir Humphrey Laird?" Lord Ryerson snorted. "A dashed loose screw, if you ask me!"

Emberland coughed. "One hopes it doesn't run in the family."

Ryerson rounded on his friend. "If you are suggesting that Lottie is a bit touched in the upper works, I must tell you you're wide of the mark. For that matter, how many of us could stand a close scrutiny of *every* branch in our family trees?" Turning back to address Sir James, he added, "And Lottie *likes* the way I dress. She gave me permission to call on her tomorrow."

"I wonder," murmured Sir Charles carelessly, "how many other gentlemen will be in attendance at the Parton house when you arrive?"

"Dash it all, Charles—" sputtered the affronted Lord Ryerson.

"Didn't mean to get your blood up, old fellow," Emberland stated. "It queers me, James, how when a man falls head over ears he loses his sense of humor. Have you noticed that?"

"I am not," retorted Sir James in quelling tones, "an authority on romance."

Emberland eyed him quizzically. "I must confess that I half believe that tale they tell of you."

"I never take any notice of gossip, Charles, nor should you."

"It's true, wouldn't you say, Robert?" Emberland went on as if Sir James had not spoken. "There was an unfortunate affair in his youth that quite dashed his faith in all females."

Sir James looked indignant. "I do not care to have my name bandied about in connection with such nonsense. Now, if the two of you can leave off bamming for a few moments, I should like to ask you a question. By chance, have you met a young lady this season named Sophia?"

Lord Emberland raised his ornate quizzing glass to observe more closely his friend's expression. Youthful affair or not, Sir James had never been known, in all of his two and thirty years, to fall into raptures over a female, however engaging she might be. What the unknown Sophia had done to arouse his interest Lord Emberland could not well imagine.

Sir Robert's brows rose. "Lord Rawleigh's niece is called Sophia, I believe. By all that's wonderful, James! Have you eluded parson's mousetrap all these years only to develop a *tendre* for that jumped-up miss? Her papa is impoverished, you know, and it's rumored her brother is a free trader. Besides, the lady is very nearly at her last prayers. Lady Rawleigh has undertaken to introduce her to society, although her parentage will not be easily overcome, I fear. If you should ask for my opinion, I would advise you to look elsewhere, for you will have that greedy old fool of a father of hers about your neck for the—"

"Stop this curst prattling, Robert," Sir James intervened. "I am not referring to that Sophia."

"My dear James," Sir Charles said with a bored expression, "the only other Sophia I have heard of among the quality is Lord Kern's eldest, but she is still in the schoolroom. You cannot mean her!"

"No, I do not," stated Sir James impatiently. "The Sophia I refer to is the possessor of red-gold curls and eyes of an unusual blue-green color."

"I know of no such young woman," Lord Emberland said, frowning, "and you know I have not missed any of the early-season festivities."

"I believe she is a great book lover," provided Sir James as an afterthought.

"A bluestocking," observed Sir Robert with distaste. "I would not have believed it, although they do say there's no fool like an old fool."

"I've half a notion to plant you a facer for that remark, Robert," Sir James muttered. His friend, being just twenty-six, evidently considered anyone over thirty to be doddering.

Lord Emberland looked shrewdly from Sir Robert to Sir James with an unsettled expression. "You might tear his coat, James!"

Apparently Ryerson had the same concern, for he crossed his arms over his chest as if to protect the fine fabric. Emberland continued, "I am convinced the lady is not of the quality, else one of us would know of her. You cannot mean, James, to make a cake of yourself over a female of the lower classes, and a bluestocking into the bargain. Only conceive how it must look!"

"You are running ahead a great deal too fast, both of you," Sir James retorted. Lord Emberland was prepared to say more, having decided that Lord North did not mean to deliver a right, after all, but, concluding that the expression in his lordship's eyes was still somewhat wrathful, made up his mind to leave further exhortation to a later time.

"I daresay," Lord Ryerson remarked reflectively, "you cannot have been properly introduced to the lady in question. Is she an actress? You must own that you have taken an interest in such females before now." He hurried on as Sir James's scowl deepened. "Whoever she is, the chit seems to have made a deuced strong impression on you. Never thought to see the day you'd fly into alt over the color of a chit's eyes! I don't suppose you'd care to say where you came upon this vision?"

Sir James's exasperation was complete. He said grimly, "I perceive I shall discover nothing here. Mother is expecting me for dinner. Good day, gentlemen."

As he turned on his heel, Sir Robert was heard to say, "Damme, Charles, have you ever known James to behave in such a smoky fashion?"

Strolling from the room, Sir James made a great effort to possess his soul in patience. Not an easy accomplishment, for he could not be said to be, by nature, a patient man. The chit's tale of visiting an aunt could have been a fabrication, he reflected rather darkly. Though why she should have taken the pains to embroider a story for a stranger was beyond his understanding. However, he had discovered that much of female logic was anything but logical.

She could not be a member of a family of quality, for she had been quite alone—without chaperon or abigail. She might be a maid in one of the fine London houses, although her speech was not that of a servant. If she were a maid, she had surely not been reared for such a lowly position in life. No, if she were any kind of servant, she was more likely a governess.

Sir James climbed into his curricle, taking care not to disturb the sleeping kitten, and told himself that he could only wait upon events. He intended to return to the Frost Fair, in any case, and perhaps there would be another chance meeting with the mysterious Sophia. It occurred to him that it was the mystery that surrounded the girl that intrigued him—forgetting for a moment the red-gold curls and blue-green eyes, for he had, in his career, known rather well several more beautiful women. However, the life of an English gentleman was often devilish dull to a man of less than frivolous interests. Tracking down the elusive Sophia promised to be more engrossing than his ordinary daily routine.

Sir James drove immediately to his house in one of the most fashionable streets in London, where he found his mother, Lady North, engaged in a pleasant coze with his sister, Lady Haverly, in the gold salon. When he entered this apartment he found the two ladies seated facing each other in handsome brocade armchairs, a fire flickering warmly between them behind the screen in the open grate.

Lady Sarah Haverly, two years Sir James's junior, married now for eleven years, and the mother of two daughters, aged ten and eight, was still a dark-haired beauty with somewhat slanting gray eyes who had broken a number of hearts during her first London season and had ended it triumphantly by becoming engaged to the eminently eligible Lord Haverly, whom she had known all her life since his country estate adjoined her family's.

Lady North, a still-handsome dowager of fifty-eight, wore a voguish russet gown generously decorated with ribbons and lace. She regarded her son, in his exquisitely cut blue coat worn with a paler blue waistcoat and a snowy cravat, and arranged her face in an expression of stern, though not unfond, reprimand.

In her richly regal voice she remarked, "So what has delayed you this time, James? I collect you promised to come in by five." She turned to her daughter, whose gray eyes were dancing, although her pretty face was properly grave. "You are blessed in having no sons, Sarah. They care nothing for society and prefer to spend their time at White's or at Newmarket when they come up to London at all. I dare say we shall learn that James is returning soon to Havenwood. He fancies himself a scholar or a farmer, though I am hard pressed to discern which calling he most favors."

Sir James exchanged a greeting with his sister and handed her a package. "A small token for your upcoming birthday, Sarah."

While Lady Haverly tore into the wrappings like an eager child, he bent to kiss his mother's remarkably unlined cheek. "You must put your mind at rest on one score, Mother. I have no immediate plans to return to the country." Favoring her with one of the charming smiles that he sometimes used to advantage, he strolled to the fire and held his hands out to warm them.

"Oh, James!" Lady Haverly exclaimed delightedly.

"Miss Austen's novel. I have so wanted to get my hands on this!"

Sir James had turned from the fire and was reaching inside his coat. When his hand returned to view, it held a small gray kitten. Both ladies were wide-eyed and momentarily speechless.

Recovering, Lady North demanded, "What is that, James? A more wretched and ramshackle creature I have never clapped eyes on!"

"A pet for my nieces," Sir James replied, smiling with suspicious warmth at his sister. "I daresay she will look just the thing after a few good meals. You must tell them, Sarah, that her name is Sophia."

"You have not answered my question, James," said Lady North roundly. "If that parcel of matted fur is not on the verge of expiring, I miss my guess. How came you by the animal?" She laughed shortly. "And Sophia! Why, I never heard such a missish name for a cat!"

"Pooh!" said Lady Haverly, rising from her chair to take the purring kitten into her arms, Miss Austen's novel quite forgotten. "The poor thing is underfed, but perky enough. Come with me, puss, and I'll soon have some warm milk inside you." She left the salon, still talking to the kitten, and Sir James could not hide a satisfied expression. He knew well his sister's weakness for homeless animals.

Lady North seemed quite unmoved by her daughter's sympathetic utterances. "James—" she began.

"Indeed, Mother, I was about to answer your question. I found the kitten at the Frost Fair. She had wandered into the bookstall in search of food."

Lady North's dark eyes narrowed suspiciously. "And how came you to know the beast's name?"

"I chose the name, Mama," said Sir James, reverting to the familiar title he had used in childhood, a tactic that usually put his mother into a docile mood.

Lady North stared at him, not the least mollified. "Lord, you are a slippery fellow," she remarked brusquely. "But we shall have done with this, for I know when I am defeated. Only do not take me for a fool, James. There is more to this pretty tale than you have chosen to relate." She eyed her son thoughtfully. "If you were not so utterly immune to feminine charms, I would believe there's a woman in this somewhere."

Sir James shrugged, grateful that, if his mother knew of the few, brief alliances he had had with women, she was discreet enough not to mention it. "Fortunately, Mama, you know I do not pass my days in dalliances. Now, if you will excuse me, ma'am, I shall change for dinner."

He strolled from the salon as his sister returned. "Mrs. Holly is quite taken with Sophia, James. She has given her warm milk, and when I left the kitchen, she was searching for a basket in which the kitten might be transported to my house."

"You have saved Sophia's life, Sister," Sir James said, patting Lady Haverly's arm fondly. "I am grateful. Give my love to my nieces."

Grimly, Lady North surveyed the empty doorway through which her son had disappeared. "Coming it much too strong, my dear fellow," she said meaningfully. "Wandered into the bookstall, indeed! You cannot suppose I believe that's the whole of the story—not with London full of homeless beasts."

"Yes, it has occurred to me," Lady Haverly mused, "that James was never overly fond of cats."

"Just so," returned Lady North pungently.

* * *

Later that evening, in the house in Bedford Square, Lord and Lady Parton were discussing their niece's direful circumstances, or rather Lady Claire was delivering a monologue on the subject while Lord Parton's uncle muttered occasionally from his chair and her indolent husband sipped his port and murmured a few disinterested responses from the chair that faced Sir Humphrey's. Neither of the gentlemen's remarks made much impression on Lady Parton in her agitated state.

"I have dragged myself from my sickbed, Randolph," wailed that plump, beribboned lady as, with one hand pressed against her forehead, she paced about the study. "Indeed, my poor nerves were in such a state after Charlotte came to me with the solicitors' report that I could not lie still another instant!"

Lord Parton, who had been listeningly silently to his wife's plaints for some minutes, stirred his rotund figure in the soft armchair and attempted to reason with the lady. "Poppycock! It's not as if we expected that brother-in-law of yours to have taken thought for the future, m'dear. A more improvident fellow I have never met! I wish you will not get into a pucker over this."

"Thought he was in trade," observed Sir Humphrey, helping himself to a sweet from the dish at his elbow. "Never knew anyone in trade who was improvident. Shrewd moneygrubbers, the lot of them."

"I am *not* in a pucker!" Lady Parton corrected her husband sharply while, from long habit, ignoring Sir Humphrey altogether. "I am concerned. Dear knows what I am to do with the girl now. If that merchant my sister married had not been all about in his head, he would have left his only child comfortably circumstanced, and I *might* have found a respectable husband for her in spite of her other faults."

"This port," said Sir Humphrey earnestly, "is better than that last lot, Randolph." He sipped appreciatively, then set his glass beside the sweets dish.

Lord Parton, looking at his wife's flushed face, pondered with some interest the realization that Lady Parton seemed to have quite forgotten that her own father had been in trade. That fact was rarely mentioned in her presence, for being reminded of it made her out of reason cross. He was wise enough not to put his thoughts into words, however, but merely remarked, "Aside from the distressful circumstance that Emma has no fortune, I cannot think what faults you refer to. She is pretty enough, certainly, and of a most equable nature. Sits a horse astoundingly well for a city girl. Deuced fine whist player, too."

"Used to play whist at the Lion's Paw till I learned every Captain Sharp in town hangs out there," said Sir Humphrey. "Avoid the place, Randolph, if you want my advice."

"Really, Randolph! You are as bad as Jonathan," said Lady Parton, referring to her seventeen-year-old son who was, at the present moment, in the billiard room teaching his cousin the game. "Truly, I can't think what Georgina was about allowing that husband of hers to fill Emma's head with history and other such masculine subjects with not a thought given, as far as I can gather, to any feminine accomplishments whatsoever. She tells me she has never held a watercolor brush or touched a pianoforte! I simply cannot credit it. What *was* Georgina thinking of?"

"I daresay, m'dear," murmured Lord Parton lazily,

"that your sister's thoughts were all of clothes and such like. She *was* a bit want-witted, you must own."

"Comes of marrying a merchant," pronounced Sir Humphrey, selecting another sweet.

"Do you know," Lady Parton went on, quite as if Sir Humphrey and her husband had not spoken at all, "Emma told me earlier that she wished to seek a position as a governess when she is out of black gloves. A governess, indeed! What respectable family would employ an instructor for their daughters who cannot even play the pianoforte? I pointed out to Emma her many lacks in that connection, thinking to give her a set-down, but the silly girl merely replied that she must needs spend the next few months learning whatever accomplishments will be required for such a situation. She said she would ask Charlotte to teach her."

"Lottie, eh?" Lord Parton laughed shortly. "If Emma can get Lottie to sit still long enough to learn anything from her, that will be the greatest accomplishment of all! But the girl's idea has some merit. Can you not find a teacher for her? Surely in a few weeks time she can learn enough of that foolishness to pass herself off as a governess, if that is her desire."

"Sounds a demmed silly notion to me," Sir Humphrey said. "Why would anyone set out to be a governess? Must have mistook her."

Lady Parton stared at her husband, pressing plump fingers against a throbbing vein in her temple. "Sometimes, Randolph, you quite amaze me! What will our friends think if we allow our niece to go into service? No, we must find a suitable husband for her. A young curate, perhaps—or someone in trade."

"Demmed money grubbers," intoned Sir Humphrey.

"Dear knows," Lady Parton went on, "how I shall find such a person. I can't pretend I don't find the prospect quite odious. Well, I shall have to cudgel my brains as to how it can be accomplished."

"I am sure this is all a hum," said Lord Parton, yawning and stirring from his chair to refill his uncle's glass as well as his own. "I have complete faith in your ability to see Emma properly set up. I am sure things will turn out well if we will wait upon events." He picked up the *Times* and began to peruse the front page.

"Had a tickle in my throat all day," said Sir Humphrey to anyone who would listen. "I believe I am going to have a demmed bad cold."

Seeing that any further conversation of hers would fall upon deaf ears, Lady Parton took herself off to her bedchamber where her abigail soaked a handkerchief in cologne and applied it to her mistress's throbbing forehead.

"Devilish glad I never married," remarked Sir Humphrey, masticating a sweet ruminatively. Being "as rich as the king" and having named Lord Parton his sole heir, that gentleman could say anything he pleased in his nephew's house and often did. "Demmed females always in a twit about something."

Sir Randolph merely grunted at this and did not even look up from his paper.

In the billiard room Jonathan was becoming impatient with his cousin's obvious disinterest in learning the game. "I say, Emma," he declared, setting aside his billiard cue, "you'll never be a match for me if you let your thoughts keep wandering off."

Emma sighed and strolled to a window to stare out into

the night. "I'm sorry, Johnny. I am a bit distracted tonight, aren't I?"

"Not like you a'tall," Jonathan agreed. "Still thinking about going out to be a governess? I should think that would be the *last* thing you'd care for. Devilish boring, if you ask me."

"I can't say I'm happy about the prospect," Emma admitted, "but I must do something."

"I shan't allow you to do it then," Jonathan announced stoutly. "I shall speak to Papa about it. I'm sure we can discover a better plan."

Emma turned to smile at her cousin, a skinny, gangling young man with auburn hair and hazel eyes. "I shouldn't think your papa will care to hear anything from you at the moment, after you were sent down from Oxford in disgrace."

Jonathan gave her a rakish grin. "I am sure that will all blow over. It was nothing but a prank. I expect it will be forgotten in a few days and I shall be allowed to go back."

"A goat in the master's office!" Emma could not suppress a bubbling laugh. "Really, Johnny, that was too bad of you."

"I didn't intend to leave the odorous creature overnight, you know," Jonathan confided sheepishly. "Only one of the fellows laid a wager on it that I *would* not. Well, you can see why I had to do it."

"Oh, quite," returned Emma, dimpling.

Jonathan sighed and threw himself into a chair. "Well, I can't expect a girl to understand about a gentleman's honor."

"I fail to see," Emma replied, tongue in cheek, "what is so honorable about being sent down from Oxford."

The young man's freckled face was pulled down into a

grimace. "That's what Papa said." He shrugged. "Oh, well, I shall stay out of his way for a few days, and he will get over his pique, I imagine." He glanced about the room with dissatisfaction. "Dashed boring around here, I must say. I almost wish I was back at school." He regarded Emma with an accusing look. "I thought I could depend on you to be a proper companion while I'm here."

Emma raked slender fingers through her short red-gold curls. "I'm sorry to disappoint you, Johnny, but I do have serious problems to consider."

"Because of your papa's taking off and you without a feather? I shouldn't worry overmuch about that," said Jonathan with youthful insouciance. "You look all the crack to me, and you're a dashed good sport, too. Not all missish blushes like most girls. I expect some man will marry you."

"Do you, indeed?" responded Emma wryly. "You can't imagine what a relief it is to hear you say that!"

"I'd marry you myself if I was old enough."

"Aunt Claire would take to her bed for a month if she heard you say that," Emma said, laughing.

"I expect so," agreed Jonathan affably. "Mama is already in a great taking over your news. I saw her going into Papa's study a while ago to harass him about it. Uncle Humphrey was there, too. What do you collect they are saying?"

"That they have been left with a niece who is like to be an ape-leader, I don't doubt," said Emma dryly.

"Well, it's good luck for me."

"Why?"

"As long as they are preoccupied with you, they won't be giving me a rake-down for being sent down."

How Emma would have replied to that, Jonathan was

not to know, for their conversation was interrupted on the instant by the housekeeper, Mrs. Tabbens, who brought the information that Lady Parton was asking for Emma to come and read to her in the faint hope that such an activity would ease, however slightly, that lady's vexing headache.

# CHAPTER THREE

Lady Parton's bedchamber was overwarm and heavy with the rose scent she used in too liberal amounts. She reclined on a satin chaise, a dampened handkerchief spread across her brow.

Emma entered the chamber briskly. "Good evening, Aunt Claire. Are you feeling better?"

"No," responded that lady in a weak voice. "I have the headache, Emma, and I've sneezed twice. I very much fear I am in for a serious setback."

Emma walked to a window, opening it a crack. "It's too stuffy in here. It's enough to give anyone the headache. Where is Genevieve?"

"I sent her away," said Lady Parton with a weak fluttering of plump fingers. "I grew weary of her unsympathetic attitude. 'Get up and work on your embroidery, my lady. Go for a stroll. Get your mind off your aches and pains, my lady.' I should like to know how I can do that when my head is pounding so wretchedly. I very much fear, Emma, that my abigail is totally devoid of compassion. If she had her way, I would be driven from my sickbed and forced to march barefoot through the snow."

"Hardhearted creature," said Emma, suppressing a smile and assuming her role as sympathetic companion, a role she had become well used to during the past eight months. In the beginning she had tried talking her aunt out of her ailments, as the abigail persisted in doing, but it soon became clear to her that Lady Parton's vagaries were best handled by accepting them with equanimity.

Lady Parton gestured weakly toward a tray on her dressing table. "I could hardly touch my dinner. Everything just seemed to stick in my throat, as if there were some sort of barrier."

Emma, taking in at a glance the scant remains of her aunt's dinner, shook her head and said, "Poor Aunt, you must be feeling wretched indeed! Only a plate of beef and vegetables and a small dish of pudding. Why, you have left half a loaf of bread."

Lady Parton, so absorbed in cataloging her ailments, failed to detect any humor in Emma's words, taking note merely of the soothing tone. She touched the base of her throat gingerly. "What do you suppose is wrong in here, Emma? One hears such horrible stories of growths and lumps."

"I am sure it is only a little swelling. You have often told me that even the slightest cold makes your throat puffy."

"Yes, that's true," conceded Lady Parton wanly. "Uncle Humphrey said he felt he was coming down with a cold, and I suppose he has given it to me. Naturally I would be the one to succumb, since my constitution is so much frailer than anyone else's in the family."

Emma removed the handkerchief from her aunt's brow, sprinkled more lavender water on it from the decanter on the dressing table, and smoothed it gently in place again. "There now, does that help?"

"You are very kind, Emma dear, but I can't feel the lavender water is helping at all. This dreadful news from your father's solicitors has made the headache worse, too. It has quite knocked the pins from under me, I can tell you. And now we are to have Johnny in the house, dashing about and falling into things. One wonders if all boys make as much noise as Johnny does. It isn't so bad when we're in the country where he can be outside riding and the like. Oh, but you mustn't think I am not fond of the boy."

"Of course, I don't think that," said Emma sympathetically. "It is quite evident that you have more than your share of distressful situations to contend with, Aunt. I wonder how you manage to bear up as well as you do."

Such misplaced consolation was soothing balm to Lady Parton, as Emma well knew, and upon occasion it even seemed to speed her toward recovery, as if having found someone who believed she was ill, she could then allow herself to get better. In spite of the impatience she often felt with her aunt's constant complaining, Emma had come to believe that the woman could actually make herself feel ill by thinking that she was. And the more others in the household ignored her complaints, the worse her state became. Getting Lady Parton's mind off herself sometimes helped, too, but one had to do it subtly and indirectly so that she didn't suspect what one was about.

"Perhaps if you would close your eyes now, I can read to you from that novel we began last week."

"Oh, I don't know whether I shall be able to concentrate on the story," whined Lady Parton. "I'll be very brave and try, but I can't promise that I will manage to follow half of what you are saying. Do you suppose I'm to have a fever of the brain?"

"I am sure it will not come to that," Emma assured her as she opened the book. "Now I shall read slowly and quietly."

Sighing heavily, Lady Parton closed her eyes and Emma began to read. She had finished almost an entire page before her aunt interrupted to inform her, in quite graphic detail, of the intensity and location of the sharp pain she had just felt in her chest. At the end of the second page, a low back pain as sharp as a rapier's thrust had to be described. But as Emma read on, the complaints became less frequent, and eventually Emma realized that her aunt had fallen asleep. With vast relief she laid the book aside and tiptoed from the room.

When she reached Lottie's bedchamber, the door was open. Lottie was standing in front of a wall glass, examining her reflection gravely. "Come and tell me what you think of this necklace," she called to Emma. "Will it be attractive with my pink silk gown? Or do you think it too elaborate for afternoon wear?"

Emma perched on the side of her cousin's satin-covered bed. "Not too elaborate, I think, if you will leave off all other jewelry. Besides, you are able to carry off rather outré fashions better than many girls your age. I think it is a certain self-confidence you have."

"Why, thank you, Emma. Then I shall wear the necklace when Lord Ryerson comes to call tomorrow. I hope Mother's headache keeps her in bed all afternoon—not that I would wish her any harm, you understand."

"Naturally," responded Emma dryly.

"It's only that for some unfathomable reason Mama has taken Sir Robert in dislike."

"An opinion with which you are not in agreement, it seems."

"Oh, I was not excessively taken with him last season, but he appears to have changed. His taste in clothes is wonderful! I mean he's not all staid and stuffy like so many of the gentlemen of the ton, and yet he doesn't wear monstrous cravats and too many ribbons on his pantaloons, as his friend Lord Emberland does. He's just dashing enough to be interesting."

Emma's eyebrows rose. "I see!"

Lottie frowned suddenly. "You are not to repeat a word of this conversation to Mama."

"No power on earth shall wring a syllable from me," Emma assured her.

"Then perhaps I shall tell you more about Lord Ryerson," said Lottie handsomely.

"Pray, do!" said Emma. "I am finding this deeply intriguing."

Lottie plopped down across her bed beside Emma, supporting her head with her hand, and said with an air of imparting a confidence, "Just last week he rode his horse through the most notorious gaming-hell in London—from front door to back—without knocking over a single piece of furniture or grazing any of the gentlemen who were there. His friends had wagered he couldn't do it without unsettling *something.* Isn't that the most amusing thing you ever heard?"

"Lord Ryerson does indeed sound like an amusing gentleman," said Emma, straight-faced.

"And—" Lottie glanced quickly toward the door, then leaned closer to her cousin. "He told me that once he actually rode out with a highwayman. He wore a mask and carried a pistol and helped take the jewelry from the occupants of a chaise and everything. And he wasn't one tiny part afraid, either." She lay back across the bed with a sigh and contemplated the intricately carved ceiling. "It was excessively romantic."

"I suppose it was," ventured Emma, "as long as he did not land in the lockup."

"Oh, but in that case, I am sure he would have managed to escape," Lottie assured her.

"Of course! Why didn't I think of that?"

"I would have helped him escape," mused Lottie. "I think I should like to help somebody escape from the lockup. I could have gone to visit him wearing a hooded cloak that covered me to the ground. I should be able to hide food and pistols and whatever might be needed beneath it. And, of course, if they caught me—but I don't believe they would—Papa would get me out. So you see, there would really be no danger in such an undertaking. And it *would* be such a romantic adventure."

"Hot, too," pointed out Emma. "I mean, if you should have the misfortune to find yourself pursuing such an undertaking in the summertime wearing that hooded cloak."

"Oh, Emma." Lottie sounded utterly exasperated. "Must you always be so sensible?"

"Forgive me," uttered Emma with a laugh. "I've no doubt if I stay around you long enough, I'll overcome that lamentable trait in some part."

"Papa might be angry, though," Lottie continued, drifting back into her fantasy. "Papa is not at all romantic. Now that I think about it, I believe I am the only person in my family who *is.*"

"That must be tiresome for you," sympathized Emma. "But perhaps there is hope for Johnny. That goat in the master's office shows some spark of imagination, don't you think?"

"Perhaps," murmured Lottie, sighing again. "Sometimes, Emma, I wish I were a man. The life of a lady of quality is quite boring a great deal of the time."

"That reminds me," said Emma, "of a favor I wanted to ask of you. Perhaps it would relieve the boredom a little. Do you think you could teach me to play the pianoforte?"

"Of course I could teach you. It is very simple, really.

But I must warn you, Emma, that it is not very amusing at all. One must start with scales and the like."

"I had expected that," said Emma, "but I am determined to learn."

Lottie turned her head to peer at her cousin intently. "Whatever for?"

"I have decided to become a governess, and for that I will need to play the pianoforte and learn a few other things that were sadly neglected in my upbringing."

"A governess!" Lottie sat up abruptly. "Why on earth should you desire to become a governess?" She shuddered at the thought. "I cannot think of anything more dull than that!"

"I shall have to support myself somehow," said Emma matter-of-factly.

"Fiddle," concluded Lottie. "If you would come to Almack's with me—I am convinced Mama could secure a voucher for you—and attend a few of the parties, I am sure we could find you a husband. You do not have to absent yourself from all festivities merely because you are in mourning. Besides, you've worn black for eight months now. I should think that would be enough for anyone. Let me ponder this. Who would be suitable for you? I don't suppose—no, fifty is too old, isn't it? Tell me, would you mind a slight limp?"

"It is excessively thoughtful of you to want to catch me a husband, but I assure you I cannot allow you to bother yourself."

"Oh, but it's no bother," said Lottie. "Actually, it might be rather amusing."

"Thank you *ever* so much, but no. Now, will you teach me to play the pianoforte? I should like to begin tomorrow, if possible."

"Well . . ." Lottie's eyes narrowed thoughtfully on her cousin's face. "We shall make a bargain. I will teach you to play the pianoforte if you will help me talk Mama into letting us go back to the Frost Fair."

"All right," said Emma, though doubtfully, "but what if she will not agree?"

"Oh, she will listen to you. I have complete faith in your ability to convince her. I do think we ought to wait until she is feeling somewhat better, though."

"I couldn't agree with you more." Emma got to her feet, smoothing the wrinkles from her black skirt as she did so. "I believe I'll go to my room and read for a while. Good night, Lottie."

"Night," murmured Lottie, fingering the necklace that she still wore clasped about her neck. Then, wandering across the room, she gazed with a melancholy expression out the window into the darkness.

In her own blue-and-white chamber Emma discovered that she was infected with some of Lottie's restlessness. Unable to concentrate on reading, she followed her cousin's example of going to the window to look out. Her chamber, being at the front of the house, overlooked the front garden and the street beyond. Although it was early yet, not a single pedestrian or carriage could be seen. The ice-paved surfaces were too precarious for anyone who had a warm house in which to take refuge to venture upon after dark.

She thought about the Frost Fair and wondered if people were still there at this late hour. Remembering the tall stranger who had taken the stray kitten, she hoped he had found a home for it as he had promised. She rather thought he was a man who kept his word, and so she tried not to worry about the kitten, who she told herself was surely snug and full by now.

Although she tried, she couldn't remember exactly what the kitten had looked like. Had he been brown or gray? On the other hand, she could recall the stranger's face quite distinctly—what she had seen of it. She found to her consternation that it would be quite easy to drift into a fantasy in which she and the dark-haired man were together, perhaps at a party. She shook her head bemusedly. How odd. Lottie, as she herself had said, was the romantic in the family, not Emma. She suspected her unusual state of mind could be credited to what had transpired during the day. Learning that she had no money had been a rude jolt to her sensibilities.

After several moments she went to the small desk that sat in the corner and took out her journal, ink, and a fresh pen. Seating herself, she began to write an account of the day's events, putting down all the details she could recall of what she had seen at the Frost Fair. Since it was a unique occurrence, perhaps her descendants—if she ever had any—might like to read about it in future.

When she had finished the entry, she took a clean sheet of paper from her stationery box and began composing a lighthearted verse, an activity that usually relieved whatever restlessness she might be feeling.

*Poor Lady P. has taken to her bed*
*A soothing kerchief atop her head.*

Pausing, Emma lifted her pen and, smiling, reflected for several long moments. Then she continued writing:

*After facing her tray with commendable zeal*

*And forcing down a five-course meal,*
*Convinced, though all of London cry nay,*
*She's at death's door for the third time today.*

Smiling again as she read over the flippant lines she had written, Emma scolded herself for having such uncharitable thoughts. Still, she did feel much better, having gotten them out of her system. And she wasn't harming anyone, for no eyes but hers ever saw her poems. They were like medicine to her spirit, much more effective than most remedies prescribed by physicians. And she had not inscribed the irreverent portrait of her aunt in her journal, so it could be destroyed.

Then, since the poem had served its purpose, she crumpled the paper into a ball and left it lying on the desk to be discarded the next day when she went belowstairs.

She slept later than usual the next morning, however, and when she did arise her mind was occupied with getting Lottie out of bed before noon, if possible, so that Emma's first lesson on the pianoforte could proceed prior to the arrival of afternoon callers. Consequently the crumpled poem remained on her desk, forgotten by its author.

Emma spoke first to Genevieve, Lady Parton's abigail, and learned that her aunt had spent a restful night and was, in fact, still asleep. She then went along the hall to Lottie's bedchamber and knocked. There was no response, but, undaunted, she entered anyway. As she had expected, Lottie was still sleeping, her tangled curls forming a dark frame for her pretty face and making an even sharper contrast with the snowy whiteness of the pillows.

Emma walked about the large chamber, opening the draperies so that the pale morning sunlight could find its way in. Lottie stirred and opened her eyes reluctantly.

"Joan, how many times—oh, it's you, Emma. Have you run mad? What are you doing opening the draperies at this hour of the night?"

"It's past ten o'clock, Cousin," Emma responded. "I asked Genevieve to instruct Joan to bring in your chocolate."

Lottie groaned. "But I don't want my chocolate. I want to sleep."

"You must become accustomed to getting up a little earlier, that is, if you really mean to keep your promise."

Lottie yawned and frowned disgruntledly. "What promise?"

"The one you made last night to teach me to play the pianoforte."

"Oh, of course I mean to keep it," said Lottie, "but I don't intend to drag myself belowstairs and face the odious instrument before noon!"

"You know very well," said Emma reasonably, "that if we don't do it before noon, we shan't find the time to do it at all. There are always afternoon visitors, or else you are making calls with your mother. After that you spend hours getting ready for whatever festivity you are attending in the evening."

Lottie yawned again and, plumping the pillows at her back, sat partly upright, leaning against the pillows. "Lud, Emma! You are a single-minded creature when you take a notion into your head. But I must tell you that I have no intention of getting up at ten every morning for months."

"Of course not," soothed Emma. "Two mornings a week should be adequate. I will spend the other mornings practicing my scales."

"Oh, lovely!" groaned Lottie. "The music room is just below my bedchamber."

"I shall play very quietly," promised Emma.

There was a light tap at the door and Joan came in with a tray. "I've brought your chocolate, Miss Charlotte, and some nice toast and marmalade." She set the tray on the bedside table. "Is there anything else?"

Lottie merely scowled at the abigail and waved her away. Emma said, "That looks very nice, Joan. Thank you." As the abigail withdrew, Emma handed Lottie the chocolate.

Lottie gazed at her over the rim of the cup. "Well, I am convinced there will be no more sleep for me this morning but, please, after this couldn't we wait until eleven?"

Emma agreed and some time later the two young women were seated side by side at the pianoforte. Lottie went through the major scales several times, then moved aside to allow Emma to try them. When Emma had done so, Lottie said, "Thank goodness, you seem to learn quickly. You must practice the scales now, and I'll just sit here and listen."

Emma nodded absently, intent on fingering the pianoforte keys.

Abovestairs a restless Jonathan had already taken his breakfast in his chamber and, dressed for the day, was wandering about in search of something to do or someone to talk to. Thinking that his cousin might consent to trying her hand at another game of billiards and knowing that Emma usually arose before the other members of the household, he went to her door, and finding it open, he called her name and stepped inside.

There was no one in the room, and thinking to wait for a few minutes in case Emma returned, he paced restlessly about the chamber, his hands clasped loosely behind him. The room, like all the others in the house, was clean and neat, except for the slightly rumpled bed which had not yet been attended to by the abovestairs housemaid. There was, in addition, he noticed now, a crumpled piece of paper on the desk.

Jonathan, more bored than curious, picked up the paper and smoothed it out. As he read what was written there, his freckled face broke into a delighted grin and a loud guffaw escaped him. Emma had caught his mother to a T. Still smiling to himself, he was thoughtful for several moments. Then he folded the paper carefully and tucked it into the pocket of his coat before leaving the room.

In the music room Emma had just executed all the major scales without a mistake. Lottie, who was chafing to be about more interesting pursuits, said, "Perfect, dear Emma. That should be enough for today, don't you think? Now, let us lay our plans as to how to approach Mama at luncheon about going to the Frost Fair. If she takes the meal with the family, I mean."

"If we include Jonathan in the outing, perhaps she would be more willing to agree," Emma suggested.

"Oh, must we? I dislike being trailed around by my younger brother—as if I can't be let out without a watchdog."

Emma smiled. "I can't think of anyone who would be less of a watchdog than Johnny! He's the one in need of watching, I fear. Besides, you don't imagine we shall be able to get off without him if he learns where we are going, which he is certain to do if we bring it up at luncheon."

"Well, I don't mean to play nurse to Johnny. I want to wander about on my own, as we did yesterday."

"I'll try to keep Johnny with me," Emma said. "Although he may prefer going off on *his* own, you know. He would be quite insulted if he thought anyone felt he needed a chaperon!"

"I suppose," mused Lottie, "taking Johnny would be better than not going at all." She pursed her lips thoughtfully. "But you must be the one to speak first at luncheon. I think we shall fare better if Mama thinks it's your idea."

"I don't look forward to this," Emma told her cousin, "but I must keep my bargain, mustn't I?" For a fleeting moment the tall stranger's face appeared in her imagination, and she wondered if she would see him again should they return to the Frost Fair. She did not like the hopeful feeling that came over her at the thought. Evidently her shunning of society the past eight months was causing her to grasp at any straw if she could entertain such a curious interest in a chance-met stranger. Perhaps Lottie was right and she ought to start going out again, at least to an occasional small gathering. Of course, that might not be so easily accomplished, for she had received no invitations since they had come to London. She doubted if many of the Partons' acquaintances even knew there was a second young woman staying in the house in Bedford Square.

When she said that she wanted to practice her scales awhile longer, Lottie left her to go and change to an afternoon gown for luncheon and the expected arrival of Lord Ryerson.

Emma soon tired of scales and fell to staring into space, a vague expression on her face, until Jonathan found her and pressed her to agree to a game of billiards.

"Oh, all right," Emma finally agreed, "but I must tell you that knowing the game of billiards is not one of the accomplishments a proper governess is expected to have."

Johnny grinned wickedly. "I can't imagine you as a

proper governess, Emma. Besides, I thought you would have given up that silly notion by now. If you must support yourself, why don't you become an actress? I will tell all my friends to come and see you perform."

"That is too kind of you, Johnny," teased Emma. "Unfortunately, I don't think I should do very well on the stage."

"Why not? You're always the best when we play charades. And when you and Lottie put on that entertainment for our guests in the country, everyone said you were the funniest chimney sweep they'd ever seen. Lottie said you wrote the entire drama yourself. You have a talent for writing. Perhaps you should become a novelist. You could use a man's name and no one need ever know." His face had become more and more animated as he talked. "I say, I believe I like that idea best of all. You must become a writer."

"I fear you can't be very objective, Johnny," said Emma with a tinkling laugh. "I do appreciate your confidence in me, but it is one thing to write a drama for a few houseguests in the country and quite another to think of having one's writings printed for all the world to read. No, I must pursue something more within the realm of possibility."

Johnny gave her a doleful look as he led the way to the billiard room. "I'll teach you to play billiards at any rate. You're already fairly competent at card games. Perhaps you could become a gambler."

"Now there's an interesting idea," Emma told him with mock gravity. "Hand me my cue and prepare to defend yourself."

## *CHAPTER FOUR*

Emma did not really expect Lady Parton to appear in the dining room for luncheon, for she judged that her aunt had not yet wrung the last drop of drama from her current "setback." Therefore, she was quite surprised, when she and Johnny were summoned to the dining room by the butler, Hemmings, to see Lady Parton seated in her usual place at the table, facing her husband, with Sir Humphrey to her right and Charlotte to her left.

Taking her own seat, Emma remarked, "I'm glad you're feeling well enough to take luncheon with the family, Aunt Claire."

"I must tell you that I am not *fully* recovered," said Lady Parton, lest anyone take the notion that she was not still to be sympathized with. "It is just that I remembered the Haverlys' dinner party this evening. There is no question of crying off from an invitation from the Haverlys, of course. I couldn't allow Lottie to miss this evening's gathering, even if it means forcing myself to smile and converse when I am feeling quite wretched. I did think that I ought to get up and simply push myself to walk about so that I might get over this light-headed feeling." She sighed heavily. "The sacrifices one makes for one's children."

"No need for you to put yourself into such a dither, m'dear," said Lord Parton. "I daresay the Haverlys will understand if you aren't feeling quite the thing. Just as lief stay at home myself."

Lady Parton peered at her husband. "I thought you liked Lord Haverly, Randolph."

"Like him well enough. Just prefer my own house and my own food."

Sir Humphrey had been following this exchange reflectively. "Have I been invited?" he asked after a pause.

"I don't think so," responded Lord Parton. "I expect the Haverlys didn't think you would care to attend since you don't go much into society anymore. Should you mind remaining here for the evening?"

"Not if we have plenty of that fine port," replied Sir Humphrey honestly. "Don't want to listen to a lot of twittering females anyway."

"Really, Mama," spoke up Charlotte, "I wouldn't mind missing the Haverlys' party if you aren't feeling well."

"Don't be a goose," snapped Lady Parton impatiently. "Lord North is sure to be in attendance, since Lady Haverly is his sister. If we cry off there is little telling when you might be presented to that elusive gentleman. He hasn't been at any of the other early season parties we've attended. I understand his mother is quite overset with his indifference to society."

"I'm not pining to be presented to Lord North, Mama," said Lottie with a sniff. "There have been a number of other amusing gentlemen at the parties we've attended."

"I am not leaving my sickbed so that you may meet amusing gentlemen, Lottie," said her mother frankly. "I am interested only in prospective husbands, and Lord North is among the most eligible gentlemen of the ton."

"Mama," protested Lottie, "I am only nineteen, not in danger of becoming an ape-leader for a few years yet."

Her mother frowned at her. "If you do not become engaged before the end of your second season, I fear people will begin to think there is something wrong with you."

Lottie drew an impatient breath. "Perhaps they will think I merely have refined tastes."

"No, they will more likely name you eccentric, too particular to be biddable. Gentlemen look for a biddable wife above all else."

"Lottie, *biddable?*" exclaimed Johnny, almost choking on his roll. "Really, Mama, I must tell you you'll not find many gentlemen who will be flummeried by that Banbury tale."

Ignoring her brother, Lottie continued to address her mother. "Well, I—" she began, but then she caught Emma's eye, saw the slight shake of her head, and fell silent, having clearly remembered that she had hoped to elicit permission to attend the Frost Fair. Engaging in an argument with her mother would certainly defeat her purpose. She picked up a spoon and dipped it into the steaming soup that Hemmings had just placed in front of her.

"Not at all sure it's safe to take the carriage out tonight," remarked Lord Parton hopefully.

"It is only a short distance to the Haverly house," said his wife, "and we shall leave in time to make the drive slowly." She tasted her soup. "I can't think when we have had such a frigid February. I understand the Thames is frozen solid."

Charlotte darted a speaking look at her cousin. Emma put down her soup spoon and cleared her throat. "When I visited the solicitors' yesterday, I heard a great deal of talk about the Frost Fair that has been set up on the ice. It seemed to be generating a lot of excitement."

"Frost Fair?" Sir Humphrey finished his soup and reached for a roll to tide him over until the next course was served. "Never heard of it. You ought not to believe everything you hear, gel."

"Oh, it's true," said Charlotte. "While Emma was in the solicitors' office, I directed Benjy to go for a short drive—it seemed warmer when we were moving—and I saw the booths on the river—from a distance, of course."

"No sense in putting them on the river," said Sir Humphrey with a bewildered look. "Much safer to put them in the park if people must have a fair in the dead of winter. Whole demmed town must have gone distracted." His attention was diverted as Hemmings appeared with petits pâtés.

"Sounds a bang-up idea to me," said Jonathan enthusiastically. "I'd like to see it myself."

"Would you?" inquired Emma gratefully. "I've had somewhat the same notion. Perhaps you will allow Johnny and Charlotte and me to go to the fair, Aunt Claire. With us out of the way, the house would be quiet enough for you to rest."

"Oh, I think Lottie is expecting some callers this afternoon, aren't you, dear? I've forgotten the gentlemen's names—"

"We could go tomorrow," provided Lottie. "I don't think anyone is expected then."

Lady Parton was shaking her head, taking a healthy spoonful of her pâté. "I don't think that would be the thing at all, Lottie. I am sure the place is frequented only by footpads and other such members of the criminal classes."

"You are quite wrong, Mama," said Lottie. "At the Massingales' rout all of the young people were planning to go."

"Freeze your feet," remarked Sir Humphrey, "walking around on ice. No sense to it." He chewed his food, a puzzled look in his eyes, then washed it down with half a glass of wine. He set the wineglass aside and turned to his nephew. "Why would people want to have a fair on a frozen river, Randolph?"

"I don't know, Uncle."

"I believe your new blue silk would be just the thing for the Haverlys' party, Lottie," pondered Lady Parton, in deep thought, "or perhaps the lavender sarcenet. On the other hand, rose brings color to your cheeks and there's that new—"

"If you won't permit Emma and Charlotte to accompany me," Jonathan interrupted, "I might as well go to the Frost Fair today. I'll take Frazier with me if it will make you feel any easier, Mama."

Lady Parton turned to her son, a displeased frown etching two deep lines between her brows. "Johnny, it's my opinion you aren't old enough to be going about town on your own."

"All my friends do it," argued Jonathan with some heat.

Sir Randolph grumbled with impatience. "Leave the boy be, m'dear. You can't keep him in the nursery until he goes back to Oxford. Besides, you know that Frazier is the soul of trustworthiness."

"Never liked him above half," offered Sir Humphrey, setting aside his empty plate to make way for the main course. "Never has any expression on his face. Don't trust a man with a blank face."

Charlotte was scowling at Emma with vexation. "If Emma and I aren't allowed to go with Johnny to the fair," she said, mutiny snapping in her brown eyes, "I doubt that I shall be feeling well enough to attend the Haverlys' party in this weather."

"Lottie," said Lady Parton, "don't throw one of your

tantrums. You know that always gives me the headache, and I am not feeling myself as it is."

Seeing the situation rapidly evolving into a battle of wills between Lottie and her mother, Emma said, "Perhaps if we took Lottie's abigail with us, Aunt—"

"Why must you pursue this disagreeable topic of conversation, Emma?" inquired Lady Parton accusingly. "It is not like you to be so stubborn."

"I should very much enjoy eating my meal in peace," protested Lord Parton as forcibly as a man of his natural indolence could be expected to. "All this bickering is enough to goad a man to madness. I see no reason not to permit Lottie and Emma to go with Johnny to the fair as long as Joan accompanies them, since they seem to desire it above all else."

Sir Humphrey had been studying his great-nephew with a faint interest gleaming in his eyes for some moments. "I say, Johnny, what are you doing here at this time of year? Shouldn't you be at Oxford?" He glanced at Sir Randolph, baffled. "This is February, isn't it, Randolph?"

"Yes, Uncle," said Lord Parton with a sigh of depression. "Johnny was sent down. I told you that the other day."

"Nonsense," commented Sir Humphrey. "Nobody ever tells me anything."

"Yes, I did," insisted Lord Parton. "There was a dust-up about a goat in the master's office."

"They don't have goats at Oxford," stated Sir Humphrey.

"Well, they had this one," said Sir Randolph. "I'll explain the whole business to you later, if you like."

Sir Humphrey sampled his meat, clearly losing interest in Jonathan. He continued eating, but added in a moment,

"If anyone should care for my opinion, this brisket is overdone."

"M'dear," said Sir Randolph to his wife, his expression that of a man beleaguered almost beyond endurance. "What do you say to permitting the girls to attend the fair for two hours tomorrow afternoon?"

"Oh, very well." Apparently Lady Parton had detected the mutiny in her daughter's eyes as clearly as Emma had. "But Joan must accompany them. And, Jonathan, I expect you to play the proper escort."

"Depend upon it, Mama," Jonathan agreed readily.

"Good." Sir Humphrey turned his attention to his plate. "Now I should very much appreciate it if we could discuss something less controversial for the remainder of the meal."

"Ruins brisket to overcook it," said Sir Humphrey. Seeing the elderly gentleman's empty plate, Hemmings served him more meat, which Sir Humphrey seemed to eat with as much appetite as the first serving.

"Tell me, Uncle," said Emma, taking pity on Lord Parton, "will you be going to your club this afternoon?"

Sir Randolph informed her that he did, indeed, intend to visit his club in spite of the hazardous streets, for there he could be assured of having peace and quiet, an utter dearth of females, and a relaxing game of cards. Lady Parton, after finishing her meal, declared herself on the verge of swooning and said she would spend the afternoon resting in her chamber in order to gather her waning strength for the evening's gala.

As soon as she could, Emma excused herself to go and practice her scales once more. Charlotte followed her to the music room, looking thunderous.

"Why did you have to suggest that Joan accompany us? You know she tells *everything*."

"It was clear that we were to have either Joan or Frazier," said Emma calmly.

"Well, I should have much preferred Frazier. That valet is the soul of discretion. When Papa tried to question him about that dust-up at Oxford, he couldn't get a word out of him except that Frazier claimed he wasn't in his young lordship's confidence, which is a Banbury tale if I ever heard one. I believe he could look upon an orgy and remain unmoved, and he would never breathe a word of what he'd seen."

Emma's blue-green eyes danced. "Surely you did not expect to engage in an orgy at the Frost Fair!"

"No," admitted Lottie, "but I have been toying with the notion of borrowing some of Joan's clothes and masquerading as a maid. Then I should be able to go about alone without anyone remarking it."

"But what if you met someone you know?"

"Oh, I should disguise myself so no one would recognize me. It would have been such an adventure." She looked crestfallen. "I shan't be able to do it now if Joan is to go with us. She would spread it all over London before sundown."

"It wouldn't have done, anyway," said Emma. "You heard Johnny promise to play the proper escort."

"Oh, I daresay he meant it at the time," agreed Charlotte, "but you know that he will be dashing off in all directions as soon as we reach the Thames. My brother loves nothing better than a fair—unless it is a cockfight, although he manages to attend those even less frequently than fairs since Mama would have a spasm if she ever suspected he'd witnessed such a barbarous event."

"Nor can I find it in my heart to blame her," said Emma with a shudder.

"Well," mused Charlotte, "I shall contrive to get away from Joan somehow." She wandered to the window and gazed out for a long moment, then turned back to say, "I believe I'll go up and change my gown before Lord Ryerson arrives. I've decided I prefer the green with this necklace." She smiled suddenly. "At least Mama is closeted in her chamber, so she won't be about when he calls."

When her cousin left her, Emma applied herself to her scales. But it was difficult to concentrate fully on her fingers, for she couldn't help thinking of the next day's outing. To own the truth, she was as eager as Lottie to return to the Frost Fair.

At the Haverly mansion a short distance from Bedford Square, Lady Sarah Haverly was hurrying from kitchen to dining hall and back again, checking on the servants' preparations for the evening's dinner party. The Haverly butler, Jessup, intercepted her in one of her trips from kitchen to dining hall with the information that Lord North awaited her in the library.

Entering that room a few minutes later, she greeted her brother with delight. "James, this is an unexpected pleasure. To what do I owe the honor of being chosen over White's and Watier's?"

Lord North's quirked mouth brushed her cheek affectionately. "You wrong me, Sarah. I have often preferred your company above my other pursuits. It is just that you are so busy with your family I hesitate to burden you with my conversation."

Lady Haverly eyed the fine figure of her brother in an exquisitely cut gray coat with brass buttons and leather breeches, a perfectly aligned cravat, and gleaming top boots. Her hazel eyes smiled at him. "Jackanapes! So you've come to tell me one of your farradiddles, have you? Well, I am all attention. Only wait while I summon Jessup to bring some refreshment." She tugged at a bell pull in one corner of the room. "It is too early for tea, but you may sample the petit fours the cooks have prepared for the party. And I believe there is a bottle of excellent wine. Dorian declares it is too good not to have been smuggled."

Sir James settled himself in a comfortable chair while his sister instructed the butler. Shortly Jessup returned, carrying a silver tray. The butler poured the wine and withdrew.

Lady Haverly offered her brother the petit fours, then sat on the high-backed settle near his chair. "Ann and Cassandra were quite taken with the kitten, James. The beast is so well fed and pampered, I've no doubt she thinks she's died and gone to feline heaven. You know, of course, that Mama believes you came by that cat in some other way than what you've told."

Sir James chuckled. "Mama has ever had a regrettably suspicious turn of mind." He sampled the wine, then lifted his glass to examine its color. "Dorian is right about this wine, I think. Where did he find it?"

"You'll have to get that information from him. He didn't say, and I didn't think to question him. He's gone to his club now, but you may ask him this evening."

"Ah, this evening." Sir James set his wineglass down and nibbled at a petit four. After a moment he said, "Actually, that is what I wanted to speak with you about. Would you be very put out with me if I absented myself this evening?"

Lady Haverly sat forward. "I shall be utterly overset!

Surely you would not be so ungentlemanly as to cry off at this late hour, James!"

"Now, draw bridle, Sister. Don't rip up at me like that. It's just that my estate manager has sent me a lengthy proposal for some changes in the crops. I must go over it carefully, and it is likely to take several hours."

"James, this is the outside of enough! You aren't deluding me for a trice with this humbug! You are bored by parties and you are regretting your promise to attend mine. But I tell you, James, I shall never forgive you if you cry off now!"

Sir James leaned back in his chair and surveyed his sister's flushed face with a rueful look. "You know me too well. I admit my manager's proposal can wait until tomorrow. I should have known you wouldn't let me off easily." He made a face and took another sip of wine. "Well, how many featherheaded man-traps have you gathered for my scrutiny?"

Lady Haverly could not but laugh. She rested her chin in her hand. "Tell me, James, what sort of woman would it take to make you contemplate marriage?"

He looked slightly startled and not very patient. "I have no plans to contemplate marriage at all. Not in the foreseeable future."

"Some people," remarked Lady Haverly challengingly, "would think that an—unnatural attitude in a man who is in his prime."

Sir James scowled at her. "That is a most unladylike thing to say, Sarah, not to mention insulting."

Her eyes twinkled. "Yes, I suppose it is. But then you know I am only bamming you. I am quite aware of that actress with whom you spent a great deal of time last year. Do you still see her?"

"I have no intention of discussing my personal affairs with you."

"Affairs?" teased Lady Haverly. "Yes, I would say that is the appropriate word."

"Do you imagine, Sarah, that I would marry a lady of quality just for the privilege of bedding her?"

She raised her brows. "No," she replied calmly. "I know there are dozens of light-skirts available for that purpose."

"This," he said sternly, "is a most improper conversation for a sister to be having with her brother."

His momentary flash of indignation died quickly, however. He said, less harshly, "Sister, I am quite aware of my duty to perpetuate my name. When I am ready, I promise you I shall make a proper alliance."

"A marriage of convenience?" inquired Lady Haverly with interest.

"Of course. I daresay I shall be able to make an agreeable enough match—sometime in the future."

"Oh, that is dastardly!" said Lady Haverly. "I suppose you will present the lady of your choice with a businesslike arrangement. Must she sign a legal paper, James? She will be asked to run your house and bear your children. In return, you will very graciously honor her with your name and pursue your alliances with actresses discreetly. I am almost convinced that you are devoid of any sensibilities whatsoever."

"You are suggesting that I look for romance in a marriage?"

"Oh, perish the notion! No, I expect you ought to look for someone who is quite plain. Otherwise, she might find opportunity to take a lover of her own. Goodness knows, that would offend your dignity! I fear you will have to settle for a modest dowry, too, for ladies with fortunes tend to be regrettably ungrateful to the men who marry them. She will have to be at her last prayers, of course. I shall begin immediately to look out the plainest, poorest lady among the quality that I can find."

"Thank you!" said Sir James.

"Luckily," pursued his sister relentlessly, "there are any number of ladies who fit your requirements to be found in town. Why, I believe I could come up with at least ten whose mamas have given up on finding them husbands."

"Really, Sarah," protested Sir James with a short laugh, "this conversation is foolish beyond all reason. I have not the slightest desire to look for a wife at the moment. And when I am ready, I shall not require your assistance."

"Oh, I am extremely sorry to hear that. I believe I have thought of just the lady for you. Of course, she does slump her shoulders terribly and cowers in corners. Just between the two of us, I fear she is not overly bright. And her hair is a bit thin, I must own. What a pity that wigs are going out of style."

"Enough!" cried Sir James.

"Seriously, you must know it makes little difference to me if you choose *never* to marry. But I promised Mama to make a push to get you more into society. If I fail, I am sure I shall be treated to a Cheltenham tragedy. Take pity on me, brother."

"Gudgeon!" he accused, but not without amusement. "Very well, I shall attend your party, and I shall bow and scrape and be a perfect credit to you."

"What an accommodating brother you are, to be sure!"

Having resigned himself to the necessity of keeping his promise, the marquis took his leave shortly, deciding on the spur of the moment to take another walk through the Frost Fair. Perhaps he would find a clue to the identity of the elusive Sophia there. Truth to tell, he had disposed of the actress his sister had mentioned some time ago, and he wondered if a governess might be a refreshing change of pace. Unhappily, all the governesses he had ever known had been extremely prudish. Which made him wonder again if Sophia were indeed a governess. She had appeared too young and too spirited to be a member of that prim and proper brigade. Yet if she were not a governess, he was at a loss as to what category to place her in. More mysteries to be explained. He admitted to himself that he had never run across a female who had raised so many intriguing questions in his mind as had Sophia of the red-gold curls.

## *CHAPTER FIVE*

The hour at the Frost Fair was wasted as far as catching even a fleeting glimpse of Sophia or finding anyone who could identify her from the scanty description Sir James could provide. By the time he had tromped through every booth, his feet, even in the well-lined boots, were cold and he was feeling somewhat disgruntled.

Why, he asked himself, was he traipsing about in weather like this in search of some will-o'-the-wisp fabrication of his own imagining? In the space of an hour he had cast Sophia in the role of illegitimate daughter of a duke; impoverished orphan of wellborn, but long-dead, parents; cruelly treated niece of a noble, though lecherous, uncle who had run away to escape an unacceptable marriage; and French émigré of the royal house (this fancy disregarding the fact that she had no French accent) who had fled from the revolution with nothing but the clothes on her back.

It all resulted from the malaise brought on by contemplating the activities available to him in London, he decided. His sister's dinner party that evening was a prime example of the sort of event that was sending his unoccupied brain on these excursions into fantasy. It was so totally unlike him. If it weren't for having to suffer the disappointed recriminations of his mother and sister, he would return within the sennight to Kent, where there were matters of substance to occupy his thoughts and his time.

The devil was in it! He would have to remain for a

two-month stay at least in order to pacify his female relatives and leave himself unencumbered by any feeling that he was a selfish oaf with too little interest in the family honor.

So . . . he would make a game of detection of ferreting out Sophia. He had always been aroused to action by a challenge, and Sophia had stirred his gaming instincts. Most females in whom he had felt an initial interest had turned out, upon further acquaintance, to be disappointingly dull and insipid, their brains continuously filled with the most trivial matters conceivable. Perhaps he had turned cynic where women were concerned, but he had little doubt that Sophia, should he succeed in clearing away the mystery surrounding her, would be no better than the others. At any rate, he would have won the game of detection, which would be a source of some slight satisfaction to him.

With these thoughts in mind, he returned to his carriage, taking the reins himself, for he was an excellent whip. When he reached his house, he called for his valet to assist him in making ready for his sister's dinner party. He had promised to be a credit to her and, by gad, he would carry it off if it bored him beyond all reason.

Upon his arrival at the Haverly mansion that evening, his sister spotted him instantly. Plainly she had been awaiting his appearance with a trace of trepidation, lest he find some necessity to break his promise, after all. She came toward him, a flattering gown of cream satin swirling about her legs.

"James, you are gorgeous!" Her glance raked his black evening coat and the lace-trimmed white shirt, its collar higher than he usually wore as a concession to the latest fashion. A reluctant concession, Lady Haverly felt sure, for her brother, although he always dressed well, had a preference for comfort over style. "So many of the matrons have already asked me to present you to their daughters. Are you going to be congenial and humor me this evening? Dorian has laid a wager with me that you will retire to the gaming tables immediately after dinner."

"Your husband has not taken enough account of my affection for my only sister," said Sir James amiably. "I am in your hands, Sarah. I collect there will be dancing after dinner? Then I shall partner several ladies of your choosing. Tell me the ones whose mamas you desire to placate. Only, pray, have a little sympathy and do not take too great advantage of my affection."

"But it is such a temptation, James," she said with a tinkling laugh. "You are rarely so tractable. No, don't get on the fidgets. I'll require your attentions to only the prettiest and wealthiest of the marriageable misses."

"I suppose," remarked Sir James wryly, as he followed his sister toward the dining hall, "I'll have to find what consolation I can in that."

"Think of it as placating Mama," advised his sister. "Truth to tell, you will reap more benefit from that than I since she is staying with you in your town house. Mama is an amiable companion when she isn't cross. Very like you, Brother, if I may say so. I've put you at table with Lord Ryerson and, because he is so obviously taken with her, Miss Parton," she added in a low voice as she moved back to take his arm. "The other young lady at your table is Lord Wallenby's youngest and the most fetching of that brood. She is just turned twenty, I believe, and has already rejected four offers for her hand. I fear you shan't charm her easily, James."

"I'll do my best," promised Sir James, but he was already feeling a tinge of weariness at the prospect of the next several hours. "I presume these are two of the ladies I must ask to stand up with me?"

His sister nodded as they approached one of the small white-clothed tables that filled the dining hall. Sir Robert Ryerson and two attractive young women were already seated there. Sir Robert got to his feet as he saw his hostess approaching.

Lady Haverly inquired after the health of the three guests, then introduced her brother to the ladies. "I should like to present my brother, Sir James North. James, Miss Charlotte Parton and Miss Letha Wallenby."

Sir James's bow was executed in a manner that even his sister could not fault. "Your obedient servant, ladies."

Lady Haverly excused herself, saying that she believed all of the expected guests had now arrived and she must tell the butler to instruct the servants to bring in the first course.

The two gentlemen seated themselves as Sir Robert remarked, "I'd almost become convinced you didn't mean to attend any of the ton parties, James. How on earth did your sister get you here?"

"Easily, Robert," replied Sir James smoothly. "I am not quite the eccentric you paint me."

"Didn't mean you're eccentric," denied Ryerson. "Just meant you ain't particularly interested in galas. You can't be said to be reclusive, either, for you are often at your club and Newmarket, and didn't you tell me you'd been to the Frost Fair?"

"Twice," confirmed the marquis, remembering his manners in time to include the two ladies in what he hoped was a congenial glance about the table.

"Have you, indeed?" asked Charlotte, her brown eyes

lighting up with interest. "Mama has given her permission for me to go tomorrow afternoon. I fear I shall hardly sleep all night because of my anticipation. You must tell us all about it, Lord North. Wouldn't you like that, Letha?"

Miss Wallenby had been following the conversation with an absentminded expression on her perfectly sculptured face. Her blond hair was piled atop her head in an intricate style that must have taken her abigail most of the afternoon to accomplish, and she wore an elegant ball gown of blue silk, with a high waistline and tiered skirt. She sat very straight in her chair, her hands folded in her lap, and held her head stiffly erect, as if she feared dislodging a curl. There was little expression in her pale blue eyes except perhaps for a trace of boredom. Sir James was struck with a sudden fancy that Miss Wallenby was likely always to be bored whenever she was not the center of everyone's attention. She was an exquisite-looking creature, certainly. She reminded Sir James of an expensive China doll.

Having been addressed directly, Miss Wallenby replied, "That would be very nice," to Lottie's question as if she were reciting a phrase from an etiquette book. There was still no interest in her expression, however.

Miss Parton's animated face somewhat compensated for Miss Wallenby's damping tone. So Sir James, remarking Lord Ryerson's worshipful gaze as it rested on Miss Parton's heart-shaped mouth, replied, "There is a bookstall with a surprisingly extensive selection. I purchased Miss Austen's latest novel there for my sister."

Miss Wallenby continued to look bored, and Miss Parton said impatiently, "For my part, I am not very much interested in reading, Lord North. Tell us about the toys—

I merely assume, of course, that there must be toy booths at the fair—and what kind of sweets are available? Surely there must be a great variety! Oh, and is there, by any chance, a mime performance or a puppet show?"

"I'm afraid I wasn't interested in the toys, Miss Parton," said Sir James with an amused quirk of one dark brow. "Nor did I purchase anything to eat. But I saw several booths offering treats. There is quite a variety to choose from. As for a performance of some sort, I believe I do recall seeing a puppet theater."

Miss Parton clasped her hands in front of her like an eager child. "I shall certainly see the puppets then." She looked at Miss Wallenby. "When are you going to the Frost Fair, Letha?"

"What?" Miss Wallenby had been examining the ruby ring on her slender white finger.

"I asked you when you are going to the fair," repeated Miss Parton with some impatience.

"I shan't be going," said Miss Wallenby with a slightly surprised look, as if she found the idea somewhat ludicrous. "I've no wish to be outside in such horrible weather. Besides, aren't you afraid of being crushed against persons of the lower classes and criminals? So dirty—and dangerous, too, I am sure." She shivered elegantly. "I can't conceive why anyone should *want* to go there."

"Lud," exclaimed Miss Parton, "they are only there to have fun, like everyone else. And if someone should pick your pocket or even strip off your coat, I am sure you will not be impoverished as a result."

Miss Wallenby was staring at Charlotte with distaste. "I hadn't thought of anyone's taking my *coat.* So violent. Sometimes you say the most frightening things, Charlotte.

Listening to you merely strengthens my desire to avoid the fair."

"Well, *I'm* going," said Charlotte, "and I shall enjoy every minute of the two hours allotted me."

"I haven't been there myself yet," remarked Lord Ryerson, "although I've been wanting to take it in. Perhaps I'll bump into you there, Miss Parton."

Charlotte gave him an arch look. "I am sure there will be crowds of people and it will be difficult to find acquaintances, but one never knows what may fall out, does one?"

Lord North had difficulty suppressing a smile at his friend's eager agreement. Fortunately, the servants arrived with the soup just then, diverting everyone's attention. Miss Wallenby, he noticed, ate as elegantly and carefully as she sat. She gave her undivided attention to lifting her spoon to her mouth, as if to spill a drop of anything on the tablecloth would be a faux pas never to be overcome.

As course followed course—salads, fillet of veal, glazed sweetbreads, prawns, pâtés, and tarts—Lord North, mindful of his promise to his sister, made a valiant effort to appear interested in the conversation, which was mainly between Lord Ryerson and Miss Parton, as well as making a suitable contribution himself from time to time. Miss Wallenby, apparently, did not feel obliged to contribute anything, except when addressed directly. Sir James became more and more convinced that she believed gracing the table with her presence to be contribution enough. She merely sat there, eating sparsely and carefully, turning her head slightly when someone spoke to her as regally as a queen.

Perhaps, thought Sir James wryly, in his younger days he might have been dazzled by Miss Wallenby's beauty and haughty demeanor. But, no, even in his younger days —except for one error in judgment—he had looked for more than beauty in a woman, and inevitably been disappointed, which probably accounted for his still unmarried state.

At thirty-two he was wise enough now to expect nothing in a future wife but good lineage, a presentable appearance, a knowledge of fashion and managing a household, and skillful performance of her duties as hostess when he wished to entertain. She must, of course, be relatively intelligent, although he did not look for more than an average amount of that characteristic. As for wit and passion—he had become convinced he must find those outside of marriage in discreet liaisons.

Before they left the table, he secured Miss Parton's promise to stand up with him for a waltz, and Miss Wallenby condescended to allow him to partner her in the first dance. He wondered grimly if she would break when he touched her. Since he would stand up with Miss Wallenby first, it seemed only polite to escort her up the curving carpeted staircase to the ballroom where the orchestra was already playing and crystal chandeliers filled with dozens of candles cast a dreamy and flickering light over the room.

An excessively romantic setting, mused Sir James, if one felt inclined in that direction. However, as he led Miss Wallenby onto the dance floor, romance was the farthest thing from his mind. Mainly he only wished to get the dance behind him, for surely none of the other ladies whom he would partner that evening would have as little conversation as that young woman.

"I must thank you for honoring me with the first dance,

Miss Wallenby," he offered after several moments of silence.

"You are welcome."

"I believe your father has his country seat in Hampshire," he struggled on. "Do you enjoy the months you spend there?"

"Not especially."

"You prefer London then?"

"If I have any preference at all, I suppose it is for the city."

"Why is that?"

"Why," she said, glancing up at him blankly, as if he had asked a very foolish question, "the dressmakers and milliners are superior here."

"Of course," agreed Sir James, accepting defeat, and remained grimly silent for the remainder of the dance. However, by the time he led her to her chaperon, he was feeling guilty about that and inquired politely, "Would you like me to bring you a glass of punch?"

Her expression did not change. "That would be nice."

He brought the punch, made his bow, and excused himself to go in search of his sister. His waltz with Miss Parton wasn't scheduled for a while, and he must discover which young ladies Sarah particularly wished him to partner. To his dismay, his sister was ready with six names. One of them was Charlotte Parton, though, so he was only required to request a dance with five others. Two of these dances were accomplished before he went to claim Miss Parton for the waltz.

He was not surprised that Robert found the chit enchanting. Her lustrous dark curls and deep brown eyes were alive, her cheeks glowed pinkly in her pretty, animated face, her rose ball gown was flattering to her petite figure and of the latest fashion, and she was an accomplished dancer. In addition, she talked naturally and easily with her partners.

"Tell me, my lord," she was saying as they began to move in time with the music, "since you don't come much to parties, what do you find to occupy your time while in London?"

"I attend the races. I go to my club. I carry on an extensive correspondence with my estate manager. I read." As Sir James named his activities, he realized that his cataloging of such mundane pursuits was disappointing to Miss Parton. "And, of course, for the time being, there is the Frost Fair where one may pass an enjoyable hour or two."

"Yes," agreed Miss Parton, perking up. "Have you galloped your horse through any gaming-hells or robbed any travelers or had any other exciting adventures?"

Somewhat stunned, Sir James replied, "I must confess, Miss Parton, that I cannot think of any reason for even contemplating either of those activities."

"Oh," said Miss Parton. She peered up at him from beneath her dark lashes, studying his face thoughtfully. "I hope you will not think me impertinent, but may I ask you another question?"

"By all means."

"Is it true that you had an unhappy romance when you were very young that has quite turned you against all women?"

"Miss Parton," said Sir James, disconcerted anew, "I must tell you that you say the most shocking things of any lady I've ever known. I am sure your mother has told you it is impolite to speak of personal matters to a gentleman with whom you are barely acquainted."

Miss Parton shrugged her pretty shoulders. "Oh, you needn't read me a lecture. Mama has told me any number of such things, so many that I confess I cannot remember them all. You must forgive me if I have offended your dignity, for if I have done that Mama will have a spasm. It is just that I think sometimes how lovely it must be to be a man and free of all the restrictions that are placed on ladies' behavior."

Good Lord, Sir James thought wryly. He must take the first opportunity to warn Robert that the man who married this chit must expect to spend his time getting her out of scrapes. Since Robert was a bit harebrained himself, there was no telling what might become of the two of them should Lady Parton actually consent to a marriage between them. In fact, he knew Miss Parton must have been thinking of that gentleman when she asked about riding a horse through a notorious gambling house. Gaming-hell, indeed! Of course, he expected Robert's tendency to fall into the briars to soften with age and responsibility, but he held less hope for Miss Parton.

"I dislike disabusing you of the notion you seem to have formed," he said, "but I must tell you that a gentleman's life is not an unending series of adventures."

"Well, of course," responded Miss Parton, "he would have to have imagination."

When the waltz had ended he returned Miss Parton to her mama with some relief. The young lady introduced him to Lady Parton, who presented her plump hand to him with a look that reminded Sir James of a terrier he had in the country who spent hours waiting patiently outside ratholes with a quite similar alert attentiveness mixed with a relishing sort of anticipation.

"Your obedient." He bowed over her ladyship's hand.

"I hope you will not think me immodest, Lord North," exclaimed Lady Parton, "but you and my daughter were a vision of grace and handsomeness on the dance floor."

"You are too kind, madam."

Lady Parton laughed. "Not at all. In fact, several of the chaperons remarked upon how lovely the two of you looked together. One of them said you put her in mind of Sir Lancelot and Lady Guinevere. A fanciful notion, of course, but you do dance well together, and your evening dress makes such an attractive contrast with the rose of Lottie's gown."

Miss Parton's cheeks were even more pink than before. "Mama, I am sure Lord North is to partner someone else in the next dance."

"That's true, madam," Sir James put in gratefully, "so you must excuse me for taking my leave so abruptly."

Lady Parton was still clinging to his hand, however. "I hope you will find you are able to accept our invitation to the ball we are giving in April, sir. I plan a few small gatherings earlier, too, and I shall be quite undone if you are unable to attend a single one of them."

He managed to extricate his hand from the woman's damp grip. "I shall check my engagement calendar, madam. Thank you for the waltz, Miss Parton." He hurried away before Lady Parton could think of other delaying tactics.

"Honestly, Mama," said Charlotte hotly, "must you be quite so obvious?"

Her mother gave her a look of chagrin. "I am sure I don't know what you mean, Lottie."

"You were practically falling at his feet!"

"Nonsense. I was merely being polite. I am convinced he will attend our ball, at least, aren't you? I believe he is taken with you. After all, you had dinner with him and the first waltz. That must mean something."

"Mama," said Lottie with exasperation, "his sister put him at my table. He had nothing to do with it. And don't forget Letha Wallenby was there, too, and she also had a dance with him."

"Oh, Letha Wallenby." Lady Parton dismissed that young woman with a flutter of her ringed fingers. "I am sure you are as pretty as she. Besides, I watched Lord North when he was dancing with her. He didn't talk as much by half as he did to you. You have done very well so far, dear. Did he request another dance?"

"No, he did not. He brought a glass of punch to Letha and he didn't even offer to bring me one. I wouldn't be at all surprised if he dances with her again, either."

Lady Parton looked extremely disappointed. "Well, perhaps he will ask you to stand up with him again later."

"I already have my programme filled," Charlotte informed her with some relish.

"What? Oh, well, if he asks you, you must make some excuse to the other gentleman. I am sure you can think of something."

"That would be impolite, Mama," protested Charlotte.

"When it comes to Lord North, there are some things more important than politeness," said her mother.

"Well, I am convinced I shan't have to be impolite, anyway, for I don't expect him to ask me to stand up with him again. Oh, here comes Lord Emberland for our dance. Perhaps *he* will be gentleman enough to offer to get punch for me."

At the house in Bedford Square Johnny and Emma

were playing cards in the gold salon when the family returned from the Haverlys'.

"Gracious, I didn't realize it was so late," exclaimed Emma as she looked up to take in the new arrivals.

"It has been a grueling evening," Lady Parton told them, "and my headache has come back. I am going straight up to bed. Johnny, it is very late for a growing boy to be about."

Jonathan made a face at this appellation. "Emma and I lost track of time, Mama. She's a right one at the card table! Beat me handily. But I demand a rematch, Emma."

"You've no notion of when to quit, have you, Johnny?" Emma teased.

"Going to bed," grumbled Lord Parton and took his leave. He was followed by his wife.

"Well, did you enjoy the party, Lottie?" Emma asked as she gathered the scattered cards and placed them in their box.

"It would have been lovely if Mama hadn't been so bent on throwing me at Lord North." Charlotte glanced at her brother, who was listening raptly. "Come with me to my chamber, Emma, and I'll tell you all about it. Good night, Johnny."

Stung by his sister's obvious reluctance to reveal a confidence in his presence, he said hotly, "If you fancy *I* have any interest in balls and such, you are short of a sheet!"

Ignoring him, Charlotte left the room, and after casting Johnny a sympathetic smile, Emma followed. Joan, a tall stick-thin woman of thirty with carrot-red hair that sprang from her head in tight, unruly curls, had fallen asleep in a chair. She stirred and sat upright abruptly as Charlotte and Emma entered the chamber.

As she helped her mistress to undress, she remarked, "I

am sure you were the loveliest young woman at the party, miss."

"Oh, I wouldn't go to that extreme," Lottie told her, "but my dance programme was filled before I even entered the ballroom."

The abigail made several other attempts to elicit tidbits that she could pass along to the other servants, but Charlotte remained noncommittal. As soon as the abigail had withdrawn, Emma, who had settled herself comfortably in a satin chaise, said, "I am expiring to know how you found the renowned Lord North! Did you like him?"

Charlotte, dressed in her nightclothes, got into bed and pulled the covers up around her. She punched at the pillows as if she were angry with them, finally succeeding in arranging them to her satisfaction. "Well," she said, regarding her cousin gravely, "I am sure he is eminently eligible, but he is horrid with it."

"Horrid? Heavens, what did he do to make you form such an unpleasant opinion of him?"

"He is pompous and arrogant and looked down his nose at everyone—besides, he is not at all romantic."

"He certainly sounds disagreeable," said Emma.

"He is! Do you know, he said that I was shocking! It was immediately following that when Mama made such a cake of herself—fawning and toadying until I wished to plant her a facer. And he didn't even offer to bring me punch!"

Emma passed her hand across her face as if to push back stray wisps at her hairline and said with a slight tremor in her voice, "But then if he behaved in such an abominable manner, perhaps he will not offer for you."

"I hope you may be right," said Charlotte, "but Mama is a determined woman. Perhaps I shall have to run away. I would do anything to avoid a marriage with Lord North.

He has no proper notion of how to converse with a lady. Moreover, he implied that *I* had no conception of good manners! That was when I asked him about that unhappy love affair in his youth."

Emma blinked at her. "Oh? But how do you know of it?"

"Everyone speaks of it. It was when he was three and twenty, an age ago. He is old, you know—more than thirty. It is my conviction, Emma, that some female threw him over and now he hates all women."

"But then why would he think of marrying at all?"

"I am sure he does not *want* to, but he must have an heir. He is very rich and is the only son. Mama is set on my becoming betrothed to him, but I will not marry a man who cannot conceive of riding his horse through a gaming-hell and spends his time reading and corresponding with his estate manager!"

"Did he say that?" inquired Emma. "He must be perfectly tiresome!"

"Yes," agreed Charlotte, casting her a grateful look, "and you may be sure he would not change his ways for any female, for he is wretchedly selfish."

"The more I hear of Lord North," confessed Emma, "the more I am convinced he is not at all the husband for you."

"Yes," said Charlotte bitterly, "but when I tried to convince Mama of that on the ride home, she almost swooned and said I was a foolish, ungrateful child and would drive her quite distracted. Then she vowed she had the headache, although she had not mentioned it once earlier in the evening and insisted that we stay until the end."

"Perhaps your papa can calm her down. And don't put

yourself in a fret. After all, it sounds as if Lord North was no more taken with you than you were with him."

"If *he* is going to begin turning up at ton parties, the season will be quite ruined for me," said Charlotte. "If I didn't have the Frost Fair to look forward to tomorrow, I am sure I should die."

"Yes, there is that," agreed Emma. "Now we had both better go to bed so that we might be rested for our trek down Freezeland Street."

This suggestion was accepted by Charlotte, and Emma left her to go to her own chamber. Once in bed, however, she lay awake for some time. It seemed to her that her aunt did not know her own children at all well. She expected them, it seemed, to be extensions of herself, to want what she wanted, to do what she would do. But if that lady thought she could bully her daughter into a marriage with a man who would not suit at all, Emma feared the lady was in for quite a brangle.

Emma had often thought her cousin flighty and immature, but in this case she could not help but sympathize with her. She wondered how she could help Charlotte avoid the fate her mother seemed determined to thrust upon her, but when she fell asleep she still had not reached any conclusion.

## CHAPTER SIX

By the time Emma and Charlotte and their two companions had reached the Thames the following afternoon, throngs of people in a holiday spirit were jostling about on the frozen thoroughfare, so many that it was difficult to find a path through them.

"Where shall we go first?" inquired Charlotte.

"I had hoped," said Emma, "to have more time in the bookstall."

"It seems we are in a hobble already," declared Charlotte, "for I've no intention of wasting a moment on books. It appears we shall have to separate."

Knowing that Joan would be immediately suspicious if she suggested the abigail come with her, Emma said quickly, "Johnny can accompany me." She glanced about, studying the booths nearby for a likely meeting place. "We'll meet you in two hours, Lottie, at the baker's booth over there."

Emma avoided Charlotte's glance as she took Johnny's arm and hurried toward what had been dubbed the Grand Mall, knowing that if looks could slay, she would probably find herself about to take off at any moment.

"*I* ain't interested in books either," complained Johnny. "I have enough of them at Oxford."

"I won't stay long," Emma promised.

"I have a famous idea," said Johnny. "You go where you wish to go and I'll go where I want. I'll meet you at the baker's booth later."

Emma hesitated. She knew her aunt would not approve

of either her or Johnny wandering about alone. But what a treat it would be to have the afternoon to do as she pleased without Johnny or Lottie at her elbow complaining and rushing her to the next booth.

"We don't have to tell Mama anything about it," Johnny added shrewdly.

"I can't feel that we ought to," said Emma finally, duty edging out desire. "I should worry that you will end up in one of those gambling establishments, and how am I to explain that to Aunt Claire should she discover it?"

"You needn't fret that I'll be fleeced," said Johnny unhappily. "My quarterly allowance ain't due for three weeks and I must make what I have last until then or Papa will be as cross as crabs. I fancy I might try the wheel of fortune for a spin or two, but nothing more than that. Truly, Emma."

"Oh—all right," she agreed reluctantly, hoping she would not come to regret the decision. "In two hours then at the baker's booth."

It took her several minutes to work her way through the crowd to the bookstall. In one corner of her mind was the farfetched hope that she might see the tall stranger again. To own the truth, that was part of her reason for wanting to go to the bookstall, for it seemed the most likely place to see him if he were at the fair. Nevertheless, she scolded herself for entertaining foolish thoughts, convinced she had built up that chance meeting in her mind until it had assumed ridiculous proportions. If she were being very objective, she would admit that the man, who had clearly been a gentleman of some consequence, had not thought of her again since that meeting. He was very likely married, anyway. This thought caused her to frown with consternation. Why hadn't she thought of that before?

Certainly he would be married. And even if he weren't, why should he have the slightest interest in a penniless orphan?

But whatever fell out, she would not let anything spoil the afternoon for her. She was wearing a dark blue afternoon dress trimmed in white beneath her gray Spanish coat, having decided that she had worn black exclusively long enough. She knew Papa and Mama would understand if she varied that occasionally with other dark hues, for they had never been bound excessively by tradition. The Frost Fair had seemed an appropriate occasion for her first small step out of mourning.

She spent a pleasant hour at the bookstall, although she left without making a purchase since she must be very careful with the few coins remaining to her. Besides, she could secure books from the lending library, which she had visited twice since her arrival in London.

After leaving the bookstall, she wandered slowly from booth to booth, watching people buy and deciding what she would purchase if money were readily available to her. She saw several ladies and gentlemen of the quality, their station evident from their dress and manner. They seemed to be taking as much pleasure from the festive atmosphere as less fortunate Londoners.

At the end of an hour Emma was growing tired and her booted feet were beginning to feel the chill from the ice. She had noticed a small makeshift tearoom not far from the bookstall, and deciding to treat herself to tea and perhaps a cinnamon bun, she made for it.

A stove blazed in one corner, and there were several small tables in front of a counter where an elderly man and two middle-aged women were filling requests. Emma paid for her tea and bun and carried them to an unoccupied table at one side of the tent. It was the farthest table from the stove, which no doubt explained its not being in use, but regardless of that it felt good to sit down for a bit. And it was warmer, even there, than outside on the thoroughfare.

She had finished eating the bun and was sipping her tea slowly to make it last when a deep voice at her shoulder startled her.

"We meet again, Sophia."

Her eyes flew to the face of the man who had stopped beside her table and widened in confusion as she recognized the stranger who had been too much in her thoughts since their earlier meeting.

All the clever things she had imagined saying should they ever meet again flew right out of her head. "How do you do, sir."

"I see you are alone," he went on, the dark eyes studying her face, "and since there are no other tables available, will you permit me to sit with you?"

"I—I must be leaving anyway. You may have the table."

He continued to stare down at her for a long moment without speaking. Then he said, "Surely you want to know what became of the kitten."

"I—yes—did you find a home for him?"

"Her," he corrected with a slight smile. "But allow me to purchase some tea. I see your cup is very nearly empty. I'll bring you another."

"No, I haven't time—" But he did not seem to hear her as he strode to the counter.

She knew that some people would consider it very improper for her to remain there alone with him. She really ought to leave before he returned to the table. But why should she allow herself to be dislodged from her place when she had meant to linger awhile longer? Besides, there were people on all sides. Further, honesty forced her to admit it, she *wanted* to stay.

He was back, setting another cup of tea in front of her and placing his own cup on the table before he sat down on her left. She gripped her cup with both gloved hands, liking the warmth that seeped through to her fingers. "You promised to tell me what became of the kitten."

His direct gaze was very disconcerting. To avoid it, she lifted her cup and took a sip. "I gave her to my nieces," he said. "My sister tells me they were enraptured."

"Oh, I am so relieved," said Emma. "This is the sister for whom you bought Miss Austen's novel?"

"The very one," he told her, smiling. She met his gaze for a moment. His sharply angled face, although it appeared somewhat stern at times, seemed less so when he smiled. Then he looked quite approachable, and Emma took some comfort from that.

"Thank you for the tea." She felt she ought to say something more, but she had no previous experience upon which to base proper behavior in the present circumstance. She applied herself assiduously to savoring her tea.

"May I inquire after your aunt?"

She set her cup down, rattling it in the saucer. Her mind raced back over their previous meeting. What had she told him about Aunt Claire? She vaguely recalled mentioning that her aunt sneezed at cats. "Oh, she is well enough."

"Did she accompany you to the fair?"

Emma wished he would stop looking at her in that penetrating way. "You seem inordinately interested in my aunt, sir," she said, more pertly than she intended, for she had the apprehensive and illogical feeling that he could somehow guess her identity by peering into her brain.

"And you, Sophia," he returned, a muscle alongside his mouth twitching slightly, "seem intent upon remaining a lady of mystery."

She smiled then, unable to stop herself, for he was so obviously poking fun at her. "That, sir, is an utterly unjust accusation. One might even name you hypocrite, for you have told me nothing about yourself except that you have a sister and nieces. You have not even told me your name."

He chuckled. "My mother was used to call me Jamie."

Emma was beginning to enjoy this. "You don't say so! I must tell you, Jamie, that I should be hard put to pick a name less suited to such an obviously proper gentleman. But perhaps your clothes and your manner are a ruse to cover up your true identity." Elbow on the table, she rested her chin in her hand. "Let me think. You are a Captain Sharp and have had a famous run of luck at the tables, which accounts for the fine coat and boots you are wearing. Am I getting close, sir?"

"Not even slightly."

"Well, never mind. I shall hit upon it in a moment."

"Pray, do not trouble yourself!" replied Sir James, eyeing her with amusement.

"It is no trouble. I have it now! You are a smuggler come up to London with your wares. Oh, excuse me, I believe the gentlemen in that—ah, profession prefer to be called free traders. I hope I have not offended you."

"Only slightly, Sophia, but I assure you I shall recover."

Emma met his look for a long moment, feeling her cheeks growing warm. Thank goodness high color could reasonably be laid to the cold. She tilted her head. "Now that I consider it, I think you are more likely a highwayman. I have been told that some of them dress as well as Brummell. I suppose it amuses them to dress like the quality after relieving them of the means to do so."

Sir James laughed outright at that. "I warned you not to read so many romances, Sophia, and I see the warning was not amiss."

"Alas, sir," said Emma, dimpling, "I fear the lending libraries in London are too conveniently available to resist. Why, the one near St. James Park has an entire section of romance novels. There must be more than a hundred of them."

Although he still lounged comfortably in his chair, there was a brief flash of alertness in his dark eyes. "Do you go there often?"

"Not often. Sometimes on Thursday afternoons I—" Emma halted abruptly, realizing that he was eliciting information from her. Oh, he was very clever! She had blithely named the lending library that she had visited, from which he might deduce the section of the city where she was staying. She still could not believe he would be the slightest part interested in where she lived, yet something in his manner told her he was.

She gave him what she hoped was an innocent look. "Usually I go to the libraries closer to my aunt's house, though. It is just that I had heard of the selection of romances at the one near St. James and coaxed my aunt to take me there." She had almost said her aunt's *groom,* but caught herself in time. From that he could infer that her aunt was likely of the quality. To own the truth, she had taken out the romances to read to her Aunt Claire and histories for herself, but it was better if he thought her an empty-headed gudgeon. In all honesty, she *had* been caught up in the tale she was currently reading to her aunt and had found herself looking forward to each new reading with some anticipation.

"I see you have finished your tea," Sir James said after a moment. "May I get you another cup? Perhaps you would like some macaroons. I find that I am hungry and I mean to purchase a bag of them."

Emma shook her head. "No, thank you, sir, I—" She faltered. Why did he persist in staring at her like that? It had just occurred to her that Charlotte or Johnny or, worse yet, Joan could be passing by this tent at any time. And what would be more likely than that they should glance inside, perhaps decide to have tea? How ever would she explain this cozy tête-à-tête with a strange gentleman? Indeed, she did not even understand herself what had possessed her to linger there, bandying words with "Jamie," although she was not so naive as to believe that to be his true name. Perhaps it was a childhood nickname. And perhaps he had plucked it from thin air.

It was clear that he was curious about her, and she thought he might very likely follow her when she left the tent. Then he would see her meeting Charlotte, whom he could probably identify, and her foolish masquerade would be over. Heaven help her, she would be in the suds then.

Well, she must be more clever than he. "Now that I consider it, I believe I should enjoy a macaroon."

He got to his feet and went to the counter. As soon as his broad back in the handsome great coat was turned to her, she slipped from the tent, pushing her way into the milling throng outside until she was certain to be hidden from anyone looking out from the tearoom tent. It must be nearing two o'clock, and the direction she had chosen would take her on a rather circuitous route to the baker's booth. However, to turn back now would require her to pass the tearoom again, so she continued in the path she had picked, hurrying as quickly as the jostling people would allow.

It was Emma's good fortune that on the drive home, Charlotte was full of having met Lord Ryerson and Lord Emberland and going to the puppet show with them. The fact that her abigail had been in attendance seemed to have dampened her enjoyment only slightly.

Sir James, upon turning from the counter with the macaroons and tea, saw that the table where he had been sitting with Sophia was now empty. He cursed under his breath and set the tea back on the counter, tucking the bag of macaroons into the pocket of his great coat.

The chit had eluded him again. Ignoring the stares from the counterman and his female helpers, he strode from the tent, leaving two untasted cups of tea behind.

On the thoroughfare he halted to look in first one direction and then another. Although his height permitted him to see over the heads of most of the crowd, he caught no glimpse of a gray cap with red-gold curls escaping from it. In spite of the fact that he traversed the thoroughfare from one end to the other, he caught no further sight of Sophia. Eventually he went to his carriage in a disgruntled mood. His driver had also returned from visiting the fair, and Sir James, deciding against taking the reins himself, instructed the man to drive to his house and climbed in.

He had learned slightly more about his quarry, he mused, unaware that he was thinking in terms of the hunt. She had a sense of humor and she definitely did not wish to identify her aunt. He relaxed against the squabs to think about that. It occurred to him that the "aunt" was nonexistent. The chit was certainly fanciful enough to have made her up out of whole cloth, no doubt to hide her own station in life. The lending library she had named was near any number of great houses. She had tried to convince him later that she actually lived some distance from there, but he had not been flummeried by that ruse.

The more he thought of it, the more convinced he became that she was employed as a companion or governess in one of those houses. So he would be at that lending library on Thursday, and he would wait all afternoon, if necessary. Actually, it would be no hardship for he would merely take one of the agricultural books he had been studying to read.

A determined expression settled on his face. The devilish chit had got his blood up.

Two evenings later Emma found herself, somewhat to her own surprise, dressing for the small dinner party her aunt had hastily planned after returning from the Haverlys' gala. She had decided to wear a dark plum-colored gown of soft sarcenet with a modest square neckline and full sleeves; flounces at the neck and hemline were its only decoration. It was subdued enough for someone in half-mourning, yet attractive enough for a dinner party. Charlotte had loaned her a string of small pearls to wear with it, and Emma had arranged her hair simply in a halo of loose curls, a plum-colored ribbon woven in and out among them.

In the beginning she had agreed to go downstairs for the party because Lottie had begged her so earnestly. "Mama has invited Lord North," Lottie had said, "and you must come and try to divert his attention from me so that I can converse with Lord Ryerson."

"I must tell you, Lottie," Emma responded, "that I am somewhat surprised that Aunt Claire invited Lord Ryerson at all. I don't think she cares for him."

"Oh, I convinced her that if she hoped to lure Lord North here she had better invite his two closest friends, Sir Robert and Sir Charles Emberland."

"Very clever," commented Emma. "But what makes you think Lord North will pay any attention to you at all? From what you said, he was not wearing the willow for you after the Haverlys' party."

"You know that Mama will throw us together," said Charlotte. "So will you come? Mama says she had worked out the table arrangement with an equal number of ladies and gentlemen, and if you cry off, we shall have an extra man. Mama would be put out with you."

Emma had sighed and relented, knowing that Charlotte spoke the truth. She did wonder, however, why her Aunt Claire so clearly wanted her at the party, too. Up until now she had not pressed Emma to go into society with her daughter.

Studying her reflection in the glass, Emma thought that she could still cry off, for Lord North had declined to attend. That had sent Lady Parton to her bed for an entire day with at least a dozen pains in various parts of her body, which was why Emma had not wished to press the matter of her appearance at dinner. When she learned one of the gentlemen was not coming, she had thought her aunt would be relieved for her to keep to her chamber, thus balancing the number of ladies and men.

Unfortunately, Lady Parton had been as insistent as ever that Emma attend, and Emma had thought it best to give in gracefully, for her aunt vowed that merely thinking of her niece's playing such an ungrateful trick on her was giving her the most vexing headache. Emma could only think that it was being opposed, even in so small a matter, that her aunt did not care for, and this accounted for her insistence upon Emma's presence at the gathering. Jonathan and Sir Humphrey had chosen to take dinner in their chambers, however, and Emma rather envied them.

The guests were received by Lord and Lady Parton along with Charlotte and Emma in the large blue salon. Decorated elegantly in blue and pearl-gray brocades and satins, with graciously full and swagged velvet draperies and a beautiful crystal chandelier, the room was rarely used by the family except to entertain guests.

Lord Ryerson and Lord Emberland arrived together, both dressed in long-tailed, heavily padded coats and matching inexpressibles with silk stockings. If Lord Ryerson had fewer satin ribbons at his knees than his friend, it was difficult for Emma to discern it. The dress of the two proclaimed them to be rather out in front of the latest fashion, and Emma could hardly suppress a smile at the way Lord Parton frowned as his gaze raked the two gentlemen.

Then Augusta Woodbyn arrived, wearing a most expensive, rather low-cut gown of ivory satin. The gown did nothing at all for the tall, spindly miss, with its low neck showing her sharp collarbones and its color, with her pale skin and thin blond hair, making her look even more washed out than she might have in a brighter hue. Miss Woodbyn, Emma judged, must be at least twenty-five, with a long, sharp nose and thin brows and lashes. Thinking that Lord North would be among the guests, Lady Parton had made certain that Charlotte had no competition for his attention that evening.

Poor Aunt Claire, Emma thought. All her careful, if

hasty, preparations had come to naught because of the rudeness of that arrogant gentleman. She found that she felt quite sorry for her aunt, and the impression Charlotte had given her of Lord North as an aloof, condescending person too full of himself to be concerned with anyone else's feelings was strengthened.

The butler served drinks and canapés, and Emma found herself seated beside Miss Woodbyn on an embroidered settee. Charlotte, looking quite beautiful in a gold ribbon-trimmed gown, sat on a velvet sofa and was quickly flanked by the two gentlemen guests.

"We are expecting two other guests," remarked Lady Parton, making a valiant effort to put a brave face on the fiasco that the dinner party was turning into since the person for whom everything had been arranged had declined to attend.

Emma turned to speak to Miss Woodbyn, who murmured a brief reply in a soft voice. Emma tried several topics of conversation, but could elicit nothing but monosyllabic murmurs in return. Not only was the poor lady unattractive, Emma decided, but she had no conversation. Her mother must be nearly distracted by now with trying to arrange a suitable match for her.

She was saved from having to think of something else to say to the lady by the entrance of the butler announcing the last two guests, Miss Hazel Lancaster and Mr. Henry Stumpover. Hazel Lancaster was a plain, but cheerfully outgoing young woman whom Emma had heard Charlotte speak of as a good friend. But Emma hardly looked at Miss Lancaster, for she was staring at the short, retiring young man whom she had caught glimpses of a few times while they were in Sussex. He looked highly uncomfortable and totally out of place. What on earth was *he* doing here?

Lady Parton was introducing him to the others, a pained look on her face. But there was also a relentless set to her jaw, as if she meant to go on with her plans to the bitter end. Leading the man to where Emma and Miss Woodbyn were sitting, Lady Parton said, "Mr. Stumpover, this is Miss Augusta Woodbyn. Her mama was a dear childhood friend of mine. And this is my niece, Miss Robinson. But perhaps the two of you have met already. Emma, you must have heard me speak of Mr. Stumpover. He's the curate at our little village church in Sussex."

Emma recovered from her shock sufficiently to acknowledge the introduction politely, and within minutes they were going in to dinner.

Finding that she was seated beside Mr. Stumpover, Emma began to get the inkling of a suspicion. As the meal progressed, conversing with the curate proved hardly less of an effort than with Miss Woodbyn. However, sympathy for the poor man, whose suit was at least five years old and could never have been called fashionable, even when new, whose light brown hair was thinning noticeably, even though he was probably not over eight and twenty, and who had probably never been in such an elegant social situation before in his life, made Emma continue to pursue a conversation with him.

Ignoring his stammering responses, she went on talking throughout the meal, and eventually he seemed to feel more at ease with her.

"Tell me, Mr. Stumpover," she said as the dessert was carried in, "what has brought you up to London at this time of year?"

He blinked his pale blue eyes at her. "Oh, didn't you

know? Lady Parton very graciously wrote and invited me to come and have a holiday in town. The Partons have provided rooms for me at the most comfortable inn."

"I see," said Emma, her suspicion becoming stronger.

"I confess," he confided in a low voice, "I did not expect to be invited to a gathering in their home with such high-born guests. You know, of course, that I have my living from Lord Parton, but this is certainly more than I could have expected. Extremely generous of the Partons, don't you think?"

"Indeed," agreed Emma. "How long will you be staying in town?"

"I—I'm not certain. The innkeeper said my rooms and meals had been provided for three weeks. If I have no further indication from the Partons, I shall return to Sussex at the end of that time."

After dinner the group adjourned to the music room where Miss Lancaster was prevailed upon to sing while Charlotte accompanied her on the pianoforte. During the performance Lady Parton pressed her fingers against her temple as if she had the headache and Sir Randolph yawned behind his hand, then dozed. The guests began to leave as soon as the young ladies finished the last selection; it was evident they were all excessively bored, except for Mr. Stumpover, who was too awed to be bored, and Lord Ryerson, who appeared to consider close proximity to Charlotte entertainment enough for anyone.

As soon as the last guest was shown out, Lord Parton heaved a loud sigh and grumbled, "The next time you have a dinner party, m'dear, I recommend you plan a few games to liven things up."

Not at all appreciative of her husband's unsolicited advice, Lady Parton declared, "I have not been up to the mark all evening, for I have the most rending stomach upset."

"Your appetite did not seem at all affected, though," mused Sir Randolph innocently. "I must tell you, m'dear, that you put a very brave face on things."

"What else was I to do, Randolph?" snapped her ladyship. "And as for livening things up, if that vexing Lord North had . . . Well, that is nothing to the purpose now."

"I'm going to retire," put in Charlotte before her mother could get properly wound up on the subject of Lord North.

"I, too," said Emma, "unless you should need me for anything, Aunt Claire."

As if she had just recalled Emma's presence at the party, Lady Parton gave her a considering look. "You were quite pretty this evening, Emma, and you seemed to be enjoying yourself with Mr. Stumpover. I have been wanting to have him up to London for an age, and I'm glad I picked this particular time."

Her husband was staring at her in bewilderment. "Never knew you wanted Stumpover in London. Never mentioned it to me. And I can't conceive why you should, either. The man looked like a fish out of water tonight, poor devil."

"That is the very reason I thought he should spend a few weeks in town," retorted Lady Parton. "I know he is only a village curate, but a little town bronze might improve his chances of stepping up in the world."

"Why should you care if he steps up in the world?" asked Sir Randolph in perplexity. "If you have been infected with a sudden desire to pursue charitable endeavors, there must be thousands of hungry children roaming the streets of London at this very minute. Concentrate on them and let Stumpover be. I daresay he would be vastly relieved to be allowed to return to Sussex."

"Oh, merciful heaven!" Lady Parton clutched her stomach dramatically and uttered several pathetic moans. Catching sight of the butler standing at attention in the vestibule, she ordered him, "Go and tell Genevieve to come to my bedchamber. I must have a posset to relieve my stomach upset or I shan't get a wink of sleep all night."

"Shall I come up with you, Aunt?" Emma asked.

Distractedly, Lady Parton dismissed her niece with a flutter of her fingers. "No, no, dear. I shan't be wanting you to read to me, and I am sure Genevieve can prepare my posset." Her ladyship left them, followed by her still puzzled husband.

"What *do* you think came over Mama to invite Mr. Stumpover?" Charlotte asked, shaking her head. "She has never given the man the time of day before. It was all I could do to keep from laughing at the way he kept staring about at the chandeliers and furnishings. And did you see him eating his peas with his soup spoon?"

"I must tell you, Lottie," said Emma, "that you are speaking of the man your mama has cast in the role of my future husband."

Charlotte stared at her for a moment, and then she giggled. "Famous! Why, Emma, I believe Mr. Stumpover is coming to agree with Mama, too. He talked to nobody but you all evening. If anyone should ask my opinion, I should say he is wearing the willow for you already."

"No one asked for your opinion," retorted Emma. "As for talking to me, Mr. Stumpover did well to answer elementary questions. The fellow was very nearly struck dumb. He had no inkling of how he came to be here."

"We can only pray he doesn't have a jumped-up opinion

of himself as a result," said Charlotte facetiously. "Poor Emma. You have no idea how persistent Mama can be when she sets her mind on something."

"But I do! It happens, however, that I can be determined, too. For the next several weeks I can use my mourning as an excuse to avoid any tête-à-têtes Aunt Claire may plan for Mr. Stumpover and me. But then I shall have to find a position. Which reminds me, Lottie, we'd better get some sleep so that we shall be fresh for my pianoforte lesson in the morning."

"Oh, lud!" groaned Charlotte. "Are you still set on that shatterbrained plan?"

"More than ever. And by the by, Lottie, I think you should give some thought to being a little less enchanting when you are with Lord Ryerson. The gentleman is already head over ears."

Charlotte smiled. "Do you really think so?"

"Any ninnyhammer can see it. But you know Aunt Claire has her sights set higher than someone of Lord Ryerson's relatively modest means."

"Pooh," said Charlotte dismissingly, "I shall have money of my own when I marry. Uncle Humphrey has promised Papa that he will settle a sizable fortune on me."

"Nonetheless," insisted Emma, "your mama wants a feather for her cap when you marry."

Still muttering her disregard for her mother's plans, Charlotte left the salon and wandered up the stairs to her chamber. Emma followed her shortly, a thoughtful expression on her face.

## *CHAPTER SEVEN*

Having failed in her first attempt to lure Lord North into her carefully set lair, Lady Parton spent the next few days in her chamber, pleading a recurring stomach upset. None of the members of the household, with the possible exception of Sir Humphrey, was taken in by this. Knowing her ladyship as they did, they suspected that, between possets and cordials, Lady Parton was carefully plotting the next step in her campaign.

When that lady did appear again belowstairs, "almost fully recovered" from her ailment, she looked rested and ready to sail into the fray again whenever she judged the propitious moment had arrived. Charlotte was particularly on guard, for hadn't she heard her mother's injunction upon more than one occasion (usually when they were discussing when to arrive at a social gathering), "Timing, my dear Lottie, is everything"?

On that first afternoon belowstairs her ladyship, to everyone's relief, seemed content to spend some quiet hours in the bosom of her family, working at her embroidery, in the gold salon.

Emma was making careful additions to the sampler in her own small frame, having cajoled Charlotte into teaching her some basic embroidery stitches. As for Lottie, she was pretending to read a book, although most of the time she was gazing out at the dreary March day with a dreamy expression on her face. Jonathan was playing a game of solitaire, frequently shuffling the cards with impatience to lay them out again.

Sir Humphrey was comfortably settled in an armchair near the crackling fire, enjoying a glass of port and making an occasional comment that seemed to pertain to nothing that anyone else had said. Lord Parton lounged in another chair, perusing the *Times*.

"I am happy to see you are taking an interest in ladylike endeavors, Emma," remarked Lady Parton, glancing up briefly from her own embroidery. "Every young woman should have a few accomplishments before she marries, even if she is to have but a modest household."

Evidently her aunt had forgotten Emma's avowed intention of learning ladylike accomplishments in order to go into service as a governess, and Emma thought it best not to remind her. "Embroidery is a pleasant pastime," she responded noncommittally.

"Don't understand why females always have to be *doing* something," commented Sir Humphrey lazily. "Why can't you sit and do nothing? Ain't a thing wrong with doing nothing, if you care for my opinion." No one bothered to respond to this, but undoubtedly they were all thinking, as Emma was, that his elderly lordship spoke from considerable experience.

"Never could see any point in dashing about from cattle auctions to gaming tables," went on Sir Humphrey, warming to his theme, "although I do enjoy an occasional game of cards. Did I ever tell you about the Lion's Paw, Randolph?"

"What's that, Uncle?" mumbled Lord Parton, not glancing up from his paper.

"The Lion's Paw. Did I ever tell you about the time I was taken by a Captain Sharp in that place and—"

"Yes," said Sir Randolph, raising his voice slightly, but still intent upon his reading, "several times."

"Lottie," remarked Lady Parton into the silence that followed, "don't forget that we are invited to take tea with Lady North and her daughter at the North house tomorrow."

Charlotte's dreamy gaze out the window had altered to one of exasperation by the time she turned to look at her mother. "Yes, Mama, I'm not likely to forget. You spoke of little else when I visited you in your chamber yesterday. I am sure you must have hinted outrageously to Lady Haverly when we were there that we would be greatly honored to take tea with her and her mother."

"I may have mentioned it merely," responded Lady Parton, seemingly affronted by her daughter's accusation. "I do not recall every word I spoke at the Haverlys' party."

"Why should anyone be honored to *take tea?*" inquired Sir Humphrey, "unless it should be at Carlton House, although *I* don't think I'd care for that, either. No, Lottie, I must tell you I think you are fair and far off there. I know your mama has some demmed foolish notions, but she ain't feather-headed enough to be honored by an invitation to tea at some Lady West's house."

"North," Charlotte corrected him impatiently, "and you are quite wrong, Uncle Humphrey. Mama considers the North establishment practically equivalent to Carlton House."

"Why should she do that?" asked that gentleman reasonably.

"Because Lady North's son is there, and she thinks he may condescend to put in an appearance at tea," Charlotte enlightened him, "but he won't. He dislikes females."

"The fellow sounds smart to me," concluded Sir Humphrey. "I shouldn't like to be invited to a female tea party myself, and I warn you, Claire, if you have any such notion, I want no part of it."

"Very wise, Uncle," said Lord Parton, having lowered his paper in time to see his wife's red face. "I am sure Claire has no such plan under consideration. Johnny, would you stop shuffling those devilish cards? I'm trying to read the paper."

Jonathan tossed the cards aside and got to his feet to roam restlessly about the room. "I hope I shall be allowed to go back to Oxford soon."

"I've sent a letter already, informing them you'll be returning at the end of the month," his father told him. "I daresay that officious schoolmaster's dignity has recovered by now. But if you are sent down again, I mean to cut off your allowance." Having delivered the direst threat he could conceive of, Lord Parton returned to his paper.

A heavy silence settled on the salon for several moments. Then it was interrupted by a loud, barking laugh from Sir Randolph. "The *Times* must have a new satirist. Listen to this verse:

*Poor Lady P. has taken to her bed,*
*A soothing kerchief atop her head,*
*After facing her tray with commendable zeal*
*And forcing down a five-course meal,*
*Convinced, though all of London cry nay,*
*She's at death's door for the third time today.*

The others were staring at him, even Sir Humphrey, who let out a gruff chuckle.

"Why that sounds like . . ." Fortunately, Charlotte caught herself before she finished the thought aloud.

Sir Humphrey, however, had no such hesitation. "Your

mama. The fellow must be someone we know. Who is he, Randolph?"

Jonathan had stopped his restless pacing and was standing very still near the door. Emma glanced at him, and in spite of her shock at hearing her private thoughts read aloud from the *Times*, it seemed to her that the young man had an odd look on his face.

"The verse is signed 'Aristobulus,' " Lord Parton was saying. "These satirists never use their true names. They'd be stoned in the streets if they did. Wait—the editor has added a note. Listen to this. 'Aristobulus is asked to come forward and identify himself to the editor of this newspaper for the purpose of discussing publication of more of his verses.' "

Lady Parton, who had been breathing heavily for several moments, said indignantly, "I think such useless drivel is a disgrace to any respectable newspaper. Nor can I conceive, Uncle Humphrey, why you should imagine those silly lines refer to me. I am nothing at all like that."

Sir Humphrey would undoubtedly have contradicted her had not his nephew intervened quickly. "Of course not, m'dear. Uncle Humphrey was bamming you, I am sure." He did not give his uncle an opportunity to disagree with this, but turned to him with a jovial tone. "Sir, I've been saving a surprise for you and I believe this is as good a time as any to tell you. I've managed to buy a dozen bottles of the finest brandy to be had anywhere. Shall we open one and sample it?"

Sir Humphrey's interest was completely caught, of course, and when his nephew had summoned the butler, he watched Hemmings's entrance and exit from the salon with clear anticipation.

Lady Parton looked watchfully about at the others, as

if daring anyone to agree with Sir Humphrey's conclusion concerning the verse in the *Times.* No one had the effrontery to do so. Emma concentrated on her sampler, Charlotte on her book, Jonathan on a figurine atop the mantelpiece.

Shortly Hemmings returned with the gentlemen's brandy. Sir Humphrey consumed two mouthfuls and said, "It's my belief this liquor never paid duty at any port."

"No," agreed Sir Randolph, "I think it was probably smuggled. All the best seems to be these days."

Emma, seeing her aunt was again applying herself to her frame, laid aside her embroidery. "I'm going up to my chamber now," she said casually, fitting action to her words as she quickly left the salon.

Safely inside her room, with the door locked, she fell to searching her desk and then the dressing table, a frown of consternation pulling at her face. The paper upon which she had written the verse was nowhere to be found. She remembered crumpling it and placing it on top of the desk to be disposed of later. She could not remember ever seeing the paper again. Would that timid abovestairs maidservant dare to have read what was on the paper? Nonsense, the child almost certainly was unlettered. And even if she weren't, the fifteen-year-old girl who slipped in and out of rooms like a shadow and jumped violently if anyone spoke to her would never have had the audacity to take the verse to the *Times.*

There was someone in this household who *did* have the audacity, however, and he had had the queerest look on his face when Lord Parton was reading that verse aloud. She made herself wait until she was certain Jonathan would be in his chamber dressing for dinner. Then she hurried along the hall and knocked sharply at his door. The valet opened it.

"Good day, Frazier. I should like to have a word with your master, please."

Frazier, his face a perfect blank, as always, moved away from the door for a few moments, then was back. "The young gentleman is still in his shirtsleeves, miss."

"Well, I have seen him in worse than his shirtsleeves. If you will be so good as to step aside."

Although the valet moved but slightly, Emma slipped past him and confronted her young cousin, her hands on her hips. "I am sure you will excuse us for a few minutes, Frazier. I must speak to Jonathan in private."

"Sir?" inquired the valet.

Jonathan, who had seen that steely look in a female's eyes before, said, "Leave us for a bit, Frazier. I am sure I don't know what has got Emma on the fidgets, but I daresay we shall have no peace until she has given me a rake-down. *I* am blamed for any variety of things I have no knowledge of, but let that pass. I've become accustomed to it."

Emma gave him a quelling look as the valet moved silently from the room. When the door was closed, she exclaimed, "Jonathan Parton, you are the biggest rogue unhung! How *could* you have done such a thing?"

"I am sure I don't know—"

"Stop trying to look as innocent as a caged dove! I can always tell when you are filling up a bag of moonshine, for your nose twitches."

"It doesn't!" Jonathan touched the offending member distrustfully.

"You sent that verse to the *Times*, and you may as well own up to it for I mean to stay here until you do. Of all the want-witted pranks you have pulled, this is the shabbiest."

Seeing that he was at Point Non-Plus, Jonathan flung himself into the nearest chair and said disconsolately, "Devil take it, Emma! I didn't think you would fly up into the boughs like this. Hang me if I did!"

"Cabbage-head!"

Affronted, he said, "Well, *I* didn't write the verse."

"No, you shan't lay this in *my* dish. It is my own business what I write in my private papers. When my intimate thoughts are spread abroad without my desire or knowledge, that is another matter entirely. To make the matter even more dastardly, you filched the paper from my chamber."

"Now that is doing it up too brown, Emma. I visited your chamber to see if you would come and have a billiard game with me. You weren't there so I thought I would wait a few minutes. I was pacing the floor when I saw that piece of paper on your desk. I only noticed it because everything else was so neat. Well, I picked it up and—I honestly didn't mean to pry."

"But you couldn't help yourself, I suppose."

"Yes, and when I read it—well, it was too amusing not to keep. Later I got to thinking about those satirical verses some of the papers use, and I thought you were as good as Peter Pindar or any of them."

"You are too generous!"

"It's true. But I didn't mean it as a prank. You have been running on about how you must support yourself, and I have always thought you could be a writer. Didn't I tell you that? And I know you should hate being a governess. I only meant to help launch your career as an author."

"Launch my career! By holding your mama up to ridicule?"

"If Uncle Humphrey had bridled his tongue," he said glumly, "she would never have imagined the verse concerned her. But I collect you can't teach an old dog new tricks, can you? I am sure Mama doesn't suspect, anyway, for you know she never listens to Uncle Humphrey. And don't you like the name I chose for you?"

"I am transported," said Emma with the heaviest of irony.

"The editor wants to have more of your verses," said Jonathan, brightening and sitting straighter. "You must go and see him, Emma."

"Wonderful! I shall merely tell Uncle Randolph that I must have the use of the carriage for a meeting at the *Times* so that I may make arrangements to insult others in addition to his wife."

He grinned. "Papa *was* amused, wasn't he?"

"A little, I suppose," admitted Emma. "But if you ever breathe a word to anyone concerning the true identity of Aristobulus, I promise you I shall wreak havoc on your head."

"I'll sign an oath in blood, if you wish!"

"There is no call for bloodletting, Cousin, *unless* you fail to keep your promise."

"Now," he said, disregarding her threatening tone and rubbing the palms of his hands together, "we must lay a plan for you to call on the editor without anyone else catching wind of it."

"Johnny," said Emma sternly, "I will have your word on it that you won't try to *help* me anymore."

"Dash it, Emma, you can't let this opportunity go by. You could be famous! Well, not you exactly, but Aristobulus. And how amusing it would be to poke fun at people without being caught out."

"I shall give it a great deal of thought, I promise you. In the meantime, your word."

"Haven't I already said you can trust me? I will never cry rope on you. If you decide to go to the *Times,* though, you will need a carriage and someone to accompany you."

"Do not concern yourself, I beg you. I am capable of supervising my own affairs."

"But you have forgiven me?"

"Only partly," Emma said with a wry look. "But if you ever do anything like that again . . ."

"Devil take it, you ain't going to ring another peal over me, are you?"

She threw up her hands and with a new burst of exasperation said, "Oh, fiddle! I will leave you to finish dressing for dinner. I may take a leaf from Aunt Claire's book and plead the headache. I am not sure I am up to facing her at table quite yet."

"Depend upon it, she will never in a million ages guess it was you."

"I sincerely hope you may be right," she retorted as she left.

Sending down word that she had the headache, no doubt from doing so much close needlework when she was unaccustomed to the activity, Emma took her dinner in her chamber. At first she had been so angry she had thought of nothing beyond confronting Jonathan. But she rather thought, after the rake-down she had administered, he would keep watch on his tongue and not let a clue to the identity of Aristobulus slip out. As provoked as she still was at what her cousin had done, she couldn't help pursuing, in her thoughts, the opportunity that Johnny's heedless act had provided.

Could she continue to write her verses for publication without anyone but Jonathan suspecting? It would be possible, she mused, to hire for a farthing one of the urchins she had seen loitering about the lending library to deliver the verses, safely sealed from prying eyes, to the *Times* editor. There was always the post, of course, but she couldn't send correspondence to the *Times* from the Parton house without someone discovering it. No, she thought a private arrangement of some sort would be safer.

But how could she learn enough about topics of popular interest to write such verses regularly? Peter Pindar already lambasted the politicians regularly, and besides, she knew little of what went on at Whitehall. There was always the ton, though, but she did not go very much into society. Still, she had access to all the latest on-dits through Charlotte, who could not be kept from passing them along in any case. Every time she returned from a party, she was so full of all she had seen and heard that she usually insisted upon a coze with Emma to discuss it.

Emma would have to be more careful to disguise the subjects of her verses, too. Had she dreamed the satire upon her aunt's imagined frailties would be given public airing, she would have named the lady "Lady Q" or anything but "Lady P." It would be greater fun for readers to be kept guessing, anyway.

Briefly, she worried about the consequences should her aunt discover what she was doing. But that possibility was so remote and the thought of someday being a woman of independent, if modest, means was too attractive to cast aside easily. Johnny was right. The verses would launch her career as an author in a small way, and later she might try her hand at a satirical novel—perhaps even a serious one.

Before Emma slept that night, she had made her decision to call upon the editor of the *Times.* It only remained for her to find a way to accomplish it in utter secrecy.

The opportunity to carry through with her intention was not given her until the following Thursday. It was the day upon which she usually visited the lending library alone, for neither Charlotte nor her aunt was interested enough in reading to spend much time making selections. Lady Parton liked Emma to read aloud to her, but she left it to Emma to choose the tales.

The Parton carriage and driver were provided for Emma's trips to the lending library. On this Thursday she informed her aunt that she might be away a little longer than on her previous visits, since she wanted to browse through the shelves that she hadn't taken the time for earlier. Lady Parton gave her grudging permission, insisting that Emma must return to the house by teatime.

Set down in the street near the library, Emma told Benjy that she planned to stay a full two hours and suggested that he drive back to the house and return for her later. The groom was more than willing to agree, for he clearly chafed at waiting idly with the carriage while Emma exchanged the volumes she had brought for different ones.

Emma left the books she carried in her arms with the librarian and returned to the street as soon as the Parton carriage was out of sight. It was a matter of only a few minutes before she was able to attract the attention of the driver of a chaise-for-hire. She settled the matter of the fare with him before she stepped inside, still begrudging the amount they finally settled on. But there was no help for it, and she would be earning more money soon.

At the rather drab-looking building that housed the offices of the *Times*, she instructed the driver to wait for her and strode through the portals, her shoulders back, although she was trembling inside. When she informed a squinty-eyed gentleman at a battered desk that she wished to see the editor, he surveyed her suspiciously and demanded to know her business.

"You may tell him," said Emma, her head held high, "that I have information for him concerning the identity of Aristobulus."

"Who?" The squinty eyes were definitely disbelieving now.

"If you will just tell him, I am sure he will see me."

Finally the fellow sauntered off, muttering imprecations. He was back shortly, jerking his head toward the door through which she had seen him disappear briefly. "He's in there, miss. Don't know who this Air-ee-stab-you-lus bloak is, but *he* does, it seems."

The editor was a slight, hunch-shouldered man with bushy brows and sharp green eyes. He offered Emma a chair near his desk with curt politeness and recommended she state her business succinctly for he was a busy man.

Therefore, she minced no words. "I am Miss Emma Robinson, and I wrote the verse that appeared in your paper four days ago above the signature 'Aristobulus.' "

The penetrating green eyes rested thoughtfully on her face. "You don't say so? Before you go on, miss, perhaps I should tell you that three persons have already been in this office proclaiming themselves to be Aristobulus. You are, however, the first female to make the claim."

Emma was momentarily stunned into silence. It had

never occurred to her that others would claim authorship, nor that she would have to prove her assertion. Finally, she stammered, "But—how did you discover that all the others were interlopers?"

"Easily, my girl. I merely asked for more samples of their versifying. None of them came even close to the verse that I printed in my newspaper. Two of them couldn't even rhyme."

Emma breathed a sigh of relief. "Oh, well, I have brought two verses with me. I suppose I could write one here on a topic of your choosing, but I must be back at the lending library in little more than an hour. You see, no one in my family—except for my younger cousin, Johnny, who posted the first verse without my knowledge—is aware that I am Aristobulus. And they must *never* know. My—my aunt would be outraged beyond all reason."

The editor took the papers she handed him without reply. As he read the first verse concerning the Prince Regent's recently acquired habit of wearing a corset, a smile twitched at the corners of his thin mouth. The second verse, an account of a harried Lord Byron dashing about the streets of London, his capes flying as he tried to elude that eccentric lady, Caroline Lamb, brought a deep-down hearty chuckle from the editor.

"I—I am aware that other satirists have written of Byron's escapades," Emma offered as the editor continued to look her over without speaking, "and the regent has certainly not been immune, either, but I wrote those rather hurriedly so that I would have something to show whenever I found it possible to come here. I should have to come up with many other subjects, I know."

"You mentioned an aunt, Miss Robinson," the man

said finally. "What of parents, brothers or sisters, a future husband?"

"I am an orphan, sir, and an only child," Emma told him. "I make my home with my aunt and uncle and two cousins. We are up from the country for my cousin Charlotte's second season. And I do not expect to have a husband for a good while yet."

"I see," he mused. "Your aunt and uncle would not approve of your doing this, I gather, from what you have said. How do you propose to go on with it in secrecy?"

At least, he seemed to have accepted her as the real Aristobulus, Emma told herself. She thought he had liked the new verses very well. "I have given that a great deal of thought, and I believe I have worked out a plan. I could have the verses delivered to you by messenger on Thursday afternoons."

"And how will I convey your wages to you if you don't come yourself?"

"I—I have thought that through, too. You could deposit my wages with the firm of solicitors who handled my late father's estate. I have written it all down for you. Then I could arrange for the solicitors to hold the money until I call for it."

The editor sat back in his creaking chair. "So, Miss Robinson, beneath that red-gold cap of hair there is an altogether devious mind."

Emma felt that this must be a criticism of her character. "I am sure you would not care to have a devious person in your employ, but I am not ordinarily devious. It is just that I want so much to earn some money of my own."

The editor laughed. "On the contrary, I think it will require a little deviousness to carry through with this plan as you have presented it to me."

"You believe that I am the true Aristobulus then?"

"I am half convinced," stated the editor with a slight shrug of his stooped shoulders. "I will print the two verses you have brought with you, and as long as the ones you send me are as good, I will print those, too. If you are not the original Aristobulus, you will do as well."

"But I *am* the original," insisted Emma, troubled by the man's suspicious nature. "I have enjoyed writing as long as I can remember, and I have kept journals and written poetry since I was very young. I've always had a secret desire to be a published author, but until now I never thought it could be possible."

The editor sat forward, his chair creaking, and propped his elbows upon the desk. "I will give you some free advice, young woman, since you seem sincere. Editors do not care a rush what you have always enjoyed doing or longed to do. Don't bother telling them. The only thing they care about is the work you give them. If that is good enough, you won't have to try to convince people that you're an author." He reached for a scrap of paper and pen. "Now if we can agree upon remuneration."

A few minutes later Emma left the *Times* building in something of a daze. The amount the editor had said he would pay her for each verse was modest, but he wanted to print two a week, and over the course of a year the sum would be a respectable amount, perhaps not as much as a governess earned, but more than most houseservants. If she could find employment as a governess, too, the combined wages, over a period of a very few years, would provide her with a measure of independence. And if, in future, she could write an acceptable novel . . .

But she was running ahead a great deal too fast, she told herself as she entered the hired chaise and directed the driver to return her to the lending library. Before she had left the office, the editor had paid her for the three verses already accepted, so she did not begrudge the chaise fare quite so much. The editor had even agreed to contact her father's solicitors and to explain to them about the money he would be depositing in her name. The solicitors would be told merely that she was writing an occasional piece for the *Times* and that the arrangement must be kept in the strictest confidence.

She was at the lending library with a half hour to spare before Benjy's expected return with the carriage. She went directly to the shelves where the romantic adventure novels were kept to pick a new volume for reading to her aunt. There would not be time today to browse among the histories for additional reading material for herself.

The romances were in a shadowy ell of the library behind a free-standing row of shelves taller than Emma herself. To read the titles on the bottom shelves, it was necessary to bend one's knees and stoop down in an extremely unladylike pose that made her skirts trail across the dusty floor. Fortunately, she had come prepared for this by donning one of her most worn gowns, a muddy brown afternoon dress that would not readily show the dirt.

As she was thus positioned, she heard footsteps approaching, and not wishing to be caught in such a stance, even by the young women who sought out this section of the library, she tugged one of Mrs. Radcliffe's novels from its place and straightened hastily. But she was too late, for the tall figure of a man stood near her, watching her self-conscious movement with amusement.

"Hello, Sophia."

Emma felt as if the breath had been forced from her

lungs. Standing before her in dark-colored coat and waistcoat, light tan inexpressibles, and gleaming Hessians, a caped driving coat over his arm and a beaver grasped in his long fingers, was the gentleman who had presented himself to her as "Jamie" at the Frost Fair. As she regarded him with enormous eyes, he took her free hand, which had flown to her breast at the sight of him, and bent over it. The gesture was perfectly polite and proper, but even in the dim light Emma thought she caught a mocking gleam in the dark eyes as he straightened.

Abruptly she withdrew her hand from his grasp. She moistened her lips. "I—I did not know that gentlemen read romantic novels."

She was disturbingly aware that he was blocking her way out of the narrow aisle. He looked even taller in that confined space, and his shoulders seemed even broader than she remembered. "In fact, I am surprised to see you here at all. I am sure you must have many books in your private library."

He smiled, his teeth flashing white in the masculine planes of his face. "I must confess, Sophia, this is my first visit to a lending library. I have been here some time, reading, and I admit it cannot compare with my own reading room. For one thing there are no servants to bring refreshment when I desire it."

"Then, why—?"

He chuckled appreciatively. "You would have me believe you haven't guessed I was waiting for you? I saw you come in a few minutes ago and followed you back here."

Emma found that her heart was pounding with a rapid and thunderous rhythm. This was the consequence of the silly game she had indulged in at their last meeting, acting as if she made a habit of clandestine tête-à-têtes with gentlemen and running on about gamblers and highwaymen in that ninnyhammer way. She had even told him that she visited the lending library on Thursday afternoons and named this one. Surely he hadn't thought she was issuing a veiled invitation for another secret meeting. Or had he?

"I must go, sir. My aunt is expecting me."

He didn't move aside, but continued to look down at her in that amused way. "Such a convenience, this aunt who always seems to be waiting for you. Ah, what a mysterious little baggage you are, Sophia. Why did you run away from me at our last meeting if not to whet my appetite to learn more about you?"

"I didn't mean—I suddenly realized that it was growing late." She had no earthly idea of how to handle the situation that her poor judgment and loose tongue had gotten her into. Her throat tightened painfully, and she looked away from his handsome, knowing face. "Please," she said in a voice that hovered just above a whisper, "I must go."

"My carriage is outside. I'll drive you to your—ah, aunt's house."

Her eyes flew back to meet his. "No!" The word was a strangled sound.

The slightly mocking look softened. "Sophia, I haven't frightened you, have I?" The tone held a touch of exasperation. "I've no wish to harm you, you know."

"No—" She shook her head, her vision suddenly obscured by mist. "I don't know anything of the kind. I can't conceive why you have come here, why you should have been waiting for me."

"You can't?" he asked, sounding rather baffled. "Perhaps I have been presumptuous then, or at least importunate."

Emma was regarding him with incredulity. "Presumptuous? I fear you may have received the wrong impression of me."

"I have no desire to insult you, for God's sake. How can I make myself more clear? Oh, Lord, you're not going to cry, are you?" He watched, fascinated as her mouth quivered uncontrollably. It stunned him and made him feel a veritable shabster, and quite as much to his own surprise as to Emma's, he caught her in his arms and stopped the trembling of her lips with his own.

Perhaps his initial intention had been to comfort her, but the kiss was certainly not comforting, nor was it brief. He kissed her thoroughly because she made no effort to pull away. It was an odd moment for both of them, a moment separate in time, as if it were happening to two other people.

When he released her and moved aside so that she could pass, she was so relieved to see that the aisle was now clear that she murmured, "Thank you," in a very soft voice.

He responded, with no trace of mockery or amusement in his tone, "The pleasure was mine, I assure you."

He watched her walk quickly away from him, clutching the book in her arms and not looking back. If he had not stood there for a long moment recalling the kiss and trying to put it into some logical frame of reference, he might have seen the carriage that waited for her outside. But by the time he thought of that and rushed into the street, there was no sight of Sophia or any conveyance at all.

## CHAPTER EIGHT

Emma was back in her own bedchamber before she would let her mind dwell on what had happened at the lending library. And even then she could hardly comprehend it. That such a clearly eminent gentleman as "Jamie" should actually wait for hours in that mundane place merely for her to appear was beyond conceiving. There was only one possible explanation for such uncharacteristic behavior, and it made Emma's cheeks flame anew as her thoughts settled on it.

She felt even more humiliation, knowing that she had only herself to blame for whatever false impression Jamie might have received concerning her at the Frost Fair. Hadn't she heard the tales Charlotte brought home of high-born gentlemen and the mistresses they kept? Even the ones who were married seemed to indulge themselves in affairs with women of the lower classes with shocking frequency. To hear Charlotte talk, one would think a gentleman was not considered quite up to the mark unless he had kept at least one mistress.

Both times she had met Jamie she had been unchaperoned, and the second time she had conversed in such a frivolous and free manner that he could not have thought her very wellborn. Since she was certain he could not possibly believe her to be a member of the quality, a shameful purpose could be all that had been on his mind in seeking her out.

The fact that she herself had misled him, albeit unintentionally, did not keep her from feeling insulted and angry.

She should have rung a peal over him that he would never have forgotten. Instead, she had been moved to tears and then had allowed him to embrace her and kiss her with the greatest familiarity. And even then she hadn't given him a set-down. To own the truth, her senses had been in such disorder that she'd been incapable of anything but to scurry away like a frightened rabbit.

The only solace she could see in what had happened was that she had, at least, disconcerted the man by taking her leave as quickly as possible. She did not think he would bother to seek her out again, and this provided a measure of solace.

A sharp rap at her door brought her out of her reverie. "Emma, may I come in for a moment?"

It was Charlotte. Emma gave her reflection in the glass a brief inspection, half fearing that something in her face might hint at what had happened at the lending library. However, her normally calm features merely looked slightly pale, which could be explained by tiredness or recently being out in the biting cold.

She opened the door and her cousin swept past her in a swirl of mauve skirts. "Ready to go down for tea so early, Lottie? Are we having special guests that you are eager to meet?"

Charlotte seated herself in a chair and surveyed Emma's worn gown. "We are having *a* guest. But hadn't you better be getting dressed yourself? I don't think Mama will approve if you appear in that old thing."

"I'll put on a more proper gown shortly." Emma took a seat on the chaise and smiled at her cousin. "Could it be Lord Ryerson that you're expecting?"

Charlotte shook her head. "It is no one to see me at all. I tried to cry off, but Mama insisted that I make an appearance. She said it would not look well otherwise. I've come to warn you, Emma. The expected guest is Mr. Stumpover."

It was a moment before Emma could put the name with a face. The shy young curate had made so little impression on her that she had forgotten him completely, hoping that her aunt, after seeing how ill at ease he had been at dinner in the house, would have done the same.

"Oh, lud!" she exclaimed finally. "I suppose I should have known Aunt Claire wouldn't be thwarted so easily."

Charlotte grimaced. "No, I fear not. But I promise you, I shall remain with you, no matter how strongly Mama hints that we should leave the two of you alone after we have greeted the man." Her brown eyes softened doubtfully. "At least, I shall try."

"Well, don't give Aunt Claire a spasm," Emma said. "I shall be able to hold my own with Mr. Stumpover, if need be."

"Good," breathed Charlotte, clearly relieved at not being asked to oppose her mother too obviously.

Emma stood and walked to the dressing table where she began to restore her red-gold curls to order. "Tell me, Lottie, did you enjoy the Simmons' party on Tuesday night?"

Charlotte's wry expression was reflected in the glass. "It was tedious beyond all things. There were place cards, and I was paired with the odious Lord North. I am sure that Mama whispered in Lady Simmons's ear before the party and somehow convinced her to do it. And Lady Haverly, Lord North's sister, was there, and she kept watching me all evening with the most calculating look in her eyes. I believe Mama has half convinced her that I would be a proper wife for her brother. I must tell you that I was amazed to see him there, for he was obviously bored by it all."

Emma turned from the glass. "Didn't you try to entertain the gentleman?"

Charlotte shrugged. "Oh, I was very civil in the beginning. But he has little interest in the latest on-dits and even less in putting himself out to be agreeable to ladies. I've never known a man with such a jumped-up opinion of himself in my life! Why so many females are on the catch for him, I cannot well imagine."

"Perhaps it is their mamas who think him so eligible," Emma suggested.

"Probably," agreed Charlotte. "Getting him to accept an invitation is like pulling teeth, though. You cannot imagine the ruses some of the mothers have resorted to in order to have him presented to their daughters." She giggled suddenly. "And then he merely looks through his quizzing glass at them with a bored expression as though he were thinking what poor deluded creatures they are to imagine that the awesome Lord North might find them even slightly amusing. Do you know, last evening he acted as if he'd never clapped eyes on me before—after I stood up with him at his sister's party!"

"Gracious, he does sound formidable!"

"And when I asked him if he had ever seen the inside of Newgate, he stared at me as if I'd planted him a facer."

Emma laughed delightedly. "But whatever possessed you to ask him such a question?"

"Well, he was being so aloof, hardly talking at all, and Mama kept staring daggers at me to remind me that I ought to be drawing him out. I have always wondered what Newgate is like and, oh, it just popped out. Maybe

I wanted to unsettle that haughty manner he wears. I don't think I succeeded, though."

"I *am* sorry," said Emma. "It does sound as if Lord North needs a good set-down, too. I wonder what it would take to give him one?"

"I am convinced that would be very difficult. I mean, the way everyone toad-eats him—his sister and his mother, and all the matchmaking mamas, and a surprising number of the gentlemen, too. Why, even Lord Ryerson admires him and says he is a good man in a turnup. I cannot conceive why men think another man is all the crack merely because he's got a right."

"Nor can I," murmured Emma very thoughtfully. But then she recollected herself and added, "I'd better get dressed now, Lottie, or I shall be late for tea and your mother will take the headache."

Charlotte took her leave and Emma dressed hurriedly in a rust-colored afternoon dress, reflecting all the while on the haughty Lord North. The gentleman sounded as if he ought to have his pride pricked, and she thought she knew just the way to do it. She was humming to herself as she descended the stairs and went toward the gold salon where tea would be served.

As it fell out, Charlotte was not as intrepid as she had painted herself in Emma's chamber earlier. At first she pretended not to take her mother's meaning when that lady suggested Mr. Stumpover might feel overwhelmed by trying to make conversation with so many ladies at once. But it took only one long, hard stare from Lady Parton to move Charlotte to follow her meekly from the salon, casting an apologetic look in Emma's direction as she did so.

It was no easy task carrying on a conversation with the

self-conscious curate, and Emma was already feeling weary from the rather extraordinary things that had befallen her that day. When Mr. Stumpover gathered enough courage to compliment her on her gown, it was all she could do to smile and pretend to be gratified. This, however, seemed to be enough to encourage the gentleman to add, while blushing furiously, "I am at a loss to understand, Miss Robinson, how a young woman of your intelligence and sensibilities could be still unwed."

"Oh, that is very easily explained," said Emma blithely. "The gentlemen who have become well enough acquainted with me to consider matrimony have discovered my dreadful secret."

The curate blinked at her, his expression one of mingled curiosity and disapproval. "Indeed? I cannot imagine that a proper lady such as yourself could harbor any secret that is too wicked."

"Alas," said Emma, "but I have the most wretched temper, sir, and can be moved to a blistering harangue by the most idle remark—if it happens to be one of my bad days."

He stared at her in bewilderment, finally inquiring earnestly, "Have you prayed about this?"

"Oh, many times," said Emma, hoping that God would forgive her for misleading a man of the cloth. "But it is no use."

He cleared his throat uncomfortably. "I have found fasting to be a great character builder."

"Indeed? Well, I'm afraid that wouldn't do for me for my temper is even worse when I am hungry."

"I see," said Mr. Stumpover, looking quite at a loss. "Then I shall pray for you, Miss Robinson."

"You are too kind. Perhaps you should return to your

rooms and begin now, for I don't seem to improve with age."

He looked at her blankly for a moment before he seemed to realize that he was being dismissed. He got to his feet with haste and watched Emma nervously as she summoned Hemmings to tell him that Mr. Stumpover was leaving and would require his coat.

When he was gone, she drew a sigh of relief and hoped that she had discouraged any interest Lady Parton's matchmaking maneuvers might have stirred in him. But Henry Stumpover was quickly forgotten as her mind went back over the happy fact that the *Times* editor had employed her to write for his newspaper. As she remembered her earlier idea of unsettling Lord North's self-esteem a little, a light came into her blue-green eyes. Glancing at the antique clock on the mantel, she saw that there was a good while left before dinner.

She ascended the stairs as quietly as she could, not wishing her aunt to hear her and to realize that Mr. Stumpover had stayed such a short time. After closeting herself in her chamber, she went to her desk and got out her writing paper and pen.

A half hour later she had finished another offering for the *Times*. She laid her pen aside and lifted the paper upon which she had written. Walking to a window, she held it in the waning light and read over the lines:

*The elusive Lord South, so the wags relate,*
*Has condescended to attend a few parties of late.*
*From the Olympian heights of a massive conceit*
*He allows the ladies to worship at his feet,*
*While he peers through his glass at the tiresome to-do*
*Tempering his boredom with a pinch of snuff or two.*

* * *

The appellation "Lord South" would mislead few of the members of the ton, Emma was sure, and she smiled her satisfaction. Then she folded the paper and secreted it at the bottom of her writing paper box, underneath the blank sheets. She would have several more ready to send to the editor Thursday next when she went to the lending library. She placed the box at the back of the desk drawer and then moved to the window again to stare out at the falling darkness.

It was in such idle moments that Jamie and the disquieting kiss they had shared invaded the forefront of her thoughts. She had been the recipient of a few kisses since her eighteenth birthday, but none of them had shaken her as had Jamie's. She told herself that the unusual effect was brought on by her shock at seeing him, and the fact that they were standing in an aisle at the library where anyone in London could have happened upon them at any moment—even one of her aunt's friends who had met Emma. She shuddered at that thought, realizing what a narrow escape she had had.

Heaven send that she never encounter the man again, for she wondered how she would manage to face him. She felt her cheeks grow warm at the mere thought.

Almost a week later Charlotte came home from Almack's Assembly Rooms and laughingly recounted to Emma, along with several other on-dits, that Lord Charles Emberland, that Tulip of the ton, had shocked the patronesses by appearing in those hallowed chambers wearing a fur-lined cloak and a sugar-loaf hat that he removed with a flourish to reveal an orange-striped coat and pea-green pantaloons with huge bunches of purple and orange ribbons fluttering at various spots on his person.

"And then," gasped Charlotte, hardly able to keep from laughing long enough to describe the scene to Emma, "he lifted a gem-encrusted quizzing glass, gave Lady Jersey a very studied look, and said, 'My dear lady, may I give you my most enthusiastic felicitations?' " Charlotte hugged herself and fell back across Emma's bed. "I thought Lady Jersey would swoon on the spot!"

Emma, who had found the described spectacle as humorous as Charlotte did, wiped the tears from her cheeks and said, "But what *did* she do?"

"She lifted a lace handkerchief to her nose, as if she had smelled something rotten, you know, and said she must go about her duties. Then Lord Emberland came straight to my side and asked me to stand up with him."

"Never say you agreed, Lottie!"

"Of course, I did! You surely can't expect me to forgo a chance for a small adventure. Adventures are not easily come by at Almack's. This blue gown clashed horribly with all Emberland's colors, which made it even more amusing. Every eye in the room was on us as we danced. Mama took a pet, of course, and I had to behave with the utmost decorum for the remainder of the evening."

"*That* I should like to have seen," murmured Emma.

Charlotte ran on for almost an hour, telling Emma who danced with whom, what couples she had observed heading for shadowy corners, and describing the ladies' dresses in some detail. By the time she had left, yawning, to seek her bed, Emma had material enough for several new verses. The first one she wrote immediately, even though it was very late, for she couldn't rest until she had on paper a caricature of Lord Emberland, whom she dubbed Lord Ashground, shocking the very proper patronesses of Almack's with his outlandish garb.

She had taken to reading the newspapers that her uncle brought into the house with greater interest and found additional material for satire there.

She rose early the next morning and penned two more verses from information found in the *Gazette.* Thus, when she made her journey to the lending library that afternoon, she had four new verses for her editor.

Upon alighting from the carriage, she suggested that Benjy might like to give the horses a workout and return for her in an hour. When the driver had acted upon her suggestion, she looked over the eight or ten urchins who were wandering about on the street and chose a bony thin boy with wise eyes. She approached him and asked if he would like to earn a farthing every Thursday by delivering an envelope to the *Times* office. The child was so grateful for the opportunity, Emma felt she had made a good choice. She handed over the envelope she had brought with her and said he would have his pay if he returned within the hour. He was back in much less time, having run all the way.

Emma took the precaution of asking him to describe the editor to her before she handed over the coin and made arrangements to meet him there the following Thursday with another envelope.

There was just time to exchange Mrs. Radcliffe's novel for another before Benjy had returned. On the drive to Bedford Square, she leaned back against the squabs and reflected upon the success of the past hour. There had been no sign of Jamie, either, which confirmed her belief that he would not try to seek her out again. He had probably forgotten all about her by now. Not that she wanted him to think of her at all. Yes, she did rather, she admitted to herself in a moment of frankness. For some years she had expected eventually to meet a man who would stir romantic feelings in her, but now that she had . . . Oh, why was she attracted to the most ineligible man conceivable? Why couldn't she feel anything for Mr. Stumpover, a retiring country curate who, no doubt, shared her interest in books and people?

It was true that a few times she had glimpsed a rare warmth in Jamie, but that did not alter the fact that his life was clearly very different from the one she had known. He must spend his time seeking new ways to be entertained—such as tracking down foolish females he chanced to meet at the Frost Fair. The two of them could not possibly have anything in common. She would put Jamie and the feelings he had aroused in her from her mind. How had she ever allowed herself to feel anything at all for such a person?

She had other things to occupy her thoughts now. She was an author, and there were the skills she must practice regularly in order to provide herself with more income by becoming a governess. Perhaps she would never marry, but she would put her heart into her career, she assured herself as Benjy reined the horses at the Parton house. Jamie was out of her life now; indeed, he had never really been in it. The thought was not as consoling as she would have liked it to be.

March gave way to a cool, but bright, April. Jonathan returned to Oxford, but not before he had taken note of the new poems by "Aristobulus" in the *Times* and badgered Emma to admit to authoring them. Emma merely smiled, however, and said she imagined any number of authors could write such verses and sign them with whatever names they pleased. When he left London for Oxford,

Jonathan was clearly still unsure as to Emma's involvement in the matter. She supposed she would have to tell him in time for, after all, she had him to thank for the new world of writing that had opened up for her. However, she decided that she should wait until he was home for the summer when he would not be so likely to forget himself and to reveal Aristobulus's true identity to his friends.

To Emma's chagrin, her aunt had not given up her efforts to marry off her niece to Henry Stumpover. The curate was invited to the Parton house on several occasions, and now, in the last week of April, he was still kicking his heels in the rented rooms provided by Lady Parton.

Mr. Stumpover had been showing more and more interest in Emma, and, in fact, as she dressed her hair in front of her glass one April evening when the minister was expected for dinner, she had the sinking feeling that tonight he would ask for her hand, although she had done her best to discourage him. At this point she had come to wish he would speak and have done with it. Then she could decline firmly and leave him no more room for hope.

Dinner was a plain meal with but five courses, for Lady Parton had learned not to confuse the curate with too many utensils and dishes. As always when he dined with the family, Mr. Stumpover was seated to Emma's left.

Fortunately Charlotte was in fine fettle and chattered a great deal, relieving Emma of making conversation with the curate.

As the main course was served, Charlotte said, "Papa, did you read that hilarious verse about Lord North in yesterday's *Times?* It's the second time the poet has attacked him."

"The rhyme was about Lord South," Sir Humphrey corrected her. "Do you know him?"

"I know the poems *say* Lord South, but everyone knows it's Lord North," said Charlotte. "Aristobulus never uses the real names of people. He referred to Emberland as Ashground!"

"Can't understand that," observed Sir Humphrey, helping himself to a generous portion of meat. "No sense to it."

"Oh, Uncle," responded Charlotte with some impatience, "Aristobulus does it to disguise his subjects, don't you see?"

"Thought you said everyone knows anyway," Sir Humphrey said reasonably.

"They do," agreed Charlotte, "but it is all a part of the satirist's sense of humor. I think the verses about Lord North are the most amusing of the lot."

Sir Randolph, hit with a sudden thought, chuckled. "That line in yesterday's paper about his being as cold as a mackerel rather struck a nerve in the gentleman, I should imagine."

"If anyone should care for my opinion," interposed Lady Parton with a disdainful sniff, "the papers these days are filled with little but refuse. I should like to know how some grimy little versifier can have the audacity to hold up to ridicule the finest members of society."

"But, Mama, it is all in fun," said Charlotte. "And, as for Lord North, it is little more than he deserves."

"Charlotte!" Lady Parton's tone was outraged. "I shan't have you speaking with disrespect about a person of such importance as the marquis!"

"But, Mama," protested Charlotte, "he does deserve it.

He is *so* very intent upon holding himself aloof from the rest of the human race."

"Nonsense," stated Lady Parton. "The man merely knows his own value."

"He is jumped up," returned Charlotte stubbornly.

"Those verses in the *Times* are the talk of the ton, it seems," put in Sir Randolph. "I hear little else but the poet's latest thrust at my club of late. And North *has* been pictured in particularly scathing terms, poor man."

"Lord Ryerson told me that Lord North is fit to be tied," said Charlotte with some satisfaction. "He has vowed that if he ever discovers who this Aristobulus is, he'll call him out."

"Don't hold with dueling," observed Sir Humphrey. "All that posturing and melodrama, and some bloke dead as mutton at the end of it."

"Oh, but I should like to witness a duel," said Charlotte dreamily. "So romantic."

"Humph!" said Sir Humphrey. "Nothing romantic about seeing your blood run out on the ground. Demmed messy foolishness, if you ask me."

Stumpover cleared his throat stentoriously. "It's in total opposition to God's law, too. Let us not forget that."

"God's no fool," commented Sir Humphrey, seemingly pleased that the Supreme Being agreed with him.

The curate's face registered shock that anyone should speak so carelessly of deity, and he very nearly choked on a bite of his roll. Emma, wishing to turn the conversation away from Aristobulus anyway, tried to cover Mr. Stumpover's strangled coughing by remarking, "Aunt Claire, you must tell Cook the haddock is exceptionally savory this evening."

"Undercooked," contradicted Sir Humphrey.

Lady Parton was observing her guest through slitted eyes. "Have you recovered, Mr. Stumpover?" Although her ladyship made a valiant effort, she could not conceal the affront she felt at having a guest at her table commit such a social blunder.

Emma suppressed a smile at her aunt's discomfort and glanced at Mr. Stumpover. Red-faced, he stammered, "Y-yes—thank you, my l-lady. I can't think what made the bread stick in my windpipe like that."

"Maybe you eat too fast," Sir Humphrey told him, all the while shoveling in his own food with amazing rapidity.

"I daresay you decided to breathe at the wrong moment," said Emma, avoiding Charlotte's glance, for that young lady was making little effort to hide her amusement.

Dessert was a gooseberry tart. When they had finished it, Sir Humphrey and Sir Randolph retired to the library for their port, and Lady Parton requested Charlotte to accompany her abovestairs on a mission about which she was vague, recommending Emma to entertain Mr. Stumpover in the gold salon until they should return.

Emma had been expecting some such maneuver but disliked the idea of being alone with the curate, nevertheless. Squaring her shoulders, however, she led the way to the salon where Hemmings served them small glasses of wine.

Mr. Stumpover was unusually nervous and repeatedly tugged at his collar, as if he suddenly found it too tight for comfort. They finished the wine and Emma said casually, "Tell me, sir, when will you be returning to Sussex?"

He squirmed in his chair. "Within the week, I believe. Of course, I have enjoyed my sojourn here, but my little flock needs my attention. I feel I have neglected them too long already."

"You are a conscientious shepherd," Emma remarked.

Mr. Stumpover's pale eyes brightened with gratitude and he sat forward in his chair. "I am honored to receive such a compliment from a lady whom I have come to admire above all things."

Here it comes, Emma told herself, trying to arrange her face in an expression of utter innocence.

The man startled her then by taking her hand in his, casting a furtive look over his shoulder to make certain they were still alone. "I have been praying daily over your bad temper, charming lady," he intoned.

"Thank you, but I cannot feel your prayers have done a great deal of good. Of course, you did tell me once that God sometimes answers 'No' to our requests."

"Indeed, but only when they are contrary to his will. I've come to know you rather well these past few weeks, and I have yet to observe the temper you warned me of. You are overcoming it, I am quite sure."

"I hope you may be right," said Emma dryly.

"Miss Robinson," he said, his face flushing of a sudden. "I—I cannot let this opportunity go by. I have come to have the most sincere regard for you. I have given prayerful consideration to what I am about to say, and I am convinced it is the Almighty's will for me—for us. I believe we should deal extremely well together. I shall forever be your devoted servant if you will consent to be my wife."

Emma would have liked to put a stop to this speech the moment it was begun, but she had been occupied with trying to extricate her hand from his moist grip. Finally, she succeeded in doing so.

"I have observed your kindness to your aunt in her illnesses," he went on, "and I know you would be an angel of mercy to the poor of my parish. Say you will be mine, most virtuous of your sex."

Emma forced herself to meet his look. "Sir, you do me great honor by your request. But my answer must be no. I'm sorry, Mr. Stumpover, but I cannot marry without deep feelings on both sides. Please do not misunderstand. I respect you, but I will never marry unless I can have love into the bargain."

"Love?" Henry Stumpover blinked at her in bewilderment.

"You have heard of it, I am sure," Emma said, trying to lighten the atmosphere.

"Why—of course—but, my dear Miss Robinson, a marriage cannot be built upon emotion. Surely you are aware that no emotion can last for long."

"Perhaps you may be right and I am a foolish romantic," Emma told him, feeling suddenly sorry for the female he would eventually take to wife. "I may even come to rue my decision, but I am set on my feckless course."

"I see." He got to his feet, fumbling with his collar. "Then I ask to be excused, Miss Robinson. Will you convey my appreciation to Lady Parton for her kind invitation and tell her I shall call upon her before I return to Sussex."

"I'll do that," Emma said, standing and going into the hall to see him out. When the front door closed behind him, a weight of restraint dropped from her shoulders. She felt oddly free, although there had never been any thought in her mind of even considering a proposal from Henry Stumpover. Perhaps she was headstrong and expected too much of marriage, but she much preferred remaining unwed to entering into matrimony for less than love. She had been raised in an atmosphere of devotion, and in spite of the flaws she had seen in her parents as she grew up, she had never doubted their deep love for each other and for her.

Of course, she would have to tell her aunt what she had done, and she dreaded that scene above all things. But she would say nothing yet. Perhaps Mr. Stumpover would tell Lady Parton what had transpired between him and Emma when he made his farewell call at the house. If she could manage to be out at the time, her aunt might recover herself somewhat before she confronted Emma.

Later when Lady Parton and Charlotte came down to the salon and Emma told them Mr. Stumpover had pleaded tiredness and returned to his rooms, her ladyship did not seem to suspect that Emma had freed the quarry Lady Parton had worked so diligently to ensnare in parson's mousetrap. In fact, she seemed preoccupied with other things, for which Emma was fervently grateful.

They were not to learn until two days later what had been occupying so great a portion of Lady Parton's thoughts. Charlotte and Emma were working at their watercolors in the gold salon when Lady Parton returned from an afternoon of making calls. She entered the salon with a spring in her step and an expression on her face that could only be described as patent smugness. She stood in the center of the room and announced, "I have just come from having tea with Lady North."

"You will forgive us, Mama," said Charlotte rather absently, as she touched a green brush to the likeness of a willow tree, "if we are not excessively transported by your news."

"But you haven't *heard* my news yet," said her ladyship, seating herself on a settee with a flourish of flounced skirts.

Something in her aunt's tone made Emma lay aside her brush and give that lady all her attention. Charlotte, however, continued to stroke at the willow tree, saying, "I suppose you were honored by having the lady's stickler of a son acknowledge you. Pray tell us, Mama, did he actually remember your name?"

"He wasn't there," responded Lady Parton without the least regret in her tone. "Which was indeed fortunate, for it gave Lady North and me the opportunity to have a nice coze. The upshot was that we are invited to Havenwood in June for a two-week house party."

At last, she had caught her daughter's attention. Charlotte was looking at her parent with horror written on her pretty face. "Havenwood! You can't mean Lord North's country seat? Oh, Mama, never say you accepted."

Lady Parton laughed at such a foolish remark. "Silly girl, of course I did. It is more than even I could have hoped for. Lady North and I had a long discussion about her son and his lamentable reluctance to wed and produce an heir. I remarked that he seems taken with you, Lottie, and we came up with the idea of a house party so the two of you might become better acquainted."

"Mama!" Charlotte had risen to her feet, her face flushing. "How could you? Lord North isn't taken with me. I doubt that he can recollect my name. I have told you before that he dislikes all females."

"Fiddle," said her mother complacently. "No man dislikes *all* females. It is merely that he hasn't come upon the right one yet, or rather he *has*, but he hasn't realized it. This house party will be just the thing to nudge him into offering for you." She glanced at her niece and added,

"You are invited, too, Emma. When I informed Lady North that my niece made her home with us, she insisted that you come."

Emma started to protest, but then thought better of it. She would be out of mourning in June and had planned to begin immediately looking for employment. She could now play simple melodies on the pianoforte and had acquired basic skills in embroidery and watercolors. She did not think, though, that this would be the best time to broach that subject again.

"We shall have the dressmaker in immediately," Lady Parton said, a calculating gleam coming into her eyes. "You must have new gowns in the latest fashion, Charlotte, and a new riding habit or two. Gracious, so much to do!"

"No," said Charlotte.

Her mother looked at her in puzzlement. "No what?"

"I won't go!"

Lady Parton stared at her offspring, the muscles in her jaw going quite rigid. "You are causing my heart to flutter alarmingly, Lottie." She laid a plump hand upon her heaving breast. "Now, have done with this shatterbrained quibbling at once. We are all going, even Jonathan, for he will have left Oxford for the summer by then." She got to her feet, still clutching at her chest. "I must find Genevieve and have her prepare a posset right away. I feel quite dreadful suddenly." She started from the room, adding, "Emma, if I am feeling a little recovered after dinner, perhaps you will come and read to me."

"Yes, Aunt," murmured Emma, frowning as the salon door closed behind her ladyship.

Charlotte still stood beside the small table upon which

her watercolors were arranged. Her hands were clenched tightly at her sides. "I won't go!" she uttered wrathfully.

"It seems that you will not be given the choice," Emma told her. "But don't fly into a pelter just yet. This might not be such a destable turn of events."

"How can you say that? I am to be thrown with Lord North for two solid weeks. Can't you imagine the humiliating things Mama must have said to Lady North to bring about this mull? I am sure she told her I'm wearing the willow for that odious man. Oh, I can't bear it, Emma!"

"Draw rein, Lottie. Think about it for a minute. If it is to be a house party, there will be other guests there as well. It may be that you won't have to spend so much time with Lord North, after all."

Charlotte relaxed her clenched fingers and looked at her cousin thoughtfully. "Do you collect Lord Ryerson will be among the guests? He claims Lord North as a good friend."

"It is quite possible," Emma said. "And there's something else to consider, too. If, as you say, Lord North dislikes females, two weeks in the company of several of them is apt to make the situation worse. From what I have heard, he is not easily influenced by his mother or his sister, for Aunt Claire says they are quite beside themselves over his failure to marry. I really do not think there is a great danger of his offering for you."

"That's true," agreed Charlotte.

"There you are then. This house party might be just the thing to convince your mother, once and for all, that her hopes in that direction are not to be realized." She paused, reflecting. "I only wish I shall have found employment by then so that I'll have a good excuse to cry off."

"Emma, no!" ejaculated Charlotte. "You can't send me to Kent alone!"

Emma smiled. "You shall be far from alone."

"But you are the only one who understands how I feel. I must have someone to confide in."

"Let us not run ahead too fast," replied Emma. "I have yet to conceive how I am to meet ladies of quality who might be seeking a governess without being recommended by Aunt Claire."

"You know she will never do that. She thinks it's disgraceful of you even to consider going into service. It would be a blot on her escutcheon from which she would never recover."

"If I can find a position before she realizes what I've done, she will have little to say in the matter."

"I shouldn't be too sure of that if I were you," Charlotte advised.

## *CHAPTER NINE*

The dressmaker was sent for the next day by Lady Parton, who had made an amazing recovery from her indisposition of the evening before. Her ladyship flew from her closet to Charlotte's all morning like a ship in full sail, deciding which of their present dresses would be suitable to take to Havenwood. After consultation with the dressmaker, it was decided that her ladyship would have two new dresses and Charlotte, five, along with two additional riding habits.

Her aunt was in such a cheerful mood that Emma was unprepared for the sight that met her when she was summoned to that lady's chamber late in the afternoon.

Lady Parton reclined on her chaise, a handkerchief over her eyes. She flung off the cloth peevishly when Emma entered.

"Mr. Stumpover has been to call, Emma. He is returning to Sussex."

Emma sighed inwardly. She had hoped to leave the house on some pretext when the curate arrived, but she'd been with Charlotte looking through fashion magazines and hadn't even been aware that he was in the house.

"I am not surprised," she murmured cautiously. "He told me the last time he was here that he felt he's neglected his parishioners."

"He informed me that he had offered for you and that you had turned him down," said Lady Parton in indignantly accusing tones. "May I ask what you can have been thinking of?"

"I do not wish to marry Mr. Stumpover, Aunt. I feel no love for him."

"*Love!* What do you know of love, foolish girl? This is more of the idiocy your parents filled your head with!"

"It is true that I know very little of love between a man and a woman," said Emma calmly, "but I shall recognize it if I find it. And if I do not, I shall remain unwed."

"Ungrateful chit!" exclaimed her aunt. "You are already on your way to being at your last prayers! Have you forgotten you will be three and twenty in May? It is my opinion that Mr. Stumpover and you would suit admirably. And I took the greatest pains to bring him to the point of asking for you. Now I learn it was all for nothing! You care not a straw for the many inconveniences I have suffered on your behalf!"

"I am sorry that you have been inconvenienced," said Emma.

Lady Parton flung her arms out in frustration. "I am sure I cannot think what is to become of you. I must tell you, Emma, that a young woman who hasn't sixpence to scratch with is in no position to scorn a respectable proposal."

Emma had already decided to visit her father's solicitors soon to collect the money deposited with them by the *Times*. Now she said, "It may be that I am not quite as penniless as we had supposed. I—I received a letter from father's solicitors asking me to come to see them at my convenience. It seems there may be a small inheritance remaining to me, after all."

Lady Parton looked at her through slitted eyes. "I know of no letter you have received."

"It came in the post yesterday," Emma improvised. "I saw it immediately and carried it up to my chamber. I hesitated to mention it to you until I knew for certain that there would be money coming to me. I expect I should meet with the gentlemen right away."

"Benjy can drive you tomorrow," said her ladyship, "although I am convinced there can't be a great sum remaining after your parents' debts were paid."

"I am sure you are right, but if I am careful with it and—" She almost mentioned her intention to seek a position, but again decided the time was not propitious. Her aunt was as cross as crabs with her already.

"Hand me my handkerchief," ordered Lady Parton, "and be so good as to dampen it with fresh lavender water first. You have given me the headache, Emma. Between you and Lottie, I sometimes think I shall run quite mad."

Emma followed her aunt's instructions, then asked, "Is there anything else I can do for you?"

"You may reconsider Mr. Stumpover's proposal," said the lady peevishly. "I told him I would speak to you about it."

"I regret it, but that is the one thing I cannot do. Perhaps there is something else?"

"Go away!" whined Lady Parton. "My head is pounding harder than I have ever known it to. Find Genevieve and tell her to come to me at once."

Feeling depressed, Emma found the abigail and dispatched her to Lady Parton's chamber. Then she came upon Charlotte in the gold salon, still leafing through an issue of *Lady's Magazine*.

Her cousin looked up as Emma entered. "There is one consolation in this house party. I shouldn't have had so many new gowns at the end of the season otherwise. Why, Emma, you look burned to the socket. What's wrong?"

"Nothing really desperate. Only that your mother just learned I turned down Mr. Stumpover's offer for me."

"You didn't tell me that." Charlotte closed the magazine and gave her cousin a consoling look. "Well, I can't say that I'm sorry. He is such a mouse, isn't he? I suppose Mama kicked up a great dust over it."

"Oh, yes. I am ungrateful and a great inconvenience, and besides, I am fast becoming an ape-leader."

"Mother's Turkish treatment is really too excessive sometimes," Charlotte commiserated.

Emma strolled to an armchair and sat down. "Lottie, I must ask your assistance."

"I'll do anything I can, you know that."

"I should like you to question your friends, see if you can discover a family in need of a governess—without Aunt Claire's knowledge, of course."

Charlotte looked reluctant. "I wish you will give up that feather-headed scheme. Anyway, I cannot think I could do what you ask without raising eyebrows." She paused reflectively. "Wait—I was riding with Lord Ryerson and Lord Emberland in the park yesterday, and I heard someone mention needing a governess. Why, yes, it was Lady Haverly. She has two young daughters."

"Haverly—isn't that Lord North's sister?"

Charlotte nodded, her face brightening. "Yes, and the Haverly estate borders Lord North's country seat. If you will give up your reluctance to go to the house party, there will be ample opportunity to speak to her—if you must go on with this."

Emma studied a floral design in the carpet without really seeing it. "It seems fate has smiled on me at last. To own the truth, I didn't know how I was to tell Aunt Claire I didn't want to go to Havenwood. This way I can appease her and pursue my own intention as well. Oh, I must look through my own wardrobe. It is imperative that Lady Haverly be impressed by my knowledge of fashions."

"Good," said Charlotte. "Lord Ryerson called briefly this afternoon, and he told me that both he and Emberland will be in attendance at Havenwood in June. Now that you are coming, too, it won't be so utterly dreadful."

"If you are finished with these magazines, Lottie," said Emma, "I should like to take them to my room."

"Pray, do. Mother and I have already decided on my new dresses. I was merely passing the time when you came in."

Going up to her chamber with a stack of the fashion magazines, Emma began mentally adding up the sum that was due her from the *Times.* Enough to have two new gowns made, she decided, and perhaps she could solicit Genevieve's assistance in making over one of Charlotte's old riding habits.

Comfortably seated on her chaise, she began looking through the magazines. After some time, she decided on two designs. One was an elegant gown with high waistline and heavily flounced skirt, suitable, with the addition of some of Lottie's jewelry, for a country ball or, with a single strand of pearls, for an evening dinner or card party. It would be lovely made up in a blue-green sarcenet to match Emma's eyes. The other design she chose was less formal and would be delightful in a fine Indian muslin, in white or perhaps a soft jonquil color. She placed markers in the two magazines so that she could find the designs easily to show the dressmaker. She only hoped there would be enough time for them along with the clothes her aunt and cousin had ordered.

She stacked the magazines on the carpet beside the

chaise and lay back to contemplate how she would approach Lady Haverly. Although it was the opportunity she had been waiting for, somehow she could not feel any anticipation over the interview. Part of her reluctance was due to her certain knowledge that it would put her in the suds with her aunt, who very likely would take to her bed. She wished she could obtain the position without Lady Parton's learning of it until after the house party. It was probably too much to hope, however, that Lady Haverly would not mention it, even if Emma asked her not to do so. It would be wise, she decided, to wait until the house party was near its end before she sought a meeting with Lady Haverly.

She pushed these disquieting thoughts from her mind and began to picture herself in the new gowns. It would take all of the sum now due her to procure them, but it was imperative to look her best at Havenwood. How much more pleasant it would be, she thought ruefully, were she going to the house party merely to be entertained.

She imagined herself dressed to the nines, floating about a ballroom in the arms of a handsome gentleman. He would have to be very wealthy, of course, to take an interest in a penniless orphan. But the man of her dreams would love her so much he would give no thought to her lack of a portion. A wry smile touched her lips, for she had come to the conclusion, from Charlotte's ramblings, that gentlemen of the ton were even more intent than others upon finding a wife with a fortune, no matter how wealthy they might be.

She closed her eyes, humming softly to herself. She and her gentleman were on a balcony now. A full moon looked down upon them, and the smell of honeysuckle wafted on the soft breeze. He was looking down at her, his dark eyes filled with admiration.

She sat straight suddenly. Her admirer had begun to look very much like Jamie. This was foolish beyond all things, she scolded herself. What had come over her that she should be so fanciful? Charlotte's influence, no doubt. She left the chaise and went to her closet, pondering what she would take to Havenwood.

The next afternoon, to Emma's vast relief, she was permitted to go to the solicitors' offices alone in the carriage. Her aunt was so engrossed in preparations for the house party that she even failed to warn Emma to return to the house on the instant she had conducted her business. Not that Emma had any thought of doing otherwise, but it was pleasant to get away from the fuss and flurry that seemed to have filled every corner of the house in Bedford Square.

However, her meeting was completed quickly, and since she had instructed Benjy to return for her in an hour, she left the brownstone with more than a half hour to spare. With May just days away, London had taken on an air of spring. Street vendors were out in great numbers, pedestrians walked with a youthful bounce, regardless of their ages. The shop windows were splashed with gay-colored displays.

On a whim Emma decided to pass the time until Benjy's return by strolling along the thoroughfare and enjoying the attractive wares that were exhibited.

The war in France was over at last, and flags of the Bourbons were displayed everywhere. The populace in general was rejoicing. Of course, there were a few dissenters. When the French king Louis had been wheeled in a grand procession through London, Lord Byron had kept to his rooms, later, to his friends, referring to the monarch as "Louis the Gouty."

The regent, however, had invested Louis with the Order of the Garter, graciously buckling the garter around a leg even fatter than his own. Peter Pindar had delighted the masses with an irreverent verse to "France's hope and Britain's heir" whom he described as "Two round tun-bellied, thriving rakes, like oxen fed on linseed cakes."

Now at the end of April it was reported that Paris already had twelve thousand British visitors, who had followed Louis when he left London. Street singers were beginning to sing a new song, "All the World's in Paris."

While a great mob of the quality had quit the metropolis, Emma could detect no dearth of pedestrians and shoppers around her as she walked from one shop to the next, enjoying the pleasant day.

Sir James North, having shortly before left his club, was engaged in the same occupation as Emma. He, however, was less cheered than she by the emergence of spring, being rather afflicted with despondency. His game of detection that had promised to redeem a little the otherwise wasted weeks he had spent in London had come to nothing. Having exhausted his sources of information, he was utterly convinced there was no young woman of quality fitting Sophia's description in town. And after his last meeting with her in the lending library, he was bound to admit that he seemed to have misread a lighthearted frivolity for something more. The young woman was not available for a liaison; in fact, he rather thought he had shocked her by giving her the impression he thought otherwise. She was a governess or a dressmaker or something of the sort—the dress she had been wearing at the library had been quite worn—but apparently she had more rigid moral standards than some of her station.

The most depressing thing on his mind, however, was not his failure to further an acquaintance with Sophia, which he had seen as little more than a diversion at any rate. It was far more chafing than that. His mother had invited a houseful of guests down to Havenwood in June without consulting him. When he had taken her to task for such disregard of his opinion, she had been affronted, remarking stiffly, "It did not occur to me to gain your permission, James. After all, we have had house parties before. I am fully aware that Havenwood is now yours, but I still consider it my home. Perhaps I have assumed too much."

Of course, he had had to reassure her on that head. Once she was mollified, he could not return to his earlier criticism without negating all his bolstering disclaimers. So he was resigned to two weeks of enduring relative strangers milling about the house and grounds, and he would have to be in attendance upon them some of the time. Devil take it, his estate needed his attention at this time of year far more than a bevy of Tulips and young females with more hair than wit.

Nor was he flummeried by this maneuver of his mother's. She had undoubtedly settled on one of the young women who would be among the guests as a suitable match for him. That giddy child, Charlotte Parton, probably. There was some consolation in the knowledge that Ryerson would be there, dangling after her, relieving James of constantly entertaining the chit.

It was at this juncture in his cogitation that he glanced down the thoroughfare and caught sight of a fluff of red-gold curls beneath a lacy blue cap. He shouldered himself through the cheerful throng and arrived at her side while she studied a lavender gown draped in the window of a modiste's shop.

"Thinking of purchasing it?" he inquired. "The color would be quite fetching with your hair."

She whirled about and regarded him with astonishment. "Oh, you startled me!" Her cheeks colored charmingly. "I—I was merely enjoying the sunny day."

"Are you alone?"

"Yes, but I must be going."

"I was considering stopping in that tearoom next door. I should be grateful for your company."

"Thank you," she said slowly, "but I cannot accept. My aunt—"

His dark brows rose. "Your aunt is expecting you. I have heard that before." He still tended to believe the convenient aunt was a fabrication. Sophia's seeming intentness upon being always at the woman's beck and call was more indicative of an employee-employer relationship than a familial one. "Aren't you allowed any time to yourself?"

"Oh, yes, but it is a particularly busy time for her."

"Sophia, I promise you I have no motive but to enjoy a cup of tea with you—and perhaps some macaroons." A corner of his mouth quirked slightly. "As I recall, the last time I purchased macaroons for you, you ran off without even sampling them."

"I felt you were—presuming too much, sir," she said primly.

Resisting a desire to shake her slender shoulders, he asked, "Will you not allow me to prove you wrong on that head?" He could see the vacillation in her eyes and pressed on. "You can't mean to deny me the opportunity to leave you with a more favorable impression than you received at our last meeting."

Her face flamed and it was all Sir James could do to suppress a laugh. Gad, she *was* innocent, but the manner in which she had responded to his kiss made him suspect there was a certain sensuousness hidden beneath that prim exterior. He rather envied the shopkeeper or merchant who eventually married her.

She dropped her eyes from his. "I suppose I might have a cup of tea," she said, though still hesitantly, "but I can stay only a few minutes."

Nodding, he escorted her into the cozy establishment where they discovered the macaroons were fresh from the oven and the tea was well-brewed.

He watched her slender fingers as they curled around the cup's handle. Glancing up at him, she intercepted his gaze and said, "I collect you are only in town for the season and will be returning to the country soon."

He watched her profile which had turned as she looked, somewhat anxiously he thought, through the door that opened onto the street. "And you?"

"We—we shall be leaving London very soon." There was an odd note in her voice which made him believe she found his question disquieting. With a slight feeling of regret, he realized that he would never solve the mystery of Sophia, if indeed there was one.

"Where do you go?"

Her eyes came back to his face, wide and somehow vulnerable. "I am not certain. I believe we shall be traveling for a while."

He had the distinct impression that she was telling an outright lie, and that she was not accustomed to lying, but for some reason his idle question forced her to it. "You don't like to talk about yourself, do you, Sophia?"

"No, I suppose not."

He attempted to discuss matters of no importance then, but she remained clearly on guard against any further prying into her personal affairs. Devilish unusual chit, he decided, who did not enjoy running on about herself. Most of them could not be prevented with a muzzle.

After a few minutes she rose to her feet abruptly. "Thank you for the refreshment. I must be going now."

Standing, he captured her hand before she moved out of reach. Gazing down into her eyes, he said, "This is good-bye then. You did say you are leaving London shortly?"

She nodded. "Yes, and there is no likelihood that we shall ever see each other again." She looked flustered. "I—I don't mean to imply that you have any interest in such a thing."

"I confess, I shall remember our few meetings with a bit of nostalgia. They brightened my days in London."

"And mine, as well," she stammered and then looked surprised, as if the words had slipped past her guard.

He bent to brush her fingers with his lips.

"Good day—Jamie." She pulled her hand from his grasp, and there was a look of sudden appeal on her face. "Please do not go out with me."

Not knowing what had put that anxious look back into her eyes all at once, he shook his head, gazing after her as she slipped through the doorway. By the time he had recollected himself and hurried to the street, hoping to catch a glimpse of her direction, he could see no sign of her.

## *CHAPTER TEN*

June burst upon London like a fireworks display that was too much for the eyes to take in with a single look. Gardens rioted with reds and yellows and purples, the parks were emerald oases invaded daily by a scattering of ladies and gentlemen who had remained in town and whose costumes rivaled the gardens for brightness, and the streets rang with horses' hooves, carriage wheels, and the cries of hawkers of wares.

The Parton cortege of three carriages left Bedford Square on the morning of the tenth, bound for Kent. Seated between her aunt and Charlotte in the family carriage, Emma settled against the squabs with a feeling of having just finished a foot race. For the past week she had spent her days overseeing the packing of the family trunks, which followed them in the third carriage behind the servants. Her aunt had been almost beside herself with anxiety over the preparations, and finally Emma had urged the lady to gather her strength for the journey by resting for the last several days in her chamber, allowing Emma to carry out her instructions.

Lady Parton's wrought-up state was an indication of the importance she placed upon their stay at Havenwood; Emma very much feared the lady had made up her mind that Charlotte's betrothal to Lord North would be imminent, if not actual, by the end of the two weeks. When Charlotte refused the marquis's offer, as she vowed she would—even supposing that arrogant gentleman could be brought to the point of offering for her—the result, as far as the family was concerned, was certain to be unpleasant. Emma shuddered even to think of her aunt's reaction. But she was too frazzled to worry about that now. Each day for the past week after leaving her aunt, she had spent additional hours at her desk composing enough of Aristobulus's verses to supply the *Times* for the next two months. It had been difficult to think of enough subjects for that many verses in such a short period of time, and she had drawn upon Charlotte's more and more uncomplimentary remarks concerning Lord North for two of them.

Wedged into the seat across from Emma, his knees pressing against hers, Jonathan fidgeted between his father and Uncle Humphrey with an impatience that boded no restful atmosphere for the journey.

"Must you squirm like a worm on a hot lid, Johnny?" Lord Parton grunted after some moments. "You'll have a hole worn through the seat if you keep on like this."

"Did I tell you, Emma," Jonathan inquired, casting his father an apologetic glance, "that Lord North has promised to teach me to box?"

"Several times," Emma replied with amusement. Jonathan had met the marquis only two weeks prior to their departure when he had gone to a cattle auction with his father. He had come back to the house singing the man's praises. According to Jonathan, the marquis was a great gun and a top-sawyer and Charlotte was totty-headed not to be grateful for any attentions he might condescend to pay her. He had always suspected that his sister was touched in her upper works, he declared, and now he was confirmed in that opinion.

Jonathan's opinion, in fact, was so at odds with his

sister's that Emma had felt a decided twinge as she had penned a verse picturing that gentleman's retreat to Kent with several determined mamas hanging precariously from the carriage. But she had consoled herself with the thought that Jonathan's admiration was apt to be directed toward the queerest objects. Only last month he had written Emma from Oxford, declaring himself head over ears for some hey-go-mad young woman he had met at a cockfight. The girl helped her father train fighting cocks, it seemed, and according to Jonathan could scream for blood with the lustiest of men. Fortunately, that infatuation had been short-lived, for Jonathan had clapped eyes upon the charmer but once, and he soon became bored with frequenting cockfights, which he confided to Emma dimmed with familiarity, for another glimpse of her.

"Lord North says I have the look of being quick on my feet," Jonathan announced, shifting his position in the seat so that Uncle Humphrey, who had been dozing in the corner, jerked awake and grunted crossly.

"I cannot conceive," interposed Lady Parton, fanning herself with an ivory-inlaid fan, "why any sensible young man should take an interest in such a violent pursuit."

"Oh, all the sporting fellows go in for it, Mama. Lord North told me he put on the gloves at Gentleman Jackson's at least once a week while he was in London."

"Demmed foolishness," muttered Sir Humphrey, still scowling at being awakened.

"Well, I daresay it is an acceptable pastime if Lord North endorses it," said Lady Parton.

Charlotte, who had been leaning forward to watch the countryside through the window, turned to grimace in disgust at her mother's remark. "I can't conceive, Mama, why you continue to toad-eat that man after he refused to attend your ball in April. But I collect it would be acceptable for Johnny to come to dinner bare to the waist if Lord North endorsed it."

"Lottie!" Lady Parton's ejaculation was shocked. "I should be excessively grateful if you will leave off speaking like some—some shop girl. I know you pick up these common expressions from Johnny, but it becomes you ill." She fanned faster. "Sometimes I think most of what young men learn at Oxford these days is in questionable taste. If I'd had my way, my son would have had a private tutor."

"We all know your opinion on that head, m'dear," muttered Lord Parton, "and it will serve no purpose to go over the ground again."

"I hope North has laid in an ample supply of liquor," remarked Sir Humphrey with disgruntlement.

"I am sure you'll not be disappointed, Uncle," Sir Randolph responded. "Living in Kent, he has access to some of the best to cross the Channel. Dover is a smuggler's haven, I'm told."

Charlotte's expression showed the first interest she had taken in the trip thus far. "How far is Havenwood from Dover, Papa?"

"It's a good distance inland, but a man could make the trip and back with good horses in a day."

"Then I don't suppose we shall be having an excursion to Dover," said Charlotte, losing interest and returning her gaze to the side window.

"I think you will not find time weighing heavily upon your hands, Lottie," Lady Parton said. "Lady North has planned several outings in the countryside for riding and picnicking and the like."

Charlotte heaved a bored sigh but did not otherwise respond.

"Don't know why we couldn't have gone straight to Sussex," Sir Humphrey said, a refrain that he had returned to frequently during the past week. The old gentleman preferred familiar surroundings with his own room and his own bed, but he had refused when Lord Parton suggested he might like to go ahead to the Parton country estate and await the family there. He didn't relish two weeks with nobody but servants for company, Sir Humphrey had declared.

"Well, I for one am dashed glad we're going to Havenwood," said Jonathan. "Aren't you, Emma?"

"I am sure we shall find the time passing pleasantly enough," Emma replied, although she herself did not expect to enjoy it much. However, she meant to present herself in a favorable light to Lady Haverly whenever that lady was about. She feared, though, that those occasions would not be as many as she would have liked. After all, Lady Haverly had her own house to manage. Lady Parton *had* said that the Haverlys would be entertaining the house party guests and local gentry at a country ball during the second week of their stay.

In the early afternoon the carriages stopped near a shaded green field where a white cloth was spread on the grass and a luncheon of cold meats, cheeses, and fruits was provided for the family by the servants traveling with them.

After eating sparingly, Emma took a brief stroll across the downs, enjoying the bucolic setting. Sheep grazed in an apple orchard near where they had stopped, and farther away a group of cowled oast-houses sat among hop fields.

She returned to the cramped carriage feeling considerably refreshed.

The day was beginning to dim into dusk when they finally reached their destination. Havenwood was a medieval manor house, with towers and battlements. It stood on a slight eminence overlooking a valley to the south. The magnificent old house and surrounding grounds had a well-kept look that indicated a large retinue of retainers and the expenditure of a good deal of money.

The Parton manservant's knock on the oversized oak door was answered by a formidable-looking butler who dispatched underlings to see to the visitors' carriages. The family was escorted into an antechamber with narrow arched windows where they were welcomed shortly by a still-handsome matron near sixty—Lady North. She was all that was gracious, and as soon as greetings were exchanged, they were shown to their chambers. The house party guests would assemble for dinner in little more than two hours.

Emma's room was of modest size and furnished attractively, the furniture in the Queen Anne style, the carpet and window dressings in shades of blue and pale gold. The chamber assigned to Charlotte was larger, but similarly appointed and could be reached from Emma's room through a connecting door.

Charlotte used the door immediately, coming to lounge in an upholstered armchair in Emma's room while her abigail unpacked for her. Emma had already opened her trunk, delivered to her room before her arrival there, and was taking out her gowns, shaking the wrinkles from them and hanging them in the wardrobe.

"You don't have to do that," Charlotte told her. "You

know Mama said Joan could wait on both of us while we're here."

"I think Joan will have enough to do looking after you," Emma said. "Besides, I've become accustomed to waiting on myself. It's not at all the difficult task we've been brought up to believe it is."

"I wonder if Lord Ryerson has arrived yet," Charlotte mused. "He told me he planned to be here for dinner this evening, so I should think he *must* have, wouldn't you?"

"Very probably," responded Emma absently.

"I'm going to wear my new sprigged muslin with the lace inserts on the skirt. Robert likes to see me in white."

Emma turned from hanging her last gown in the wardrobe. "So it's Robert now, is it?"

Charlotte's dreamy look gave place to a slight uneasiness. "That just slipped out, Emma. You must go on as if you didn't hear it."

Emma's look was dry. "I hope it doesn't slip out in front of your mother. We shall be treated to a stern lecture on decorum in that case."

"Never fear. I'll watch my tongue when Mama's around." Charlotte's brown eyes rested pensively on Emma's face. "Emma, I have been bursting to talk to you about something. I—I think I am falling in love with Lord Ryerson. But I've never been in love before, so I'm not sure how it should feel."

Emma glanced at the connecting door and was relieved to see that Charlotte had closed it. "I'm not an authority on that subject," she said lightly, but her cousin's serious tone sent a ripple of disquiet through her. Her aunt had made it abundantly clear that she had set her sights elsewhere for a match for her daughter.

Charlotte had shifted her gaze to the hands clasped

lightly in her lap. "When I am with him," she went on, "I feel excited and comforted at the same time. He is so amusing, but it's more than that." She brought her gaze back to Emma's face. "How do the heroines feel in those romances you are always reading to Mama?"

"They seem to swoon a lot," said Emma, smiling and coming to sit near her cousin in an armless blue-cushioned chair.

"Well, I've never felt at all like that."

"Lottie," Emma said gravely, "I do hope you have not encouraged Lord Ryerson. You know he is not acceptable to Aunt Claire."

Her cousin's chin thrust forward stubbornly. "I shall speak to Papa about it. I do not think Mama was ever in love, not that I can imagine Papa falling head over ears either. But at least he will listen to my opinion."

"Have you and Lord Ryerson already discussed a betrothal?"

She shook her head. "No, but I am sure that is only because I have always turned the conversation when I sensed he was about to speak. But, Emma, the more I am with him, the less inclination I have to turn the conversation."

"You must not show him the least partiality while we are here," Emma warned. "If you must speak to your father, wait until we are back at home. Two weeks is not a long time. But we'd better change for dinner now. I wouldn't want either of us to be late the first evening."

Charlotte got to her feet reluctantly. "It could be such a lovely house party since Lord Ryerson is here, if that odious Lord North would only fall ill or tumble off his horse or something."

"What an unappreciative guest you are!" Emma chided her.

Charlotte smiled ruefully. "If only he will take a liking to Hazel Lancaster, though I don't expect *that* to happen." She giggled suddenly. "I wonder if he even wants to have guests. I'd lay a wager on it that this whole affair was stewed up by his mother and mine. Well, I'm off to see what Joan can do to make me stunning. I must make Mama proud, mustn't I? I'll knock on the door when I'm ready and we can go down together."

Emma, out of mourning now, wore a two-year-old gown of lavender muslin that she had remade to give it a more fashionable look. When she and Charlotte went downstairs, the other guests were already assembled in one of several salons that opened off the wide entry hall. Having already met lords Emberland and Ryerson, as well as Hazel Lancaster, in London, she was presented to Miss Lancaster's parents, a tall, stately-looking pair who appeared to be about the age of Lord and Lady Parton.

Then Lady North said, "I was just explaining to the others that my son will be unable to join us for dinner." There was a forced quality to the lady's smile that made Emma suspect she was not at all happy about this development. "He is closeted with his estate manager and tells me he must remain there all evening. He has promised to be available for horseback riding tomorrow, however. He feels that he's neglected the estates while we've been in London, and I am sure you will all forgive his absence this evening."

The guests murmured assurances and, in fact, almost everyone present appeared to believe themselves capable of going on quite well without their host. Jonathan was, of course, disappointed, but he told Emma he had learned

Lord North breakfasted early and meant to have a long conversation with him in the breakfast parlor the next morning. Only Lady Parton and Lady North gave evidence of being indignant over the news, but Lady North was carrying things off with good grace. Lady Parton's manner, on the other hand, indicated a sharp irritation. Fortunately, she kept her thoughts on the subject to herself as they went in to dinner.

Somewhat to her own surprise, Emma found herself enjoying a lively conversation with her near companions, Lord Emberland and Miss Lancaster. Although Lord Emberland's purple coat and ivory satin waistcoat, from which numerous fobs and decorations dangled, were rather shocking to the sensibilities upon first glance, Emma found him an interesting enough conversationalist.

Miss Lancaster remarked, "Lord Emberland, if you assault our eyes with any more coats like that one during our stay, I am half convinced to send detailed descriptions to Aristobulus at the *Times.*"

"You may do as you wish, Miss Lancaster," said Emberland good-naturedly. "I don't mind being the talk of the ton. Rather like it, in fact. I don't take offense at finding my name in the newspapers as James does."

"But you must admit, sir," returned Miss Lancaster, "that Lord North has had rather more than his share of being the brunt of the poet's humor. I find Aristobulus's verses quite hilarious myself, but I am not at all sure I should feel the same were I in Lord North's shoes."

Emma glanced across the table to see Lady Parton frowning at the back of her daughter's dark head, which was bent toward Lord Ryerson. Whatever that gentleman was saying must be highly amusing, for Charlotte laughed frequently. Charlotte, it appeared, had decided not to heed

Emma's warning concerning her attentions to Lord Ryerson. Emma thought she had better speak to her cousin again as soon as they were alone. She frowned slightly, thinking that the two weeks at Havenwood might not pass so pleasantly, after all. If Charlotte and her mother were to be at odds and the host meant to ignore the guests, it could turn out to be a rare mingle-mangle.

When she did speak to Charlotte much later that evening, after they had retired to their chambers, that young woman retorted, "But Sir Robert sat down next to me, Emma. Would you have had me ignore him?"

"You know that isn't what I meant," returned Emma. "I only wanted to point out to you that Aunt Claire was scowling disapproval in your direction all during dinner."

Still on the defensive, Charlotte said, "I suppose *she* thinks it's acceptable behavior to leave your guests to their own devices on their first evening in residence, as Lord North did! Have you ever come across such a rudesby in your life?"

"It would behoove us not to judge him too quickly, Cousin," Emma said, attempting to soothe Charlotte's ruffled feathers. "He *has* been in London for some time, and I am sure there are estate matters that need his immediate attention." Seeing the irony in "Aristobulus" defending the marquis, she smiled slightly.

"Now you are sounding like Mama," Charlotte declared. At which point Emma gave up trying to reason with her cousin for the moment and went to bed.

Lady Haverly called upon her mother early the next afternoon. The two ladies were having a coze in the informal salon where Lady North spent a good portion of each day. There the same arched windows found throughout the old house were set into two of the walls, and the sofas and chairs were upholstered in gay melon-pink satin that matched the floral design in the carpet. The salon gave an effect of warmth and welcome.

"I couldn't wait any longer to find out how all goes here," Lady Haverly was confiding to her mother.

"The guests arrived yesterday," said Lady North. "I believe the young people are going riding this afternoon."

"Mama," said Lady Haverly with great impatience, "I want to know how James and Charlotte Parton are going on."

"Don't run ahead so quickly, Sarah. They haven't even seen each other yet."

"But I thought you said the guests arrived yesterday."

"That's true, but James was out at the time, and he did not see fit to put in an appearance at dinner. Oh, Sarah, I must confess I am put out with him. He wasn't at all eager to have guests from the beginning. You know how he always pleads business interests to excuse himself from society. But he *promised* to play the dutiful host."

Lady Haverly looked thoughtful. "James isn't one to be purposefully rude. I can't but think there *were* pressing matters that kept him from dinner. Besides, I have never been at all certain James is as enchanted by Charlotte Parton as her mother says."

"But I thought he stood up with her at your party."

"Oh, he did, and with several other young women as well—all the ones I asked him to honor."

"You *asked* him to stand up with her?"

Lady Haverly chuckled. "You know how James is. I almost had to beg to get him to come to my party at all. And then he told me to give him a list of the young women I thought he ought to ask for a dance, as if he couldn't be bothered with looking them over for himself. I named six, I believe, and he asked them all to stand up with him once, and then he retired to the game room, as I recall."

"Such a romantic gentleman!" said Lady North dryly. "However, Lady Parton assures me he stood up with Charlotte at other gatherings in London. And she *is* such a pretty little thing and will have a great fortune, too. I can't believe James is totally immune to her charms."

"If she has been here since yesterday and he hasn't even seen her yet, it is my opinion that he isn't top over end for her either," commented Lady Haverly with an amused smile.

Lady North shook her head regretfully. "No, I fear you are right, dear, and I should have taken Claire Parton's broad hints with a grain of salt. Now that I think back on it, I believe this house party was *her* idea from the start. And I allowed myself to get caught up in it, I am afraid, because I would so like to see James wed and setting up his nursery."

"Don't despair," her daughter advised. "Who knows what may happen in two weeks?"

"Well, I can tell you one thing. The Lancasters are bored already. They hardly said a word at dinner, and finally, afterward when Lady Lancaster tried to lecture me upon the architecture in Kent, Sir Humphrey kept interrupting and contradicting her. She was quite upset, I could tell. They retired early, and neither of them has set foot belowstairs yet today. Ah, well, Hazel seems to be having a good time."

In another salon across the broad entry hall, the young people were gathering for the planned outing. Charlotte was wearing one of her new riding dresses, a fetching creation in a muted rose shade. Emma had appropriated an old habit of Charlotte's and altered it to fit. She had been well pleased with her reflection in the glass before leaving her chamber. The dress was a rich wine color, trimmed with black braid, and there was a brimmed hat to match with a saucy feather curling halfway down one cheek. She had been looking forward to the ride ever since arising; she had had no chance to ride while in London, and she had missed the enjoyment that particular form of exercise gave her. Too, she admitted to herself as she and Charlotte descended the stairs, she had grown quite curious about the gentleman upon whom her cousins held such differing opinions. At last she was to meet him.

As she and Charlotte entered the salon, Ryerson, who had evidently been watching the door for their arrival, came immediately to Charlotte's side. "Your servant, Miss Parton. And yours, Miss Robinson."

Charlotte gave him a dazzling smile. "It looks as if everyone is here. Are we ready to leave now?"

"Almost," Ryerson told her. "Charles and James are discussing the best route. I believe they've decided to visit some Roman ruins not far from here. There's a pleasant meadow there where we may have refreshment before riding back."

Emma was gazing across the salon to where Lord Emberland stood in animated conversation with a tall gentleman, who must be Lord North. His back was turned to Emma, however, and all she could see of him was a set of very broad shoulders in a finely tailored camel-colored riding coat and a head of thick black hair worn short in the popular Brutus cut and curling at the neckline.

"Miss Robinson, I understand you haven't yet been introduced to our host," remarked Ryerson. "If you ladies will come with me, I'll do the honors."

He escorted them across the salon. They had reached the two gentlemen before either of them became aware of the trio. Lord Emberland smiled broadly. "Ah, I see our latecomers have arrived."

The man with Emberland turned his head toward them then. A pair of dark eyes fell upon Emma and widened in shock. Emma experienced a moment of numb disbelief before she felt all the blood leave her face and her heart began to pump furiously. Unconsciously, she reached out and clutched at Lord Ryerson's coat sleeve for support.

"Miss Emma Robinson, may I present our host, Sir James North? James, this is Miss Parton's cousin. I believe I mentioned her to you earlier."

Emma's mind was a whirl of confusion. She must be dreaming—or suffering delusions. This could not actually be real! What was Jamie doing at Havenwood? Had she just heard Lord Emberland introduce him as Sir James North?

She was aware of a feeling of release as sharp as a gasp when his dark eyes broke contact with her own and he bowed over her hand. "Your obedient servant, Miss Robinson." But momentarily he was searching her face again in that penetrating way. In fact, Charlotte and Emberland seemed to have sensed something odd in the situation, for they both glanced questioningly from Lord North to Emma. "Forgive me for staring, Miss Robinson," he went on coolly. "It is just that you don't look like an Emma to me."

A bark of laughter escaped Lord Emberland. "Now there's a deuced queer remark if I ever heard one, James. What does it mean, old fellow?"

Lord North's gaze remained frozen on Emma's face,

chilling her to the bone. "I should say she looks more like a Sophia, Charles, wouldn't you?"

Emberland chortled again. "Been at those estate books too long, James. A brisk ride will set you up, though, I've no doubt."

Emma had bethought herself enough to remove her fingers from Ryerson's coat sleeve. She managed to tear her gaze from Lord North's and glanced at Charlotte, whose raised eyebrows spoke volumes.

"Sophia is Emma's second name," Charlotte remarked. "What an odd coincidence that you should have chosen it."

"Indeed," responded Lord North with another quelling look in Emma's direction.

Jonathan came bursting into the salon then and rushed to Lord North's side. "I say, sir, the grooms have the horses ready. Shouldn't we be on our way?"

Lord North quirked an inky eyebrow at the boy. "There you are, codling. I was wondering where you'd got off to." He raised his voice so that the others could hear him. "Ladies and gentleman, shall we go?"

There was a general bustle as everyone began to move toward the entry hall. Charlotte murmured an excuse to Lord Ryerson and hung back to walk beside Emma, who was amazed to find that her legs would carry her at all.

"What was *that* all about?" Charlotte peered into Emma's face.

"I'm sure I don't know what you mean," Emma murmured, clasping her hands together in front of her to keep them from trembling.

"You looked as if you'd seen a ghost! And Lord North! Well, I've said all along he's not in the ordinary run of gentlemen—not to my taste certainly—but I must tell you

I've never known him to talk gibberish before. Saying that you looked like a Sophia. How eccentric! And that look could have sliced bread!"

"You are being too dramatic," Emma murmured, only half hearing what her cousin was saying.

"Why are you clenching your hands like that? The man is a total stranger to you, and yet you actually seem frightened. He may be odious, but I don't believe he bites. If you should care for my opinion, I think the two of you have run quite mad. I only hope it's nothing in the drinking water."

They had caught up with the others and moved through the open front door toward the grassy verge where the grooms held the horses. There was no opportunity for Emma to reply to her cousin's final remarks, which was fortunate since she could not think of any rational explanation for what had transpired in the salon. She had not yet fully taken it in herself. The only thing that was clear to her was that Jamie and Lord North were one and the same gentleman, a fact that she could not have imagined in a thousand years, had it not been forced upon her awareness.

Emma's mind searched frantically for a reason, any excuse to stay behind. But she had made such a point of saying at dinner last evening how much she anticipated riding again that it would look very strange indeed should she change her mind now. She was only vaguely aware that the groom had spoken to her and had to ask him to repeat his words. He was offering to help her mount, and she allowed him to do so since there seemed to be no credible way of avoiding the afternoon's ride.

Lord North and Jonathan rode out briskly ahead of the others, and Emma held her mount back to ride in the rear next to Hazel Lancaster. It was but an hour's leisurely ride to the meadow where the ruins were located. When, after tossing out several conversational gambits, Miss Lancaster concluded that Emma did not care to talk, she urged her mount forward to chat with Lord Emberland.

During the ride Emma kept a wary eye on the broad shoulders in the camel-colored coat. Several times Lord North glanced back over his shoulder at the other riders, and each time he did, Emma pretended to be engrossed in the passing pastoral scene. But she could feel him staring at her, just the same, and prayed for the afternoon to end quickly.

Upon reaching the meadow, they dismounted and strolled to the crumbling walls of an ancient Roman fortification, while two grooms led the horses to a nearby spring. Another manservant accompanying the group spread a cloth upon the grass and took small frosted cakes and chilled punch from a large hamper. The collation was spread picnic style, and the guests wandering back from the ruins helped themselves.

Emma ate a cake and swallowed a few sips of punch, then discarded her glass to stroll off alone toward the wooded copse bordering the meadow. She was sure her imagination was running wild and exaggerating things completely out of proportion, but it seemed to her that every time she glanced toward Lord North she intercepted another dark look. She felt that if she could get away from the others for a few minutes, she could gain some perspective before the ride back to the manor house.

In the deep shade of the woods, with the others lost from sight, Emma halted and took several deep breaths. She bent to pluck a tiny white wildflower and held it to her nose, but the only scent she could detect was that of damp earth. She wandered to a low bent limb and leaned her back against it, twirling the stem of the flower idly between her fingers. She still could not make her memories of Jamie coincide with the cold, austere man who was the master of Havenwood. What thoughts had run through his mind, she wondered, when he realized that Sophia was Miss Parton's cousin?

She drew in a sharp breath and told herself that she was the victim of a cruel quirk of fate, but it had happened and the world would not come to an end. She would probably be able to look back in later years and laugh at her discomfort today.

She heard footsteps approaching and started upright from her half-sitting position against the tree. Her worst misgivings were realized as she saw Lord North coming toward her, his riding crop dangling idly from one hand. He bowed slightly, a movement that was somehow mocking.

"Are you enjoying the outing, Miss Robinson?"

"Y-yes," she stammered.

He just stood there, looking down at her as if he were waiting for her to say something more. She fingered her collar nervously and finally blurted out, "I—I had no way of knowing, sir, who you were before I arrived here. If I had known, I would have found a reason to excuse myself. I am sorry if I have put you in an—embarrassing position." She felt her cheeks flaming and could not go on. After all, what else was there to say?

"I am puzzled. Was it a wager? Or did you merely find it entertaining to masquerade as a female of the lower classes while you were in London?"

Emma bit her lip and did not dare to meet his gaze. "It

is understandable that you should think that, my lord, but I assure you it was never my purpose to deceive you."

"I beg leave to doubt that," he stated flatly, "since you did not even give me the name you are called by."

"I—I know how it must seem, but it all just happened. You see, the first time we met Charlotte and I had gone to the Frost Fair without my aunt's knowledge, and there we had separated. I couldn't tell you who I was, for fear word would get back to Aunt Claire. Later I suppose I was committed to what I had said the first time. And Aunt Claire would have a spasm if she ever knew Lottie and I had wandered about on our own in a public place, not once, but twice."

"An understandable reaction."

"Yes, I am sure you did nothing to contribute to the misunderstanding." She was beginning to chafe at being put so utterly in the wrong, and an edge had come into her voice. "I suppose it is customary for you to accost strange women and introduce yourself as Jamie."

"Our actions are in no way comparable."

"No, of course not. Women haven't enough sense to look after themselves in the world. Everyone knows it has been given exclusively to men to go about as they please and strike up acquaintances with whom they wish." Emma lifted her eyes and met his stony look. "I have said I am sorry for any embarrassment I may have caused you, Lord North. No doubt you will take into consideration the murky muddle that is the female mind and not condemn me too harshly. Now I believe I shall go back to my cousin." Her hands were clenched tightly at her waist as she walked stiffly away from him, and in her agitation she did not know when he moved to follow her.

## *CHAPTER ELEVEN*

Tea was served to the riders in the melon-pink salon upon their return. Lady North wanted to hear the details of the outing, and Charlotte and Hazel Lancaster were happy to oblige her. Sir James managed to possess his soul in patience and portray a somewhat interested bystander as the conversation flowed around him. This was no small achievement, for he had been fuming inwardly ever since Miss Robinson had given him a trimming in the woods and then had the audacity to walk away before he could respond in kind. All the way back to the house he had rehearsed the wilting sarcasms he might have delivered, had he been given the opportunity.

Every time he looked across the salon and saw her sitting so primly beside Emberland on a settee, his ire was rekindled. He was not so angry, however, that he did not realize the thing that most rankled was that she had pulled the wool over his eyes, had him traipsing all over London trying to track down somebody's servant, even had him toying with the inane notion of attempting to establish a discreet alliance with her. The chit had made an utter fool of him. And then she had the effrontery to fly up into the boughs because he didn't care for it! His dark thoughts were interrupted by Jonathan Parton, who spoke beside him.

"I was wondering, sir, when we can have the first boxing lesson."

He attempted to ease the scowl from his face and not bark at the boy. "Has your mother given her permission?"

"Mama don't like the idea above half," replied Jonathan honestly, "but she says it must be an acceptable pastime if you endorse it. Mama admires you above all things."

"I am flattered," muttered Sir James.

"Oh, yes, sir," Jonathan went on blithely, unaware of the truculence in the marquis's tone. "She's forever remarking upon your good points, especially when Lottie's around."

Sir James looked rather grim. "Lady Parton is all kindness, I am sure. But she mustn't put herself out to defend my character, since I am told she is not always in the pink of health."

Jonathan grinned sheepishly. "Mama is frequently ailing, but Emma says she is one of the strongest females in the country. Emma is the only one who can cope with Mama when she takes to her bed."

"Indeed? And how does the inimitable Emma manage that?"

"She reads to her. Emma is a great book lover. Not that she acts like a bluestocking, you understand. She can play whist better than most men, and she ain't bad at billiards either—I've been teaching her the game. Sits a horse well, too, but I expect you noticed that today."

The marquis was looking at his young friend with wry interest. "I collect you are a firm admirer of your cousin."

"Yes, sir," confirmed Jonathan. "Pluck to the backbone, Emma is. Too bad she ain't got sixpence to scratch with. Mama says she will never find a husband for Emma, especially after Emma turned down Mr. Stumpover."

A corner of the marquis's mouth twitched slightly. "Stumpover? I don't believe I know the man."

"Ain't surprised at that since I don't expect you get to

Sussex often. Mr. Stumpover is curate at our village church."

"Ah," murmured Sir James, "and your mama thought he and your cousin would suit?"

"I daresay she did! Brought him up to London, had him rack up at an inn, paid his shot for weeks. But Emma said she wouldn't have him because she didn't care for him. Gave Mama a spasm, I can tell you. She warned Emma she was very nearly at her last prayers."

"What did your cousin say to that?"

"I don't know what she said to Mama, but she told *me* she'd as lief marry one of Papa's horses as Henry Stumpover, and have a better companion for it, too."

"Do you collect she said that to Stumpover?" inquired Sir James with curiosity.

"As to that, I couldn't say, but the curate told her he will continue to pray for her bad temper. So I suppose he forgave her for throwing him over, although *I* don't think Emma is as cross-grained as all that."

A slight smile tugged at the marquis's mouth. "Magnanimous of him, I must say. Well, Jonathan, as to the boxing lessons—if you will meet me for an early breakfast tomorrow, we'll have the first one shortly thereafter."

"That's famous," the young man declared eagerly. "I'll see you in the breakfast parlor before eight."

Lady North made her way to her son's side. "James, may I have a word with you?" She drew him aside slightly. "I am sure Jonathan Parton is a fine young man, but you have been talking to him for some time."

"Have I? The time got away from me."

Lady North brushed a hand across her eyes. "Forgive me if I spoke shortly. It is just that I have had a distressful afternoon. Sir Humphrey and Lady Lancaster had a dreadful argument at breakfast over the artistic merits of the Gothic Conservatory at Carlton House, although I am sure neither of them has ever clapped eyes on it. The outcome of it was that the Lancasters have departed for Sussex."

"But they've left their daughter," pointed out Sir James.

"Claire Parton offered to carry Hazel back with them. They travel very near the Lancaster country seat. I suppose she was trying to appease the Lancasters, make up somewhat for Sir Humphrey's rudeness. I've just told Hazel that her parents have gone home, and it didn't seem to trouble her at all as long as she has been allowed to stay for the remainder of the two weeks."

"I can see you are upset. What may I do to help?"

"I don't mean to nag, James, but you *are* neglecting our guests. Why don't you take the place I just vacated in the chair on Charles's left?"

"I am sure I shouldn't know how to go on, Mother," Sir James told her, "if you didn't continue to point out my duty to me."

"Now don't fly into a pelter."

His dark brows rose. "Nothing of the kind. I'll do as you ask without quibbling." In spite of the fact that he wanted nothing more than to retire to his study with a brandy, he sauntered to the chair his mother had indicated and sat down. His gaze raked Emma, who was still seated on Emberland's right. She had stiffened perceptibly at his approach and refused to meet his look.

"Well, James," said Ryerson, who was seated on the sofa between Miss Parton and Miss Lancaster, "shall we have the honor of your company at dinner this evening?"

"Certainly, Robert," said Sir James, trying to keep his impatience at his friend's gentle chiding out of his voice.

"I must apologize to all of you for not being able to welcome you yesterday—and for missing dinner, of course."

"We forgive you," drawled Emberland lazily. "Your friends know your preference for more—ah, serious pursuits, old fellow. Frankly, I'm amazed you stayed in town as long as you did, although I can't think how you managed to pass the time while there. You were not often in attendance when the ton gathered."

"I was busy with other things," Sir James told him.

Ryerson laughed. "You waste your time trying to get more than that out of him, Charles. He is always otherwise occupied. More than that, he will never reveal."

"Perhaps," put in Charlotte, a wicked twinkle in her eye, "Lord North has a secret life."

"You have a wonderful imagination, Miss Parton," retorted Sir James with some asperity. "But I fear I must be a disappointment to you. The only secrets I possess have to do with new strains of barley, and I shan't bore you by revealing them."

"Sir, I wonder if you protest too much," Charlotte said, realizing that she was irritating him and rather enjoying it. "What do you think, Emma? Does he have the look of concealing something?"

Emma felt her face flushing as several pairs of eyes turned toward her. "I am sure Lord North's secrets are all quite mundane."

"Are you, indeed, Miss Robinson?" said the marquis stiffly.

"Oh, ho!" exclaimed Ryerson. "I believe you have offended him."

"Why on earth should I be offended by Miss Robinson?" asked Sir James, his gaze never straying from

Emma's hot face. "I assure you, Robert, I am not so easily unsettled."

"How pleasant for you," Emma said, forcing a stiff smile to lips that felt frozen.

Sir James was momentarily paralyzed by an overwhelming desire to shake her. Emma Robinson was undoubtedly the most exasperating female it had ever been his misfortune to come across. Not satisfied with playing him for a fool in London, she came to Kent and made him the brunt of her sharp tongue! Gad, what a devilish mismanaged affair this house party had turned into. "I must ask to be excused now," he said curtly, getting to his feet. "I'm scheduled to meet with my manager before dinner." And before that with a brandy bottle, he added grimly to himself.

When he was gone, Emma made her excuses also and retreated to her chamber. Tossing aside her jaunty little hat, she sat down on the chaise, a heavy depression enveloping her. The house party had become a dreadful trial for her. How could she go on smiling and engaging in activities with the others with Lord North's disapproving visage confronting her at every turn? Yet how could she avoid it? The wretched thought of the coming days filled her with such misgiving that tears came to her eyes. She heard Charlotte entering the adjoining room and quickly swiped at the betraying moisture with the back of her hand.

Charlotte sauntered into the room, a teasing twinkle in her eyes. "Emma, I must tell you that Lord North seems to have taken you in particular dislike. What a withering look he gave you downstairs. Why, Cousin, what is wrong? Surely you can't be cast down over that pompous man's rudeness?"

"I'm merely tired from riding," Emma said, forcing a faint smile to her lips. "Fortunately you had already warned me that Lord North dislikes females."

"Do you know," Charlotte said thoughtfully, "it must be true that there was a tragic affair with some woman in his youth. I wonder if she was a member of the quality. Do you suppose I know her?"

"I've no notion," Emma said a little impatiently. "I *am* tired, Lottie. Besides, it is quite useless to speculate about our host. And I'd like to rest a bit before getting ready for dinner."

Charlotte looked disappointed, as if she had anticipated indulging in a gossipy coze with her cousin. No doubt, Emma thought, she wanted to relate the amusing things Lord Ryerson had said to her during the outing. However Emma did not think she could endure any more of Charlotte's chatter at the moment, and she breathed a sigh of relief when her cousin withdrew to her own room without protest.

Left alone, Emma got out her journal to write an account of her arrival at Havenwood. With the book open in front of her, she attempted to concentrate her attention on penning a description of the medieval manor house, but her mind would not remain on the matter at hand. When she had accidentally written "Jamie" instead of "Lord North," she crossed out the word, snapped the journal shut, and pushed it aside. Her gaze wandered to a chamber window, from which the curtains were drawn back, and beyond to the rolling landscape. Crepuscular shadows dimmed the brilliant green of grass and shrubbery and lent a brooding atmosphere to the scene. Or perhaps it was merely that she was seeing nature from a more melancholy point of view than before.

She acknowledged to herself that Lord North had disconcerted her terribly in the salon earlier. Certainly he was handsome in a rugged sort of way, and he possessed considerable charm when he chose to use it, as he had when he knew her only as Sophia. But for all his breeding and social finesse, he had not the smallest capacity to see a situation involving himself from another person's point of view, particularly when that person was a woman.

She had seen his type frequently since she had come to live with the Partons. Sophisticated men who dressed with the proper elegance, looked upon women of their own class as creatures to be tolerated and treated with just enough politeness to keep them intrigued until the necessity of taking a wife could no longer be avoided, and kept a mistress on the side. Men who boxed well enough to spar with professional fighters and drove their carriages with consummate skill and reckless daring. Men who took more interest in their racehorses than they did in their families. Men who could be appealingly romantic when they wanted to be, as she well knew, but were selfish sybarites underneath it all.

It was foolish of me, she thought as she fingered her pen absently, to prolong those accidental meetings with Lord North with frivolous conversation and, even more, to allow him to kiss me without protest. But I do not think he is totally without blame in the affair, and his condemning attitude toward me is too much to stomach. In his scheme of values, well-born women are not permitted to make mistakes or indulge themselves, while he may engage in the most shocking behavior and be admired by his friends for it. A most unjust circumstance, indeed! Well, he will overcome his affronted sensibilities, and I shall hold my head up while I remain at Havenwood and show him I am not at all concerned about his feelings. It does not matter in the least that he has misjudged me.

Somewhat bolstered by this decision, she rose to choose a gown for dinner, settling at last on one of the two new ones she had had made for the house party, a soft Indian muslin in pale yellow. It was cut low enough at the neckline to be fashionable, but not low enough to be considered daring, and the color emphasized the golden highlights in her hair. She took more time in arranging her tresses than was her custom, entwining a yellow ribbon intricately among the curls.

She had become quite adept at styling her own hair since her parents' death, she told herself as she stepped back to study her reflection in the glass. Upon her arrival at the Partons' country seat, Lady Parton had mentioned finding an abigail for Emma, but she had quickly demurred, saying that since she was in mourning she wouldn't be going into society often enough to need the services of a personal maid. She hadn't wanted to be any more of a burden to the Partons than was absolutely necessary, and her aunt had not pressed the matter. Nor had she mentioned it again since.

Emma suspected this was due to the fact that Lady Parton had come to think of Emma more as her own personal companion and less as a niece. A circumstance that made Emma more determined than ever to find a position by which she might support herself. She had begun to think seriously about starting a novel, which the *Times* editor had agreed to consider for serialization in his newspaper. Until she should make enough from her writing to have a measure of independence, she would pursue a career as a governess.

Lady Haverly had been in the house that afternoon, she

knew, but there had been no opportunity for Emma to speak to her. If such an occasion did not present itself during the next two weeks, she told herself resolutely, she would pay a call on Lady Haverly at her house on the last day of her stay and ask to be considered for service in her household.

A small frown drew her brows together as she suddenly recollected that, should she obtain employment with the Haverlys, she would have to remain in the same vicinity as Lord North. Yet she couldn't let that dash her plans. As a governess she would not be seeing him socially and, in fact, would probably rarely even see him at all. She was willing to allow that he might be fond of his nieces, for he had said he'd given the stray kitten to them, but she doubted he was in the habit of visiting their schoolroom.

At dinner she requested Jonathan to escort her, thus ensuring that she would be seated next to him and at some little distance from Lord North, who had been maneuvered by Lady Parton's high-handed insistence into sitting beside Charlotte. That young woman was plainly chagrined by this, since Lord Ryerson was thus required to sit across the table from her.

Emma herself was too grateful to be separated from their host to spare much sympathy for Charlotte. As it happened, Hazel Lancaster sat on Lord North's left and engaged him in conversation throughout most of the meal so that Charlotte's unwillingness to put herself out to be pleasant went almost unnoticed.

Emma was not so fortunate when they adjourned to the game room after dinner for whist. Her reluctance caused her to dawdle several steps behind the others, and when she arrived in the room the only chair left vacant was at a table with Hazel, Sir Humphrey, and Lord North.

She took it with the air of one approaching the gallows and tried to lay the groundwork for an early leave-taking. "I'll sit in for a few hands, but I'm a poor card player."

Lord North fixed her with a slanting look that seemed to pin her to her chair. "But Jonathan tells me you play whist with admirable skill."

"The gel's a deuced good player," Sir Humphrey confirmed gruffly. "Takes me, more often than not."

Lord North smiled coldly at this remark, and Emma felt herself flushing. North dealt the cards, and Emma found it difficult to keep from fixing her eyes on his strong, agile hands. When he caught her staring at him, he commented, "You mustn't hold back now, Miss Robinson, for fear of showing up Sir Humphrey and me."

Bristling at his mocking tone, Emma retorted, "That notion never entered my head, I assure you."

Hazel laughed. "If you gentlemen keep prodding her, you will confirm Emma and me in our determination to best you."

North's dark brows rose and his gaze flicked to Miss Lancaster, then back to Emma. "A challenge, Sir Humphrey!" he declared. "We accept, ladies."

They all fell to examining their cards then. The game began, and with a furtive glance from beneath her lashes, Emma saw that Lord North's face was impassive. As she had suspected he did not permit anything to show in his expression. She attempted to look worried as she scanned her cards, hoping to outfox him. However, he soon resorted to a ruse of his own. He fixed his dark eyes on her face in a frankly suggestive manner, allowing his glance to move caressingly across the low neck of her gown and slowly up to her cheeks. Within a short time her heart was beating too loudly in her ears, and she was playing cards with no thought for strategy.

Little wonder that she and Hazel were defeated hand after hand. Emma was vastly relieved when Hazel exclaimed, "I don't know about you, Emma, but I've had enough for one evening."

Mystified by Emma's lamentable card playing, Sir Humphrey shook his head. "Never saw you make such a mishmash of a whist game, gel. Must be coming down with something."

"I am sure that is not the case," she said stiffly as she caught a glimpse of Lord North's sardonic eyes. "I am only a little tired from our ride this afternoon. I hadn't sat a horse in some time before today."

"I knew there had to be a good reason for your lack of attention to your cards, Miss Robinson," North offered magnanimously. "Sir Humphrey and I will be glad to give you a rematch whenever you are feeling up to it."

"You are all generosity," she retorted, brushing nervously at a stray curl on her cheek. "It's late, and I am sure you will understand if I retire." Without waiting for a reply, she left the table, her yellow gown whispering about her legs as she hurried from the room.

Hardly aware of the direction she was taking, she shortly found that she had bypassed the staircase. She entered a salon where a few guttering candles provided dim light. In the far wall French doors stood open on a side garden to allow the access to the night air.

Passing outside, she stepped into a small paved area with shrubbery and flower beds beyond. Light from the house provided enough illumination for her to see the narrow stone walkways that meandered through the garden.

She strolled along one of the paths. Numberless pinpricks of stars glittered in the night sky, and a faint scent of rose blossoms filled the air. Emma drew several deep breaths and felt the tension leave her body.

"You shouldn't be wandering about outside at night on your own."

The deep voice behind her sent a jolt of apprehension along all her nerves, and she whirled about to confront Lord North, his shadowy face looming above her, blotting out the stars.

"I—I only meant to take a few steps into the garden. Surely it's safe enough this close to the house."

She caught the lift of his shoulders as he shrugged. "One never knows when a poacher might be about."

"I hardly think I am the sort of game a poacher would be interested in, sir."

She sensed rather than saw his sardonic smile. "And what sort of game are you?"

Emma had started to tremble, for she had suddenly discovered that she did not trust him in this seemingly amiable mood. "I don't know what you mean, my lord."

He uttered a deep chuckle. "I think you do," came the mocking reply, somehow caressing in the darkness. "And my name is James."

Emma's heart clogged her throat as the dark head came closer and strong arms reached out to pull her against the hard length of his body. A breathless gasp escaped her parted lips the instant before his mouth covered them. Until that moment she had never dreamed how sensuous a kiss could be. She felt herself go weak as water and her arms groped blindly for his broad shoulders, clinging there as she tried to steady herself. His lips were at once demanding and coaxing on hers, drawing out the kiss like spun sugar, until Emma lost all sense of who she was and where she was and, with a new longing for the unknown stirring to life inside her, she returned the kiss with abandon.

It was some moments before she came to her senses, and shocked and undone by what was happening, she pulled away from him. Half choking on a sob, she ran past him, back through the salon, along the hall, and up the carpeted stairs.

The marquis stood dead in his tracks for a long moment and stared after the fleeing figure in yellow. He was startled, puzzled, and confused. Instead of frightening the girl by demonstrating what could befall a young woman who engaged in unseemly tête-à-têtes with strange men, he had felt her slender body respond with fire and passion until *he* had been left shaken and feeling like a bumbling schoolboy.

His amours had always been with experienced ladybirds; indeed, he had ever thought such women were placed on the earth for that purpose. Having been led to believe by his father and an extremely staid uncle that passion was foreign to gently reared females, the marquis was having great trouble understanding what had just passed between him and his house guest. What sort of woman *was* she?

Realizing that mobility had returned to his legs, he strode back into the salon. "Sophia!"

At that moment, however, his pursuit was blocked by his mother. She entered the salon from the hall and, after glancing about the room in some perplexity, returned her mystified gaze to her son.

"I thought I heard you speaking, James."

Sir James tugged rather savagely at his cravat. "You

must have heard voices from the game room, Mother. As you can see, there is no one else here."

She looked at him, troubled. "No doubt. Perhaps you ought to retire. The card playing is about to break up anyway, and you look a bit weary, dear."

He muttered his agreement with this idea and, bidding her a curt good night, strode from the salon. Lady North looked after him with some dismay. She had distinctly heard him call out "Sophia." Knowing there was no one of that name in the house was troubling enough, but to find him utterly alone was even more disquieting. Suddenly she remembered that stray kitten he had brought home last winter for her granddaughters. He had called the beast Sophia. It seemed her son had a strange affinity for that name. Indeed, such unfathomable behavior from a much-loved offspring was most upsetting.

Shaking her head slowly, she bethought herself of her duties and returned to the card room to say good night to the guests remaining there.

As for Emma, she lay sleepless in her bed that night for some time. Why did she allow Lord North to have such a disturbing influence on her? It was as if, when she was with him, he exerted a power over her that she could not comprehend, with his searching dark eyes and his compelling manner. She could no longer deny that she was attracted to him as Lord North—the man her aunt had chosen for Charlotte—just as strongly as she had been when she had thought of him merely as Jamie. To make the matter more tangled, he was far above her socially and could not possibly see her as anything more than a brief diversion. Indeed, should he ever so forget his station as to consider her in a more serious light, his family and the Partons would probably be scandalized. She could not give in again to this attraction for him, she thought despairingly.

Her sleep, when it finally came, was troubled by dreams in which Lord North alternately made love to her and scorned her. Consequently, when she left her bed near noon the next day, she hardly felt as if she had slept at all.

Upon going downstairs and finding the small dining parlor unoccupied, she helped herself to the nuncheon buffet that was spread on a long side table. None of the other guests appeared while she ate, for which she was thankful, for she did not relish the thought of making polite conversation.

After eating, she went to her chamber, took the box containing her writing supplies, and left the house through the French doors in the salon that she had discovered the previous night. She crossed the garden hurriedly, not wishing to be seen by her Aunt Claire and to be called back to perform some trifling favors. Beyond the garden she entered a wooded area where she slowed her pace so that she could enjoy a leisurely walk.

Sometime later, she found a bare brown stone beneath an oak tree and, settling herself upon it, opened her box. She took out ink and pen and several sheets of clean paper. Then using the box as a writing surface, she began jotting down ideas for new verses for the *Times*. She struggled for some time with an attempt to caricature Lord North's house party, but she found it difficult to write humorously when she was feeling so despondent.

Her long walk had not freed her from the unhappiness that had settled upon her since coming to Havenwood; although she made several attempts at the verse, none of them was quite right. She was staring at a fresh sheet of paper, determined to try again, when she heard sounds in the trees behind her. Glancing over her shoulder, she beheld Lord North dismounting from a chestnut stallion. He walked toward her with an unreadable expression on his face.

"It appears that you enjoy solitary walks, Miss Robinson."

"Yes—I do," she stammered.

He propped one black-booted foot carelessly on the stone beside her and looked down into her face. "You may take a mount from the stable whenever you wish. One of my grooms will accompany you."

"Thank you. I may avail myself of your generous offer later, but today I felt like walking. Ordinarily, it clears my head."

Dark brows rose questioningly. "Ordinarily? But not today?"

"No—I have a slight headache, which no doubt explains it."

He continued to survey her ponderingly for a long moment. Then, as if he had suddenly recollected himself, he remarked, "I see you are catching up on your correspondence."

Emma gathered her scattered wits and reached quickly for the stack of papers upon which she had been writing, stuffing them into her box with shaking hands. Lord North removed his boot from the stone and bent to pick up something from the ground. "You've lost this one." Then, as Emma watched, horrified, his hand stopped in midair as something caught his eye, and his gaze scanned the sheet.

Watching his expression change from mild curiosity to bewilderment to hard-eyed outrage, Emma longed, for the first time in her life, to possess the ability to fall into a dead faint at will.

"I should greatly appreciate an explanation for this amazing swill." His tone was rigidly controlled.

"I—I was merely scribbling—to pass the time—I—"

"Indeed?" he barked. "And are you in the habit of signing yourself as 'Aristobulus'?"

"I fear you have misunderstood."

"Oh? Well, I am waiting for you to explain."

"I—I've seen the verses in the *Times*, and I suppose I was indulging in a daydream. I've always wanted to be an author, you see."

"Hell's teeth! You really are the most outrageous female I've ever known! But you've flummeried me for the last time. Not to dress it up in clean linen, madam, *you* are the infamous Aristobulus! Look me square in the eye and tell me I am wrong."

Emma tried. She lifted her pained gaze to meet his eyes, which seemed to have turned into two black coals, but her cheeks flamed and she could not maintain the contact and quickly looked away.

"Let me explain, please," she said in a small voice. "I had to make some money, but truly I never thought of publishing my verses until Johnny sent one of them to the *Times*. And the editor printed a request for more—it seemed the answer to my prayers." She dared another darting glance at his unyielding face.

"This is the outside of enough! I beg leave to inform you that I am not without influence in London, and I give you fair warning, if any more verses attacking 'Lord South' appear, I shall take action."

The blood left Emma's face as she recalled the two verses even now lying on the editor's desk. "Sir, try to have a little compassion. No attack was intended. It was all in fun."

"I collect *you* have not been the subject of published sarcasm, madam, else you could not pass it off so lightly." He crumpled the paper he held and tossed it aside with disgust. "To think I was prepared to believe our meetings in London were accidental! But the innocent-looking Sophia was gathering material for her slanderous verses!"

"No!" Emma gasped. "That isn't true!"

"I very much doubt that scheming brain of yours knows truth when it comes upon it. You will be very well advised to set your scathing imagination upon other subjects in future. Good day, Miss Robinson." Without another word, he stalked back to his horse, mounted, and rode off.

Emma sat on the stone, watching his retreating figure, almost overcome by mortification. When she could think with relative coherence again, she penned a hasty letter to the editor, begging him not to print the verses concerning "Lord South." She would explain more fully when she saw him again, she wrote, but her request was most urgent.

Sealing the envelope, she hurried back to the house, fervently praying that the butler would know how to get the letter on the next post chaise going to London from the nearest village.

# CHAPTER TWELVE

Lord North was not in attendance at the entertainments arranged for the young people during the remainder of the week. When his mother attempted to take him to task for his abominable rudeness, he informed her he could not neglect his estate duties at the most crucial time of the year and reminded her, rather curtly, that he had not been in favor of the house party from the beginning. He continued to instruct young Jonathan Parton in the techniques of boxing, but except for the boy he more or less ignored the other guests, as far as his mother could see. Although he was usually at table for dinner, he often brooded in silence throughout most of the meal.

After three days of this behavior Lady North was beside herself and summoned her daughter from the neighboring estate to pour out her embarrassment and perplexity.

"Sarah, what *am* I to do?" Lady North was pacing back and forth across the flowered carpet in the pink salon while her daughter looked on from a comfortable chair. "I've tried to reason with James about his inhospitable actions, but he merely brushes it all aside and remains unmoved. I've never known him to disregard so blatantly the feelings of others or to take so little notice of appearances." She stopped her pacing to add forebodingly, "He's becoming an eccentric!"

"You're overwrought, Mama. I'm certain James is no more eccentric than he ever was."

"Oh? Well, James has always had a look about his eyes of your Uncle Claremont. Don't you remember him, your father's eldest brother? He lived to be past seventy and never married, and in his latter years he said and did the most bizarre things."

Lady Haverly looked amused. "But we always suspected he was short of a sheet. I remember Papa's recounting curious behavior in Claremont when they were still in short coats. Most people don't undergo a character change when they reach maturity, but merely become more set in their ways as they grow older. I am sure it had nothing to do with the fact that Uncle Claremont never married either. We don't know that circumstance was as he preferred it. Probably no acceptable woman would have him. Nor have I ever heard that one could predict behavior from a look about the eyes."

Lady North shook her head doubtfully. "I am convinced the unmarried state is unnatural and, therefore, impairing. Consider Sir Humphrey Laird if you need more evidence."

Lady Haverly giggled. "Actually, I think Sir Humphrey is quite amusing. But I don't think you need worry that James will turn out like him."

Lady North moved to take a chair near her daughter and said in a confiding tone, "The other evening I found him in the blue salon, and just before I entered, I heard him call out, 'Sophia.' "

Her daughter's eyes widened, then narrowed with thought. "Sir Humphrey?"

"No, *James,*" said her mother impatiently.

"But there is no one here named Sophia, is there? Who was with him at the time?"

"That is precisely my point, dear. He was alone. When I asked if he had spoken, he said I must have heard voices from the game room where the guests were playing cards —all except Miss Robinson, who had retired early."

"Sophia," mused Lady Haverly. "That's the name he gave Ann's and Cassandra's cat."

"Exactly. Can you fathom it?"

Lady Haverly continued to look puzzled. "No, but I am sure there is a perfectly logical explanation. Perhaps he had fallen asleep in a chair and called out in a dream."

"No, he was wide awake. I think he had been outside just before, for the French doors stood open."

"Then maybe there was someone named Sophia in the garden—although I can't think who it could have been. Is one of the maids called that? Or someone in the surrounding area?"

"Sarah!" Lady North looked shocked. "There is no Sophia here, I tell you. And it was quite dark out. Surely you aren't suggesting that James had arranged a clandestine meeting with some highflyer from the village!"

"Of course I'm not," soothed Lady Haverly. "I was merely thinking aloud. Besides, if James arranges such meetings, I am sure he would not choose Havenwood as the rendezvous."

"Sarah!"

"Forgive me, Mama." Lady Haverly tried not to smile. "I shouldn't tease you when you are in such an anxious state."

"No, you shouldn't," said Lady North worriedly, then glancing toward the salon door she added, "Oh, Claire. I didn't know you were stirring yet. Have you gone in for nuncheon?"

Lady Parton came into the room. "Yes, and very delicious it was, too. Your butler told me I might find the two of you here. I hope I'm not intruding upon a private conversation."

"No—no," Lady North assured her. "Come and sit with us. I am sure it will be no surprise to you that we were discussing my son and his exasperating absences from the house this past week. I've no idea why he is behaving this way, but I beg you not to judge him too severely." She frowned her consternation. "I must confess that the male mind, particularly James's, is often a mystery to me."

"I've given considerable thought to our situation," said Lady Parton, "and I've concluded that Lord North must have momentous things on his mind. He is absenting himself so that he might reach a decision."

"Well, his estates *are* quite large," murmured Lady North, grateful that her guest did not appear to be contemplating leaving Havenwood in high dudgeon.

"I know he is a conscientious landlord," said Lady Parton, "but I am convinced something else is weighing more heavily on his mind at the moment."

The other two ladies looked at her without comprehension. "I mean," Lady Parton went on in a confidential tone, "that perhaps we may have a betrothal on our hands sooner than any of us expected."

Lady Haverly looked quite dubious, but her mother's face cleared instantly. "Do you mean—oh, Claire, you don't mean to say that Charlotte has confided something to you?"

Her guest was looking quite pleased with herself. "Not in so many words, but then my daughter has never been wide in the mouth. However, there are signs that any experienced older woman can read. Sometimes I catch her staring dreamily into space and smiling a little secret smile. And her spirits, which I must tell you were somewhat low upon our arrival here, have risen remarkably. She breezes into her chamber and then out again to be off to some other place. In short, I believe I know when my own daughter has romantic intrigue on her mind."

"You think they are meeting secretly?" asked Lady North with avid interest.

"That is my conviction," said Lady Parton smugly. "Oh, I hope you won't think me derelict in my duty for not quizzing Lottie, but I assure you I trust her completely to know how to comport herself with a gentleman. And there are so many other people around."

Lady North looked at her daughter. "This is wonderful, isn't it, Sarah?"

Lady Haverly cleared her throat and said cautiously, "I hope the two of you aren't running ahead a great deal too fast. It is possible that Charlotte is merely having a pleasant time with the other young people. I wouldn't assume so much if I were you."

"No, Sarah," her mother said, "I believe Claire may be right. James has seemed preoccupied, as if he were endeavoring to reach an important decision."

"I don't wish to sound immodest," stated Lady Parton, "but I have never known a gentleman yet who can resist my daughter's charms for long."

"What are charms to one person can be irritations to another," Lady Haverly pointed out dampingly.

"Sarah!" exclaimed her mother. "Don't be rude. Charlotte is a lovely girl."

"I didn't mean to imply otherwise," said Lady Haverly. "I merely wished to remind you that it is impossible to predict what sort of female will attract a man. You must admit, Mama, that James has managed to resist some formidably determined and beautiful young women during the past few years." Glancing at Lady Parton, she saw that the lady did not at all appreciate her observation. "Of course," she added hastily, "I shall be as happy as either of you should Claire's deduction prove correct." She stirred from her chair. "Now, I must get back to the girls. I still haven't found a suitable governess and must leave them in care of the housekeeper. Mrs. Hanks is very patient with them, but she has her other duties to see to."

"Haven't you even a prospect for the post?" inquired her mother.

"One or two," said Lady Haverly, "but no one who has impressed me excessively with her qualifications. We are thinking of placing an ad in the *Times.* There is no great hurry, for I've promised Ann and Cassandra a summer holiday from the school room." She left the two matrons to their eager contemplation of a marriage between their offspring, still quite doubtful herself that Lady Parton had interpreted her daughter's behavior accurately.

Meanwhile Charlotte had had a tray in her room so that she could be alone and relive the exciting interlude that had transpired between her and Sir Robert on the previous afternoon when they had eluded the others and ridden back to the meadow on the pretext of viewing the Roman ruins again.

Robert had been so dashing and romantic that he had quite taken her breath away. Upon lifting her from her mount, instead of setting her immediately on her feet, he had carried her to a grassy little knoll and set her down amidst a blanket of wildflowers. He had teased her, saying she was Venus and he a faithful worshipper at her shrine. Then he had vowed he would kidnap her and carry her away to the Continent.

She had responded with more lighthearted flirtatious banter. But suddenly they were no longer teasing, but were staring longingly into each other's eyes just as the young lovers in stage dramas did. And then Robert—oh, most amorous of gentlemen—had knelt at her feet and delivered an impassioned declaration of his love for her. Charlotte was convinced that even Mr. Kean could not have done better. Robert had begged her permission to speak to her father, and Charlotte, after confessing her own love and being swept into his arms in a passionate embrace, had come down to earth long enough to suggest that a wiser course would be for her to make the first approach to her parents.

She would have liked to confide in Emma first, but Joan had said that her cousin had gone riding with Jonathan and might not be back for some time. Setting aside her tray, she arose to dress with Joan's help, having made up her mind to speak to her father immediately.

Lord Parton was found in the sitting room provided for guests on the second floor. He and Sir Humphrey were having some port and Sir Randolph was looking through the London newspaper that had arrived the day before.

"I say, Uncle, listen to this," Lord Parton was saying as Charlotte entered the room. Then he read from the *Times:*

*A beleaguered Lord South has left London behind,*
*Whipping his horses with determined mind,*
*His carriage turned in the direction of Kent;*
*But, alas, there are mamas of relentless bent*
*Who, uncovering this foul trick, gave pursuit,*
*Heedless of propriety and manners that suit.*

*For marriageable daughters are in abundant supply,*
*So do not condemn them if you see them pass by.*

Sir Randolph laughed uproariously. "Gad, North will have a fit of the blue devils when he sees this."

"Papa," said Charlotte, coming to stand in front of the couch where the two men sat. "I must speak with you."

"Oh, hallo, Lottie. I'm reading the paper now, as you can see."

"Please, Papa, it's important."

Her parent glanced up at her absently. "Then perhaps you had better speak to your mother."

"No, I prefer saying this to you."

Sir Humphrey lounged in his corner of the couch, looking over the rim of his glass at her. "Looks white about the mouth, Randolph. Must have had a dust-up with Claire."

Charlotte cast him an impatient glance. "No, I haven't—not yet."

Her father laid his paper aside and, folding his arms across his rotund middle, sighed. "Very well, Lottie. I see I shan't have any rest until you've said what you came to say. I collect it's more new dresses you're wanting."

"If she gets any more," muttered Sir Humphrey, "we'll have to move out of the house and turn the whole place into a wardrobe."

"I don't want any new gowns," Charlotte declared.

"Extraordinary," commented Sir Humphrey, draining his glass with relish. "Must be sick."

Charlotte glared at his elderly lordship before turning back to her father. "I—I wish to be married, and I—have reason to believe the gentleman in question will offer for me at any moment. I wanted to prepare you."

Sir Humphrey grunted. "Shouldn't think he'd need any more preparation than he'd had for the past month. Ain't that the purpose of this demmed silly house party?"

A smile of sweet relief wreathed Sir Randolph's face. "Well done, Lottie! Your mama will fly into raptures. Now maybe we can return to Sussex in peace." He beamed at her. "Upstanding gentleman, Lord North. Surely you aren't worried that I will say no to him, silly goose."

"Not if he wishes to remain in the same county with Claire, he won't," observed Sir Humphrey from his corner.

"You don't understand," said Charlotte, distressed. "I do not wish to marry Lord North."

"Balderdash," observed her father. "Your judgment has been overdone. I'm sure you are in a state over making such a fine match and will come to your senses directly."

"Thought she said she *wanted* to get married," put in Sir Humphrey. "I've always known you can't depend on anything a female says. Change their minds with the wind."

"Uncle Humphrey, will you please permit me to carry on a conversation with Papa without interruption?" cried Charlotte, tears of frustration coming into her eyes. "I *do* want to wed, but not Lord North. Sir Robert is the gentleman who has won my heart, and he means to speak to you soon, Papa."

"*Ryerson!*" Sir Randolph almost choked on the word. "This is preposterous!"

"Papa, try to understand," Charlotte pleaded, twisting her hands together. "I love him. He is everything I ever dreamed of in a husband."

"This is a devilish hum, Lottie," declared Sir Randolph,

with great anxiety in his tone. "Why can't you be biddable like other girls?"

"Wasting your breath, Randolph," Sir Humphrey advised. "She's already thrown her hat over the windmill, or I miss my guess."

Pulling herself up as tall as possible, Charlotte announced, "I shall marry Robert or no one. That is my last word on the matter, Papa."

Sir Humphrey chortled. "I've yet to hear the *last* word from any woman."

"Dear me, what are we to do?" muttered Sir Randolph.

"Better get Claire up here, if you want my advice," said Sir Humphrey blandly. "Then take shelter behind the nearest chair."

"Yes, yes," mumbled Sir Randolph distractedly. He lumbered to his feet. "I expect we'd better send for her. I'll find one of the servants to take the message."

Before the agitated Lord Parton returned, Jonathan and Emma entered the sitting room, still dressed in their riding clothes.

"I'm giving up on you, Emma," Jonathan was saying. "Been trying to cheer you up for the last two hours, but you are determined to have the megrims. You are starting to behave like all other women."

"I told you that I preferred riding alone," responded Emma tiredly as she relaxed against the padded back of a chair. Charlotte had seated herself also and was gazing out a window, an occupation Emma had noticed her engaged in a number of times during the past week. She turned to Sir Humphrey. "How are you today, sir?"

"*I'm* in high croak," said the old gentleman.

"Where is everyone?" inquired Jonathan, looking

around. "This place is starting to remind me of a mausoleum. No excitement at all."

"Give it a few minutes, boy," advised Sir Humphrey, an anticipatory gleam in his eye.

Before he had a chance to expand upon this remark, Lady Parton was escorted into the room by her husband. She looked extremely cross. "Of all the times to interrupt me, Randolph," she sputtered, "when I was having such a cozy chat with Lady North. I thought you were reading the papers. Well, what is so urgent that you must send a maid to hurry me so rudely away from our hostess?"

Lord Randolph left her standing in the center of the room and retreated to the couch beside his uncle. "Tell her, Lottie. This mingle-mangle is all of your doing."

Under her mother's bewildered regard Charlotte came to her feet slowly, as if she felt at a disadvantage to be seated while her mother stood. "I want to marry Lord Ryerson, Mama."

For a moment Lady Parton merely gaped at her. Then she clutched her head with one hand. "I cannot have heard you correctly, Lottie. It is Lord North who is on the point of asking for you."

Charlotte drew a long breath. "I know that you have convinced yourself of that, but it isn't true. Besides, if he *should,* I will never agree. It's Robert whom I love."

Jonathan was looking at his sister with admiration. "Now I understand why you and Ryerson are always going off together."

"*Going off together!*" Lady Parton's face had gone chalk white. "You've gone distracted, Lottie! Oh, my poor head. I feel as if I might faint." Clutching her head with both hands, she staggered to a chair and fell into it.

"Lottie," murmured Emma, "I told you to wait until we were back in Sussex to bring this up."

Lady Parton lifted her head and stared at her niece. "*You* knew what was afoot?" Emma's silence was all the confirmation she needed. "Vipers!" she shrieked. "Vipers in my bosom!"

"Now, m'dear," put in Sir Randolph uncomfortably, "try to remain calm."

"Might as well tell her to be a Chinaman," said Sir Humphrey reasonably.

"Calm! Remain calm while my daughter announces her desire to enter into a disastrous marriage? And after all I have done to make a respectable match for her. I—will—not—allow it, Lottie. *Never!*"

"Then I shall *never* marry," stated Charlotte, her own face gone as pale as her mother's.

"Ryerson ain't such a bad sort," offered Sir Randolph hesitantly.

Lady Parton's head jerked back as if she had been struck. "Mad! The whole lot of you are as mad as the king! The dandy is *impoverished.*"

"Oh, that's doing it a little too brown, m'dear," said her husband. "The man has a comfortable living. And Lottie will have her portion from Uncle Humphrey."

"Never knew a female yet who would listen to reason," stated Sir Humphrey emphatically. "Ain't in their nature."

"Well, he ain't the top-sawyer North is," observed Jonathan cheerfully, "but he's slap up to the mark in other ways. It's not as if she wants to marry the butler, Mama."

"No one has asked for your opinion, young man!" said Lady Parton, her jaw set rigidly. "Now, Lottie, if you will think about this for a day or two, I am sure you will see that it is quite impossible. This bizarre impulse will pass."

"I have thought about it for months," Charlotte told her, "and I mean to marry him or die in the attempt."

"Spoken like Claire's daughter," said Sir Humphrey with a cackle.

"It would be a good idea for all of us to think it over," suggested Sir Randolph, grasping at a way of postponing the confrontation, at least for a few days.

"There is nothing to think over, Randolph," retorted his wife. "My decision is final."

"And so is mine!" exclaimed Charlotte, her brown eyes flashing mutiny.

Lady Parton groaned pathetically. "Now my stomach is becoming upset. I am going to be quite ill. I have always known my frail constitution could not survive to old age, but I thought I had a few years left to me. I reckoned without taking into account my caper-witted daughter. Oh, where is Genevieve? I must have a posset." Holding her stomach with one hand and her head with the other, she tottered from the sitting room, calling weakly for her abigail.

"She'll be in bed for the rest of the summer now," predicted Sir Humphrey.

"I will have your answer, Papa," said Charlotte in a grimly determined tone. "Will you accept Robert's offer when he comes to you?"

"Now, Lottie," pleaded her father, "let's not rush into anything."

"So be it," said Lottie, her teeth snapping shut. "Two can play at Mama's game. I shall take to my bed and stay there until I have your permission to wed. If it is not forthcoming within a few days, I shall elope. I am sure that would be more romantic anyway." She stalked from the room, her head held high.

Sir Randolph wrung his hands. "Mercy, what am I to do?"

"Simple," his uncle told him. "I suggest the two of us retire to Sussex immediately and let them come to cuffs."

Having reached the end of his tether, Sir Randolph turned on his uncle in an uncharacteristically scathing fashion. "Will you be quiet! I daresay I can handle my own family's problems without your idiotish advice!"

Getting to his feet, his jaws puffing out with indignation, Sir Humphrey gave it as his opinion that *that* was a matter of considerable conjecture since his nephew had shown no marked facility in that direction in the past twenty-five years. Then he recommended them all to go to the devil and left them to get on with it.

## CHAPTER THIRTEEN

"Wait'll I tell Lord North what has fallen out," said Jonathan into the silence that had followed Sir Humphrey's incensed departure. "In case he *is* thinking of offering for Lottie, he ought to know. No sense in setting himself up to be thrown over."

Sir Randolph slumped back against the couch in a defeated pose and offered no word of protest as his son dashed from the room.

"Perhaps I should go and see if I can soothe Aunt Claire a little," said Emma, preparing to leave.

"You're a good, biddable gel, Emma," murmured Sir Randolph. His niece's ironic expression was lost on him as he began trying to locate the port decanter.

Jonathan went first to the pink salon where he found Lady North and Ryerson, but not the gentleman he was looking for.

Lady North left her chair and came toward her young house guest. "Jonathan, I thought I heard someone screaming a while ago. I can't think who could have been in such distress. Did you hear it?"

"I rather think I did!" said Jonathan, sauntering into the salon. "It was Mama. You ain't seen a pelter until you've seen one of hers, I can tell you."

"Gracious!" Lady North's eyes were startled. "But she was in such a mellow mood when she left me. What on earth set her off?"

"Lottie."

Ryerson, who was seated in a melon-pink chair, came

to sudden alertness. "She must have told her. Hell's teeth, I wanted Lottie to let me make the approach. I should have borne the brunt of her mother's rage."

Lady North was looking from Jonathan to Sir Robert. "I don't understand any of this. Lottie is *such* a lovely girl. I can't believe she would do anything to upset her mother."

"Ha!" observed Jonathan. "Shows you don't know my sister very well."

Affronted, Sir Robert said sternly, "I must ask you, my boy, not to cast aspersions upon the woman I love."

Lady North blinked at her guest. "The woman *you* love? Are you speaking of Charlotte Parton?"

"I am," confirmed Sir Robert, straightening his intricately folded cravat and smoothing the oversized lapels of his sunburst yellow coat.

"Lottie declares she's top over end for him, too," Jonathan expanded for Lady North's benefit. "Says she'll marry him or die. She's taken to her bed. So has Mama—*she* hinted we might as well start digging her grave. Shouldn't be at all surprised if they both refuse their food, but I don't imagine *that* will last long enough for anybody to get into a fret over it. They enjoy eating too much. Shouldn't care to lay a wager on which of them will hold out longer, though. They are both in a great taking!" His youthful face took on a deliberative expression. "I've witnessed some grand turnups between Lottie and Mama," he added seriously, "but I believe this one is the rarest yet."

"Where did you leave your father?" Ryerson asked. "I should waste no time in laying my request before him."

"He's in the sitting room abovestairs, but I'd give him

a while yet," advised Jonathan. "Let him finish that bottle of port he and Uncle Humphrey were sampling."

Lady North began to run her hand across the back of a chair in a distracted manner. "I can't conceive what has come over everyone. Lottie and Claire closeted in their chambers. Randolph going at the port so early in the day. And James wandering about in a brown study calling for someone named Sophia."

"Sophia?" asked Ryerson. *"Odd!"* He shook his head, then, much struck, mused, "I wonder if it is possible to go senile at two and thirty."

"Robert, you are not at all helping my state of mind," chided Lady North.

"I ask merely because of something that happened when I introduced James to Miss Robinson."

"Well, I suppose you might as well tell me," said her ladyship. "I doubt that I can be any more worried than I am already."

"He had the strangest expression on his face and said she looked like a Sophia. Now what do you make of that?"

"I make nothing of it," responded Lady North, "except that my son is beginning to put me in mind of his late eccentric uncle."

"Where is Lord North now?" asked Jonathan, recollecting his mission.

"As to that," she said, "I wouldn't care even to speculate."

"I thought I saw him walking around near the stable a while ago," said Ryerson. "He may have been getting ready for a ride. More likely he was returning from one since he is usually up at the crack of dawn. That's another aberration in his behavior."

"I hope I find him there," said Jonathan. He excused himself and quit the house in a dead run.

The young man was not disappointed. He found Lord North sauntering along next to the stable stalls, talking to his racehorses. Hearing Jonathan's clambering approach, the gentleman took in the boy's haste and said, "Sorry I couldn't meet you for our boxing lesson this morning, but I had an urgent matter to take care of. Don't get all Friday-faced, though. We'll have the lesson later this afternoon."

"I ain't worried about the lesson," said Jonathan, gasping for breath and coming to an abrupt halt before the marquis. "I have something to tell you so you won't make a cake of yourself."

The marquis's mouth turned up at the corners. "I am excessively grateful for your interest, Jonathan. How am I about to make a cake of myself?"

"I ain't certain you are," amended Jonathan, pausing to draw down several gulps of air, "but in case you are considering offering for Lottie, as Mama thinks—well, I wouldn't, if I were you."

"What has turned you to that opinion, halfling?"

"Lottie just told Mama she wants to marry Lord Ryerson. Said she'd give Papa a few days to agree or she'll elope."

"An excitable young woman, your sister," observed Sir James dryly.

"Well, that ain't the half of it, sir. Lottie and Mama have both taken to their beds, and Papa's going distracted over some of your liquor."

Sir James tried to suppress his laugh, but it came out sounding like a strangled cough. "Poor devil."

"I hope you're not too disappointed. I am fond of my

sister and I don't mean to sound disloyal, but I must tell you that she's more trouble than she's worth. You're probably just as well out of it."

"Thank you, Jonathan," replied the marquis. "I am sure I shall manage to recover my spirits in time."

"I was certain you could," said Jonathan with some relief. "The world's full of pretty misses."

"I've observed that myself." Sir James put an arm around the young man's shoulders, and they left the stable together. "I intend to go up to the house and see if the London newspapers have arrived."

"I believe they have," Jonathan told him. "Papa was reading them before Lottie interrupted him. I'm sure he's in no condition to be reading now. Would you like me to get them and bring them to you in your study?"

"I'd appreciate that very much. And if you'll keep it to yourself, perhaps we will have a small glass of brandy together."

Jonathan grinned broadly. "I'll not utter a word to anyone."

On his way to the abovestairs sitting room Jonathan passed his cousin in the hallway. She was carrying a small box in one arm.

"I suppose Mama still declares she's on her deathbed this time."

Emma's smile was wan. "Yes. I tried to soothe her, but she ordered me from the chamber. She says I've betrayed her goodhearted trust as badly as Lottie. Not only have I turned down the man she chose for my husband, but I've abetted Lottie in an underhanded scheme to make what Aunt Claire insists on naming 'a shocking misalliance.' She may never forgive either of us."

"I'm sorry, Emma," commiserated Jonathan, "but you

know Mama won't listen to sense when somebody opposes her. And Lottie's not much better. Do you collect she'll be just like Mama when she's older?"

"Heaven send," commented Emma, "that the man she does marry will take her in hand so that will not happen. Lottie is a sweet girl under it all. Well, since I can be of no help here, I'm going for a long walk. I'd ask you to come, but I really would like to be alone for a while."

"Don't want to come, anyway. I'm having a br—er, a meeting with Lord North in his study."

"I'll probably see you at tea then," said Emma, making for the stairs. She was glad to know that Lord North was in the house, as she needn't worry about running into him in the woods. Since their last unsettling confrontation, he had avoided being anywhere near her. In fact, he seemed to have forgotten that he had house guests at all and had been spending his days going about to his several estates in the area with his manager, or so his mother gave out. It was clear that the lady was embarrassed over this turn of events, but Emma could only thank the fates for keeping him away from her. After the last time any meeting with him could only be strained and unpleasant for them both.

She took the path through the garden and into the copse, sometime later finding herself at the oak tree with the bare stone beneath it where she had sat before. She settled herself on the stone, but instead of opening her writing box immediately, she leaned back against the tree trunk and stared into the deep greens and browns of the woods surrounding the small clearing where she was. But very soon the colors blurred and ran together, and she had to wipe her eyes with the hem of her muslin gown.

Lud, she was turning into a weepy female, and she had never had any patience at all with the type. For the past few days, however, she had noticed her throat aching and her vision blurring at the most unexpected times. Of course, she knew the reason, and she might as well be honest with herself. She had fallen in love with a man who could not stand the sight of her. It really was the most distressful thing she could have done; and she had always thought herself too sensible for anything so positively smacking of martyrdom. Well, there was nothing for it now but to overcome this weakness in her character.

Drawing a long, shuddering breath, she sat straight and opened her box. For the better part of a half hour she tried to pen a verse about the first meeting between the Prince Regent and Grand Duchess Catherine of Oldenburg, sister to the Russian czar, who had arrived in London in March with the Russian advance guard to prepare the way for a state visit of Alexander in June. The regent had called on her at Pulteney's Hotel, arriving too soon so that she was not dressed. This did nothing to create a friendly atmosphere, and when she finally did receive him, the two took an instant dislike to each other.

It was the kind of subject she had treated humorously in previous verses, but mirth was now far from her sensibilities. After she had discarded several false starts, she took a clean sheet of paper from her box and began to write in a more serious vein. The words flowed now through her pen and onto the paper with unconscious ease; it was almost as if she were merely setting down dictation from another person.

A while later her pen stilled, she read over what she had written with some surprise and a fresh blurring of tears:

* * *

*You have bewitched me, Lord Jamie, my love,*
*You've plundered and stolen my heart.*
*Dreaming and waking, you're oft in my mind*
*'Twill e'er be the same when we part.*

*I wish your station were of less import*
*Or my position of higher degree.*
*Alas, I seem destined to sadness and tears,*
*For your love can't belong to me.*

Sounds penetrated her misery. Realizing that someone was coming through the woods, she guiltily folded the poem and, without really thinking of what she was doing, pushed it out of sight beneath the edge of the stone upon which she sat. She straightened and looked over her shoulder.

Lord North emerged in the small clearing and strode to her side. He looked extremely angry.

He thrust a folded section of newspaper under her nose and demanded, "How can you have the unmitigated gall to stay in my house while going on with this?"

"I have wished ever since I first saw you here," she retorted, "that I didn't have to endure the full two weeks! Unfortunately, I have been unable to convince the Partons that I am worth the inconvenience of sending me back to Sussex early." She had not seen the papers that had been delivered to the house recently, but judging from his smoldering expression, she had a suspicion of what had happened.

Her hand shook as she took the sheet he was holding out to her. She read it quickly. As she had feared, it was one of the poems she had sent to the editor before leaving for Kent.

She raised stricken eyes to his face. "I sent a letter to the editor begging him not to print any more verses about Lord South. Your butler put it on the London post chaise for me."

"It seems you have little influence with the man."

"I—I can only think that he received my missive too late to stop the publication of this verse. I am sure that is what happened."

She was dressed in a soft pink muslin gown that was unexceptionable, but her face was pale and her eyes, especially when they rested on him, looked haunted. He just stared at her for a long moment. Finally she asked weakly, "What do you mean to do?"

"I am considering," he said gruffly, turning away from her to glare into the trees.

"My lord, please don't do anything to sever my connection with the *Times.*" Her voice sounded strangled, and she paused before going on. "It is the only chance I have of ever becoming a woman of independent means. The editor has promised to consider a novel for serialization. I'm going to start working on it as soon as I am settled some—er, as soon as we've returned to Sussex."

He looked back at her then, his dark eyes narrowed and reflective. "You are an unusual female, Miss Robinson," he said exasperatedly.

She regarded him with huge eyes. "Is it so unusual," she burst out, suddenly impatient with him and with her own precarious position, "for a woman to want a life consisting of something beyond playing sympathetic companion to a relative in her imaginary ailments?"

A corner of his mouth twitched once. "You are referring to Lady Parton?"

Already Emma regretted her words. She must sound

like an ungrateful wretch. "It isn't that I am unaware of the Partons' generosity to me."

"But it is chafing always to have to be on the receiving end of your relatives' charity. It makes you feel you are under obligation."

"Yes," she murmured unhappily.

"That, at least, I can understand. As for the other . . ." He plucked the piece of newspaper from her hand. "I shall reserve my decision as to what action to take until I see if any more of these insults appear. And about your novel, madam, I trust there will be no Lord North, South, East, or West among the characters."

"Oh, no," she assured him. "There shan't be anyone who resembles you even remotely."

He looked down at her thoughtfully. "Tell me, does anyone else know Aristobulus's identity?"

"Only Jonathan," she admitted reluctantly. "I could hardly keep it from him since he is the one who sent the first verse to the *Times* and signed it with that name. I *tried* to throw him off, but I am sure he knows. He has sworn an oath never to reveal the secret, though."

"I hope your confidence in that young man's discretion is not misplaced," he observed darkly.

Worried that he might be thinking of reversing his decision to reserve action against her, she slid from the stone, taking her box in her arms. "I beg you to excuse me. I must get back to the house and see what I can do for Aunt Claire. She—she is having one of her spells."

"So young Parton informed me," he said, his lips twisting awry. "He wanted to prevent my making a cake of myself by offering for his sister. It seems she will have no one but Ryerson."

Emma looked up at him intently for a moment, trying

to fathom his thoughts. Had he really been thinking of offering for Charlotte? Was he hurt by this news? But it was impossible to deduce anything from his enigmatic look. "Good day, sir." She turned away from him and walked quickly back the way she had come.

Sir James watched her until her slight figure was lost from sight among the trees. She didn't glance back. He sat on the stone she had vacated, looking grim. Devil take it, it wasn't that he had no sense of humor. But insults were a bit too much to swallow, coming from a chit who hardly knew him. Where had she received such a biased opinion of him?

"Here you are, sir!"

He looked up to see Jonathan Parton coming toward him. "I've been looking everywhere for you. You did say we'd have the boxing lesson this afternoon, didn't you?"

Sir James got reluctantly to his feet. "So I did."

Jonathan, facing him, was looking at the ground. "I say, what's this?" He stooped to pull a small piece of paper from beneath the stone. "Looks as if someone tried to hide it. There was only a corner sticking out." He unfolded the paper and read the words written on it. His mouth turned down with distaste. "One of those goosish love poems. Probably written by some neighborhood chit. Do you know anyone called Lord Jamie?"

With a quick alertness that surprised Jonathan, the marquis snatched the paper from his fingers. He read it over silently, his brows drawing together and his mouth settling into a narrow line. Then, without comment, he tucked it into a pocket of his waistcoat. "We'd better return to the stables if we're to have your lesson before tea," he said curtly.

Jonathan followed him from the clearing, almost running to keep up with the marquis's long strides. Even Lord North was starting to behave in an odd manner. He wondered what the remaining days at Havenwood would bring, with everyone going about in a fit of the blue devils. He suspected Lord North was irritated because he didn't really want to go ahead with the lesson. He probably had more important matters to see to. Perhaps he felt Jonathan was making a nuisance of himself. Well, Jonathan thought dismally, he wouldn't remind him of the lessons after today. He admired his host above all things and didn't want the marquis to take him in dislike.

Emma managed to avoid seeing much of Lord North during the next two days. Mostly she kept to her own chamber and that of her aunt, who had relented enough to allow Emma in the same room with her. Not that she had forgiven her niece, but Emma was the only one who seemed sympathetic to her illnesses, and besides she liked the girl to read to her.

Contrary to Jonathan's prediction, neither his mother nor his sister refused food. They kept to their vow not to leave their chambers, however, and meals were brought up to them on trays. Charlotte had had no contact with anyone but the maids and her abigail, except for the long, impassioned note smuggled into her chamber by Sir Robert, who bribed one of the maids to deliver it.

He had spoken to her father, he said, and had not been summarily dismissed. Therefore, he still held to the hope that they would receive permission to marry in time. Charlotte had sent him a return note by the same maid, saying they would wait until the day before they were scheduled to leave Havenwood. If her father hadn't relented by then, they would slip away together in the night and elope.

Emberland and Hazel Lancaster had been left, more or less, to their own devices, but they seemed to be bearing up well. They rode together twice a day accompanied by one of the grooms and had their luncheons picnic style out-of-doors. Lady North suspected there might be a budding romance afoot, but she couldn't enjoy watching the beginning of what might turn into a match between Emberland and Hazel. She was too distressed by the shambles created by Lady Parton and Charlotte. It would be a very long while, she told herself, before she planned another house party.

On the third day of the second week Lady Haverly came to call on her mother, having gotten word, through her servants who had it from the North servants, concerning what had been happening at Havenwood.

"I am going ahead with the plans for my ball on Saturday," she told her mother after they were seated comfortably in the pink salon. "The guests have been invited, and I am sure we can have a pleasant evening, even if Claire and Charlotte decline to attend. I trust James can be persuaded to be there."

"I shan't give him a moment's peace until he agrees," Lady North said. "I have tried to make the best of his eccentric behavior these past days, but I shall never forgive him if he absents himself from your ball, Sarah, I promise you."

"I don't believe he would be so shabby as that."

"Then you have more faith in his remembering what is acceptable behavior than I do," stated Lady North. "After this week just past I tell you I am very nearly at my wits' end."

"Poor Mama," sympathized Lady Haverly. "I have

been wondering if this bleak mood of James's could be the result of his having taken a fancy to some woman."

Her mother stared at her. "To whom, may I ask? Certainly not Charlotte Parton, for he apparently didn't turn a hair when he learned she had given her heart to Ryerson. As for the other young women in the house, if he is more than fleetingly aware of their presence, I shall own myself amazed."

"I am probably indulging in wishful thinking," murmured Lady Haverly.

"Anyway, I have a growing suspicion that Emberland and Hazel Lancaster will make a match."

"Indeed? Well, your house party hasn't been an utter failure then, has it? Will the Lancasters approve, do you think?"

"I can't conceive why they shouldn't. Charles has a fine living and a respectable title, and I am sure he will get over his flamboyant manner of dress as he ages."

"One might say the same for Robert, but Claire clearly doesn't think him good enough for her daughter."

"I must confess, Sarah, that I've come to know Charlotte Parton much better this past week than I ever did before. There is something in her character that I never suspected. She has a stubborn streak as wide as her mother's. If I cared to lay a wager on the outcome of this battle, I would put it on the daughter."

Lady Haverly chuckled. "Good. I hope things fall out as you believe they will. Everyone should marry for love provided, of course, the match isn't totally unsuitable. I hope I can remember that when Ann and Cassandra are of marriageable age."

The two ladies were interrupted by the butler's discreet

cough. "Miss Robinson is requesting permission to speak to you, Lady Haverly."

"To me? Oh, you must have misunderstood. I've only seen her once. Undoubtedly she wants you, Mama."

"No, madam," said the butler. "She specifically asked for you."

"Send her in, man," instructed Lady North with an impatience that was far too edgy. The strain of her house party was showing on her.

Emma was ushered into the salon, and the butler withdrew.

"Hello, Emma dear," Lady North greeted her. "You have met my daughter, I believe."

"Yes," said Emma, straightening her shoulders and walking farther into the room.

"Sit here." Lady North indicated a chair beside her own. "You wish to speak with Sarah?"

Emma nodded, turning her blue-green eyes upon Lady Haverly's attractive face. "I hope this is not an inconvenient time."

"Nonsense," Lady North answered for her daughter. "Shall I leave the two of you alone?"

"No, please," Emma responded quickly. "I shouldn't like to dislodge you from your own salon. But before I say what I came to say, I must ask both of you to keep silent about the nature of this visit. At least until my aunt and uncle have returned to Sussex. If you do not wish to give your promise, I'll leave immediately."

"Gracious," said Lady Haverly with a laugh, "you sound so grave, Emma. I may call you Emma, mayn't I? I am certain you can depend upon us to keep your secret."

"Thank you," said Emma gratefully. "I have heard,

Lady Haverly, that you are seeking the services of a governess for your daughters."

Lady Haverly's eyes widened in surprise. "That's true, though I can't think where you heard it."

"That is of no importance. What I should like to say is that I would be ever so grateful if you will consider me for the post."

"You!" Lady North interrupted, her response loud and sharp in the salon. "Oh, my dear girl, have you any notion what being a governess entails?"

"I—I have no previous experience," Emma said, wanting to be perfectly honest, "but I can play the pianoforte and know enough fancy needlework and watercolor painting to instruct your granddaughters in the rudiments of those arts. And, what I am sure is of more importance, I was given an unusually broad education. My father provided me with a tutor until I was seventeen. I've studied history, philosophy, Greek and Latin, and can converse fairly well in French. I am told, also, that I write a very ladylike hand."

The ladies North and Haverly were regarding her with some amazement. "But, Emma," protested Lady Haverly finally, "you can't be seriously considering going into service. I am sure your aunt and uncle will never hear of it."

"They will not approve," confirmed Emma, for she knew it would be useless to do otherwise, "which is why I have asked you not to mention this to any of my relatives. If—if you should agree to give me a trial, Lady Haverly, I'll tell them myself. But I must be allowed to choose the time and place."

Lady North shook her head at Emma, a look of incomprehension still on her face. "I cannot understand this at all. Don't the Partons treat you well, dear?"

"They have been very generous," Emma assured her. "It is just that I feel I have been a burden on them long enough. My—my father did not leave me anything for a portion. He was kindness itself, but not very practical, I'm afraid. At any rate I want to support myself."

"Dear me," murmured Lady Haverly ruefully. "I don't know what to say. It's not that I shouldn't be willing to give you a trial were you a person of lower birth. But, in the circumstances, I am sure your aunt will kick up a dust. I am not at all certain I wouldn't myself in her place. Coming as this does after Charlotte has shocked her so, I can't think *what* I should do."

"Will you at least give my request careful consideration," Emma said urgently, "and give me your answer before I leave Havenwood?"

"I think that would be the best course," said Lady Haverly, relieved at being given a reprieve of a few days. "I'll discuss it with my husband, and I'll let you know our decision."

Emma got quickly to her feet. "Thank you, Lady Haverly. Now, I expect I should go and read to Aunt Claire."

When the girl was gone, Lady Haverly looked at her mother and broke into a laugh. "Have you ever been so stunned in your life? Claire will be in a grand pucker when she learns of this!"

Lady North was still staring at the open doorway through which Emma had just disappeared. "It's as I've suspected all along. Everyone in this house is running mad, one by one. I am not at all sure of my own sanity at this point."

"Mama," said her daughter with another laugh, "have no fear. I should be hard put to find anyone more rational than you. If things go on in this way, I urge you to consider coming to me for a week or two. Let these feather-heads work it out among themselves."

Sir James ambled into the room at that point. "Am I to assume that you are throwing me into the same pot with the other feather-heads, Sarah?"

"I certainly am! Mama tells me you are no help at all in entertaining your guests."

"I'm sorry, Mother, for being so derelict. Now I hear that Lady Parton and her daughter have very nearly come to cuffs over poor Robert."

"Well, Mama believes Charlotte will have the best of that tangle," said Lady Haverly, smiling.

"I certainly hope so, else we will have a broken Ryerson on our hands."

His mother was looking at him with a deeply thoughtful expression. "Are you very cast down by Charlotte's choice, James? I hope not, for since I have become better acquainted with the young woman, I cannot feel the two of you would suit."

"I agree wholeheartedly," her son assured her.

"Do you suppose you could speak to Lord Parton on Robert's behalf? It is quite unreasonable of Claire to insist he is unsuitable."

"If it will put you in better sorts, I'll have a talk with Parton at the first opportunity."

Lady North sighed. "If we can induce Claire and Charlotte to leave their chambers, that will be one less problem for me to deal with. What we shall do about Emma's strange request, however, I have not yet hit upon."

Sir James's dark eyes sharpened abruptly. "Miss Robinson? What request has she made?"

Lady Haverly said, "She wishes to be Ann and Cassandra's governess."

Sir James glared at her. "A crack-skull notion if I ever heard one!"

"Don't rip up at *me,*" Lady Haverly said. "I assure you I had nothing to do with it. I don't even know the young woman. I was as shocked as you seem to be when she asked about the post."

"Then you said no?"

"Not exactly," admitted Lady Haverly. "She seemed so earnest about supporting herself. I told her I would speak to Dorian and give her our decision later. And, James, we promised not to mention this to her relatives, so please don't say anything to them."

"It will not do at all," stated Sir James emphatically. "I should like to ask a favor of you, Sarah. Permit me to be the one to explain the impossibility of such a course of action to Miss Robinson."

"But you will frighten the girl, James," interposed his mother, troubled. "After all, she is hardly acquainted with you, and you *can* look so stern when you disapprove of something."

"I promise you, Mother, I shan't look stern when I tell her."

"I don't mind if you wish to be the bearer of the tidings," said his sister. "I quite agree that I can't hire a governess who is a niece of family friends, but be careful not to offend her unnecessarily."

"I'll do my best," promised Sir James.

## *CHAPTER FOURTEEN*

The next morning Sir James left Havenwood and rode to the house of his brother-in-law, Sir Dorian Haverly, a man four years older than James and one whom he respected greatly. He had always been thankful that it was Haverly who had married his sister. Although they had not had many conversations of a personal nature through the years, Sir James suddenly felt the need of Dorian's counsel on something that had troubled him during the past few days.

The marquis reined in his horse, dismounted, and, tossing the reins to a groom who had materialized from the back of the house, strode up the steps to the front door. He found his brother-in-law in the conservatory bent over a fern, inspecting the fronds for disease.

"Hullo, Dorian," said the marquis.

Lord Haverly straightened, his ruddy face peering up at Sir James curiously for a few seconds, and then his calm gray eyes cleared in welcome.

"James," said Haverly with enthusiasm. "You haven't come around for so long I was wondering if Sarah or I had done something to put you out of patience with us."

"You wondered nothing of the sort," said Sir James amiably. "The both of you have always been kinder than I deserve."

"Well, well, well. Sit down. I'll have Jessup bring some refreshment."

"Not for me, thank you. I just had breakfast." The marquis sat in a wicker chair. "Actually, I can't stay long, but I should like to talk to you about something—er, rather delicate, if I may."

"Anything, James, you know that." Haverly moved another chair closer to Sir James and sat down, smiling. "Now we can be cozy."

Sir James sighed. Had it been a mistake to come to Dorian with this? Would he sound like a deuced idiot? It was not in his nature to go whining to friends for advice; he had always felt it might lower him in their esteem.

Lord Haverly gave a gentle cough, bringing James back to the matter at hand. "Dorian," said the marquis in a decisive tone.

Haverly looked upon his wife's brother with fondness, realizing that he was having difficulty saying what he had come to say. It was rather unusual to see James at a loss for words. "I am all ears," said Haverly kindly. "If it's money you want, you know you are more than welcome to some of mine."

"I have considerable money of my own," Sir James reminded him.

"I only thought that you might have had a run of bad luck at the tables while in London. Glad to hear you weathered town with your usual good sense. What do you wish to speak to me about then?"

Sir James squirmed in his chair. "I am beginning to think I shouldn't be here."

"No, no, you can ask me anything."

"All right," said Sir James. "I would like to know something about your life with my sister—the intimate moments."

Haverly stared at him in amazement. "But, James, I have always supposed that your experience with females has been—ah, varied."

"With a certain class of females," said Sir James uncomfortably. "I know little of gently reared women such as my sister."

A smile of understanding broke upon Haverly's face. "Are you thinking of marriage at long last?"

Sir James looked startled. "The thought has entered my mind. But about you and Sarah—"

"Ah, yes." Haverly gazed for a moment through the glass of the conservatory with a rapt expression. Then, looking back to James, he said, "Sarah may seem flighty, even undemonstrative to some people, but she has never been so with me."

Embarrassed, Sir James gazed at his hands, which were curled over the arms of the wicker chair.

"Warm and loving and passionate," Haverly said, his face softening with memories. "That's how she's been with me from the first. I have always considered myself to be the most fortunate of men for having the wisdom to ask her to marry me. The match was most suitable, of course, but it was a love match, too. No man could wish for more. I have a charming hostess when we have guests, a fine mother for my children, and when we are alone in our bedroom, I have an enticing lover. I've never been tempted to look at another woman since the day we wed." He looked at Sir James squarely, utterly unabashed by this disclosure.

"But Father always said—that women—women of quality were too well-bred to—er—abandon themselves to the pleasure of the flesh, even with their husbands," said the marquis in a husky voice.

Haverly chuckled, observing his brother-in-law's discomfort. "Your father had a number of mythical ideas. He must have got them from his own father. But why any reasonable man should believe that women of quality are any different in that regard from others, I can't think. Have you known so many women and not learned that they are all basically alike?"

"I have always paid for my pleasure," said Sir James dryly. "I have never thought much about having that sort of—delight with a wife. Those other women—well, it was their profession. From the woman I wed, I expected nothing more than that she should know how to comport herself and provide me with an heir."

"James, I am disappointed in you. I fear your knowledge of women of our class has been limited to pale milk-and-water misses. You have but to look a little farther."

A feeling of humiliation began to steal over the marquis. "I wish you had told me this earlier."

Haverly shook his head wonderingly. "How was I to know your education had been so neglected?" he countered.

"Just so," muttered the marquis, getting to his feet. "I'll take my leave, Dorian. Thank you for indulging me."

"Any time, old fellow," said Haverly, returning to his inspection of his ferns.

James claimed his horse and rode slowly back to Havenwood. It was unnerving to discover that he was not the man of the world that he had always thought. He had been rather a fool, in fact.

The following afternoon James found an opportunity to speak to Lord Parton alone. Encountering that gentleman in the garden, he invited him to have a brandy with him in the study.

When they were closeted there, James poured a double

portion of the liquor for his guest, for the man looked excessively pale and drawn.

Parton accepted the drink gratefully and sank into a comfortable padded armchair. He took a long swallow, then remarked apologetically, "I daresay you will be glad to see the back of us, North. Had I known my wife and daughter would make such gooses of themselves, I would have taken them directly to Sussex from town." He drew a long breath and applied himself once more to his brandy.

"I am slightly acquainted with the troubles females can cause when they set their minds to it," Sir James told him. "Takes a firm hand on the reins to keep them on course, I am sure."

Parton glanced unhappily at him. "There's where I've fallen short, I fear. Should have sat Claire down years ago and told her how the hare ate the cabbage."

"It may be," suggested Sir James, "that it is not too late to remedy the situation."

Parton sighed, greatly depressed. "Maybe I'm getting old, but I dread a set-to with my wife above all things. As long as I can be left in peace, I prefer to allow her to go her own way."

"From what my mother has said, sir, you are not likely to be left in peace this time. I believe your daughter has threatened to elope?"

Parton nodded glumly. "Claire declares she'll set a guard on the girl." He looked hopefully at his host. "She's convinced you mean to offer for Lottie and that the girl can be brought to see the good sense in such a match."

"Sir, your daughter is charming, but to be perfectly frank I do not think we should suit. In fact, I believe she and Ryerson were made for each other. The man is distracted over her." He pushed down his reservations concerning a marriage between two such impulsive romantics. Age, he had noticed, tamed almost everyone in time. "I urge you to give them your blessing."

"Seems a good enough chap," conceded Parton, "but I've no hope I can make my wife see it. She insists upon holding out for someone more eligible—in a word, you."

"I feel I should confide in you, Parton. I have chosen the woman I want to marry, and she is a very different kettle of fish from your daughter. If she will have me, I believe we shall go on quite well together."

Parton was all surprise. "Indeed? Why, I haven't heard any rumors to that effect."

"I have kept my own counsel. You are the first to know, and I must ask you not to spread it around until I have a chance to discover if the woman in question is willing to enter the matrimonial state with me. I give you permission, however, to tell your wife. Perhaps when she realizes she can't have her way in this, it will cause her to see Ryerson in a more favorable light. Here, let me pour you more brandy."

His glass refilled, Parton seemed to brace up a little. "I am half convinced that you are right. A steady hand, that's what Claire needs. When I leave you, I shall speak to her." He looked worried. "I hope she doesn't start throwing your vases around."

Sir James shrugged. "Vases can be replaced. Don't allow her to intimidate you."

"Yes, you are right. Should have taken a stand years ago."

What passed between Lord Parton and his wife, Sir James was never to know. It was clear, however, from the shrieks and shouted threats of expiring that issued from the lady's chamber a while later that she did not take at all well to her husband's suggestion. Quite some time after that Parton found him still in his study. The man looked as if he'd been through the French war. He fell into a chair as if his legs would no longer support him.

"If I may have another dash of that brandy, North—"

Sir James honored the request at once and waited for his guest to compose himself.

At length Parton said, "I expect you heard some of the commotion, but I stood by my decision. Told her I would give Ryerson permission to marry Charlotte if she swooned every hour on the hour for the rest of her life." He drew a shuddering breath. "Afraid she smashed one of your figurines, a shepherdess with blue flowers in her hair. Unpleasant business."

"Don't fret over the figurine," Sir James said. "Never liked it above half anyway."

Parton finished his drink before adding, "As soon as I've gathered my senses, I'll speak to Ryerson. I'll suggest we have the ceremony as early as propriety will allow. The sooner the knot's tied, the sooner Claire will accept that she cannot have her way in this. Once Lottie is out of the house, she will calm down, I'm sure."

Sir James commented with wry amusement, "I think I can tell you that Robert will agree wholeheartedly with your plan. Once your daughter has presented your wife with grandchildren, I am certain any trace of resentment that is left will disappear. Never knew a woman yet who could resist falling head over ears for her grandchildren."

Holding courageously to his intent, Sir Randolph commanded an audience later that day with his daughter and Ryerson. The two young people appeared in the above-stairs sitting room promptly, according to Sir Randolph's instructions. Wasting no words, he informed them that he had decided to grant permission for them to marry as quickly as may be, adding that Charlotte's mother, though still somewhat indisposed, had agreed to the decision.

After the announcement was made, Charlotte and Ryerson forgot Sir Randolph's presence in the room and fell to gazing deeply into each other's eyes. Not thinking it worth the effort to try to expand upon his decision to two oblivious people, he retreated from the room, leaving them alone.

Sir Robert took his betrothed in his arms and kissed her, laughing at her disbelieving gaze. She said earnestly, "I cannot imagine Mama gave in so easily. Do you suppose she has another scheme to separate us? I love you so much that I shan't believe you are mine until we leave the altar."

He laid his cheek against her hair. "Your father would not give his permission and then withdraw it. Don't worry your pretty little head another moment. We will be married, and very soon. I am very glad, however, that we shan't have to elope. Your mother would likely never have forgiven us that impropriety."

"It wouldn't have mattered to me. I want only to be your wife. It matters little how that is accomplished."

He hugged her tighter against him. "Are you aware that you are marrying a man who sometimes disregards wisdom and acts recklessly?"

"Of course I am aware of it. That is one of the things I love in you."

On the night of the Haverlys' ball Emma dressed with some misgiving. Her appearance could not have been better, except for a slight paleness in her face. She wore the new blue-green ball gown that deepened the color of her eyes. The misgiving was not caused by what she saw in the glass, but by the thought of meeting Lady Haverly again. She was certain the lady had made her decision as to whether to give Emma a trial as governess to her daughters, for the Partons were scheduled to leave for Sussex the next day. In a very few hours she would know if she had a position or must look elsewhere for her living.

Sir Randolph, Sir Humphrey, and Jonathan were, to their relief, not required to attend the party, since Emberland and Ryerson would escort the ladies. At the last minute Emma herself was strongly tempted to stay behind, too; only the knowledge that this would probably be her last chance to apply to Lady Haverly sent her down the stairs to the antechamber where the others were waiting.

Lady Claire, having emerged from her chamber on the previous day, seemed to have accepted the betrothal of her daughter to Sir Robert. In fact, she was chatting with Lady North about the wedding dress when Emma appeared.

Observing Charlotte's and her fiancé's blatant happiness as they settled into the carriage for the short drive only served to depress Emma further. It wasn't that she begrudged her cousin her joy, but merely that it served to emphasize the improbability of Emma's ever making a love match herself. She only hoped Charlotte appreciated how very blessed she was.

The ball was a gay occasion with the guests laughing and talking and exchanging partners frequently. After standing up with Emberland, Ryerson, and two young gentlemen of the neighborhood, Emma's spirits were still so downcast that she sought a few minutes' escape in a small salon near the ballroom.

There she wandered restlessly across the carpet, wondering why Lady Haverly had not sought her out. She had been very friendly and polite as she greeted Emma's party, but since their arrival Emma had caught only fleeting glimpses of her as she moved from one cluster of guests to another and once when she had danced the waltz with her tall gentle-eyed husband. Perhaps Lady Haverly did not want to give Emma the post and was avoiding her because she didn't like to disappoint her. That seemed the most likely explanation, but Emma was determined to make a direct approach before she left the house if the woman didn't take the initiative.

She sighed and dropped into a velvet chair, running her fingers idly across the smooth pile on the arm. Having to watch Sir James moving on the dance floor with other young ladies in his arms had made the party even worse for her. She didn't know whether she dreaded more the possibility that he might ask her to stand up with him before the night was over or that he might ignore her altogether. Neither prospect was at all cheering.

She laid her head back against the high padded back of the chair and closed her eyes. She was wearier than she had thought, for within minutes she was on the verge of falling asleep. She would have dozed the next moment if she hadn't heard someone in the salon with her. She opened her eyes to find Sir James observing her relaxed pose.

"Oh, it's you!" she said faintly, sitting straight.

"So it is."

"I never meant to fall asleep, but merely to sit down for a minute."

"You are not enjoying my sister's ball?"

"It isn't that. I—I'm a little tired. It is always a strain to spend an extended time in someone else's house—even when the hostess is as hospitable as your mother. But then I shall be leaving tomorrow."

"I know. Are you wondering why my sister hasn't spoken to you?"

Her eyes widened. Had Lady Haverly told him that Emma had applied for the governess's post? "She greeted us warmly when we arrived."

"I mean about your ridiculous request that you become my nieces' governess."

She closed her eyes briefly, saying with dignity, "I do not think it at all ridiculous."

He sounded amused. "She has left it to me to tell you that we have decided you will not do."

Emma regarded him with misgiving. "There is no hope that she will change her mind?"

"None. Whatever made you conceive such a cork-brained notion in the first place?"

Affronted, she regarded him indignantly. "It is no more cork-brained than your contemplating marriage with my cousin."

He looked not very pleased. "You assume falsely. It was my mother and Lady Parton who contemplated the match, not I."

She did not know why a sudden wave of thanksgiving washed through her. "I must say that your judgment was better than theirs, for the two of you would never go on together."

He nodded, then walked a little away from her, resting one arm along the mantelpiece. "May I ask you a question?"

"Yes."

"How did you arrive at the assessment of me portrayed in Aristobulus's verses?"

She flushed guiltily. "This is most embarrassing. I see now that I judged precipitously from the tales carried home by Charlotte."

His brows shot up. "What did she say?"

Her depression lifted a little and she smiled at him. "You have no conversation."

"The little termagant!"

"Yes, and you are not romantic."

"Hummmm."

"Furthermore, at your first meeting you did not bring her any punch, and then, to add insult to injury, you had the odious effrontery to behave, at your second meeting, as if you had never clapped eyes on her before in your life."

A sardonic smile tugged at his mouth. "I am beginning to understand the young lady's aversion to me."

"Well, I think that even such a chain of disappointments might have been overcome, but it was really too much to stomach when you admitted that you had never seen the inside of Newgate."

He laughed gruffly. "Poor Robert!"

"Lord Ryerson seems very pleased with his bargain."

"Oh, he is. Only I pray the two of them will grow up before they become entangled in some scandal together."

"I shouldn't worry if I were you. Lottie longs to have children for whom she can buy toys. I have noticed that children seem to make a couple recollect their duties faster than almost anything."

"Yes," he agreed musingly.

"I confess I am a little surprised, though, that you have been totally immune to my cousin's vitality and beauty all along. But then perhaps that is the result of your having been disappointed in love in your youth."

He frowned at her. "Where did you hear that?"

"Someone mentioned it in passing."

"That old tale will never be laid to rest, it appears. Well, it happens that I did offer for a young woman when I was three and twenty and had very little wisdom in such things. She was as beautiful as a marble statue, and just as cold. My heart was never involved, although she did bruise my pride. I have thanked heaven ever since that she turned me down."

"Oh." Suddenly self-conscious, she stared at her clasped hands.

There was a long silence. Then he uttered one word in a low voice. "Sophia."

She looked up at him, but he said nothing further, merely studied her face, the nervous gestures of her fingers and the rapid rise and fall of her breathing.

"Are you still furious with me for deceiving you?"

"No, as long as you never do it again. I apologize if I was too harsh. I do not possess the most even of tempers."

"I've noticed that, but then I have been known to fly up into the boughs, too."

She saw a teasing light in his dark eyes. "You, at least, have Mr. Stumpover praying for you."

She stared at him, then exclaimed, "Jonathan Parton! I'll have his neck for running on about me to others."

He laughed. "He admires you greatly." He walked slowly toward her and, bending down, took her hands, urging her to her feet. "I am beginning to understand why."

In a strangled voice she said, "Ar-are you?"

He released one of her hands to run a finger gently across her hot cheek and down to the pulse beating out of control in her throat. Then he curled a red-gold lock of hair around his finger. "I have always liked your hair."

She forced herself to meet his gaze. "Th-thank you," she whispered.

His eyes held hers for a long moment before he pulled her into his arms. He kissed her brow, her eyelids, her nose, and her chin with a tenderness that she would never have suspected he possessed. Her eyes were huge as he lifted his head to gaze into them. She had never felt so vulnerable in her life.

"Will you marry me, Emma?"

The words vibrated in the air between them until she, at last, took them in, realized that she had not dreamed them. His eyes glowed with a warmth she had not seen in them since she had known him merely as Jamie. "I—I am not good enough for you—for your position."

"But you love me."

She nodded helplessly, her heart in her eyes. "Yes—oh, yes! But your mother—"

His lips came down to touch hers lightly; then they moved slowly, deepening the kiss until Emma clung desperately to his hard strength. She was breathless when he, with clear reluctance and a soft groan, released her mouth. His breathing was ragged, and feeling faint, Emma touched her forehead to his chest. When she spoke the words were muffled.

"I—I should not like to marry anyone who kept a mistress."

He lifted her chin, forcing her to look into his eyes. He smiled at her. "I can't imagine your husband ever having any desire for one."

She returned his smile faintly. "I suppose you must marry someone to have an heir."

He pressed her head against his chest again, running his hand lovingly over her hair. "I could have married a number of women before now, sweet girl. I am so very glad that I did not. I never thought to have romance in marriage, but I've fallen in love with you. I need you so much, my heart. Please, say you'll have me."

"Oh, James." She lifted her face and smiled at him through a blur of joyful tears. "I would be honored to be your wife. You are everything I have ever dreamed of in a man. Only I don't know how we are to tell Aunt Claire."

He silenced her with a finger laid on her lips. "I'll take care of that. And I'll call upon your uncle tomorrow and gain his permission."

He prepared to kiss her again, but at that moment they heard a startled gasp behind them. Turning, they saw Lady North regarding them with owlish eyes.

James smiled at her. "Come in, Mother. Miss Robinson has just agreed to be my wife. I'll send for Jessup, and we will have a toast together before I publish my good fortune to the world."